Jeannette Maree

PLUM

BLOSSOM

A transition of one's life

Acknowledgements

My many thanks must go to the
Wynnum Historical Society,
Elizabeth Guntrip, Diane Hill and Janeen Kolb,
and to Peter Guntrip.

A special thanks to Gabriella Tedesco
for the cover design.

Also by Jeannette Maree
(under Louise Ayden)

I Belong To Me

Remember To Breathe

The plum blossom is a symbol of winter and a harbinger of spring. The blossoms bloom most vibrantly amidst the winter snow, exuding a certain ethereal elegance, while its fragrance subtly pervades the air even at the coldest time of the year. The plum blossom symbolizes perseverance and hope, but also beauty, purity, and a transition of one's life.

If ever you lose love,
it will return
in some other way

1

Sunday evenings, Wynnum Creek was the core, bustling with the hundred or so robust, weather-worn mariners getting ready to set off for their five-day fishing trip around Moreton Bay, once the heart of the fishing industry. It is shallow, and lies on the east coast of Australia, covering an area of 13,000 square kilometres encompassing Caloundra to the Gold Coast.

Skipper Daniel Larson was one of the last to steer his fishing boat 'Lusty Lady' away from Wynnum Creek, towing two dinghies. Jacko Swan, Kev Ruby and Gabe Connor were the crew.

Although fishing equipment had vastly improved by the mid-sixties in comparison to bygone days, and manageable lightweight nylon nets had replaced the high-maintenance heavy cotton, tar-dipped nets, a fisherman's life was still not one for the fainthearted.

There was no room on board the Lusty Lady for a galley so the men brought their own tucker, mainly consisting of sandwiches and tinned bully beef. They boiled the billy for tea on a primus stove and slept on their swags in cramped conditions clustered around the engine, ingesting diesel fumes. They were tough brave men with a strong preference for the solitude of a seaman's life, adaptable to harsh weather and to the ever-changing tides.

Superstitions took on an atavistic form of fear, much the same as religion. Just as any seamen would, Jacko and Kev believed disaster would befall anyone who denigrated the lore of the sea, for example: setting out on a fishing trip on a Friday, whistling on board and stepping onto a boat with your left foot. Daniel, neither religious nor superstitious, respected the tales passed down for generations. Gabe Conner, a young lad about twenty, was a sceptic who believed in nothing.

"We make our own luck!" He adamantly declared.

The crew were not talkative during the trip. There was no point in trying since the roar of the diesel engine drowned out every word they uttered, so they usually dozed until they arrived at the favourite fishing spot.

As he steered the boat, Daniel kept a vigilant eye on Gabe as well as on the sonar. The lad puzzled him. He was mostly jovial, but at times isolated himself from everyone on board without provocation or warning – speaking only when he had to. Gabe was also one of the best crewmen Daniel had ever had. The lad was dauntless. He worked gruelling hours beside the other men, hauling heavy nets bulging with tons of fish into the boat; he would stand neck deep in freezing, shark-infested waters in winter without complaint.

Two hours after leaving Wynnum Creek, Gabe climbed up onto the bow to scan the surrounding waters. His stance was defiant and proud. There was a time when he had wanted to bellow a lung-busting scream into the wind, *'I'm free now, and you bastards can't touch me!'* A tear of gratitude escaped from the corner of Gabe's eye in his elation at being rid of is childhood captors. A quick swipe of his hand dried his face, tension released with a heavy sigh. The score was settled. He has never looked back

Gabe's sustained enthusiasm for fishing was extraordinary. He scrutinised everything Daniel and the other men did, eagerly soaking up knowledge like the proverbial sponge. Daniel gladly shared with him all that he knew about fishing.

"Ya gotta keep a look out for signs for the different types of fish, mate," Daniel said in earnest, "Learn to trust your eyes because every one of 'em 'as their own callin' card. Mullet in the mangroves give off an oily smell. Get familiar with that smell. Ya gotta keep a look out for large dark shadows in the water too. It could be fish or it could be bloody sharks!"

Gabe cracked a half smile as Daniel convulsed with laughter at his own joke. "In time, mate," Daniel continued, "ya just might be able to identify fish from miles away by the ripples in the water. But that takes lots of experience. Only know of a few blokes doin' that around 'ere after workin' years with indigenous crews."

Gabe was usually calm and easy going on board. On land, it was a different story. It baffled Daniel why a young fella with movie star looks could be so fearsome. The lad was probably more dangerous than any man he had met.

The men were all very wary of 'the kid', as they called him. Daniel often wondered if Gabe possessed a conscience – too many times that he cared to count he had to rescue some poor bugger from Gabe's explosive temper and vice-like grip. The unpredictability of his mood swings caused havoc and yet Gabe still managed to beguile those he infuriated with his charismatic charm. Gabe Connor was an enigma and had exhibited no intention of talking about his past. Whenever asked, he would usually shrug nonchalantly. "No point in lookin' back ... there's only now."

No one knew anything about Gabe, except that his back was horribly disfigured with old, small, round, dark scars and raised white striped criss-crosses with long, twisted tentacles winding around his torso. Daniel had seen a lot in his lifetime, but nothing like the carnage of those scars. When he asked Gabe what had happened to him, Gabe's eyes burned with a rage that sent a chill down Daniel's spine, before he casually shrugged. "Nothin' I couldn't handle."

The skipper looked up at the sky. It was clear except for a few scattered powder-puff clouds. His gaze drifted to the horizon. He grinned with satisfaction. The weather was ideal for another profitable week.

It had been two years since Gabe had first wandered up alongside the Lusty Lady, where Daniel was crouched down working on the engine and asked where he could find the skipper. Daniel stopped what he was doing to look over his shoulder and replied in a warm baritone, "You're looking at him, mate."

Gabe smiled broadly, "G'day, I'm Gabe Connor," he chirped. "I hear you're looking for crew."

"Ah, that's news to me," Daniel responded cautiously, slowly straightening his hefty frame to its full six-foot-three inches turning around to face the stranger, wiping his hands on an old rag. "Where'd ya hear that?"

"Over at Fisher's pub," Gabe grinned, mischievously lifting an eyebrow, "where rumours usually start."

The skipper knew the stranger was lying, but he was mesmerised by Gabe's striking blue eyes, square jaw, perfect mouth and jet-black hair. He guessed the lad was about 18 or 19.

"You didn't hear that at Fisher's, did ya? 'Cause I'm not lookin' for crew." Daniel challenged.

"Nah mate," Gabe smiled unflinchingly, looking Daniel directly in the eye. "Just overheard some of the blokes talkin' 'bout how good ya catch was and figured a man as busy as you would need an extra hand. So I asked 'em where I could find ya."

"Got plenty of crew. Where do ya come from?"

"Thereabouts," Gabe replied, with his eyes still fixed on Daniel's.

"Are ya in trouble?"

"Nup!"

Daniel lifted his cap and slowly scratched his head, thinking that a face as good-looking as this one could not be all that bad.

"OK," he finally said. "I reckon I'll give ya a go. But if ya stuff up, ya gone!"

The sonar sounded just as Gabe saw a huge dark circle moving in the crystal waters.

"OK, this is it!" Daniel yelled, "Drop anchor!"

The engine fell silent and the boat gently rocked in rhythm with the waves slapping its sides. Jacko moved at lightning speed to the stern and grabbed hold of the line to the dinghies and dragged them in towards the boat. Jacko, Kev and Gabe climbed in. Daniel dropped nets from the stern. Kev grabbed the oars and rowed as fast as he could to make a circle. Gabe and Jacko each secured a corner of the inside net and dragged it in slowly to the back net already attached to the other dinghy. Hundreds of plump fish fought frantically to escape as they were scooped up into the other dinghy and quickly covered with ice.

By Thursday evening, Wynnum Creek was alive with the symphonic sounds of men shouting directions, trucks backing into position to load up fresh cargo, clanging of tools, idling engines of the boat waiting to be unloaded, hawkers and a few locals bantering among themselves. The community welcomed the opus, a life source of the industry. Some of the catch went to the local fish market and fish-peddlers, but the majority was shipped in trucks to Brisbane's Stanley Street fish markets and from there to interstate and overseas.

The last few weeks had been profitable for the fishing fleet. Just as Daniel had predicted, this trip had proven lucrative for all of them, which was not always the case. Many times in the past, the catch was minimal due to bad weather and other unforeseeable circumstances. The 'not so good days' were an ever-present punitive trend of the fishing industry. Since they were all currently experiencing 'good days', the air was full of good humour, crews ragging one another and arguing over who had won the bet for the largest catch and who was shouting the first round of beers; but everyone agreed to be at Fisher's pub that night to celebrate their good fortune.

2

Once work for the day had finished, Jacko and Kev headed home to their families, promising to catch up later in the evening. Gabe watched the clock as he gathered his gear together.

"Goin' somewhere?" Daniel asked when he noticed Gabe was anxious to leave.

"Could be," Gabe replied, shrugging his broad shoulders.

"Here," Daniel smiled broadly, handing him a small brown envelope.

"Ya betta take this then. I reckon ya've earned it ... don't go spending it all at once ... and stay out of trouble. I'll break ya bloody neck if I've got ta come 'n get ya out of the lock-up tonight."

Gabe smiled innocently, shaking his head as he walked away backwards.

"Ah mate, ya can be cruel. I'm not goin' to the pub tonight. I'm havin' meat pies instead."

Daniel's forehead creased into several thick folds as he scratched his head, trying to grasp what Gabe meant. Before he could ask, Gabe was sprinting homeward to shower and change.

An hour later Gabe was freshly scrubbed and reeking of Old Spice, attired in blue jeans, white tee-shirt, white socks and black pointed shoes. He walked briskly along Bay Terrace, patting his Brylcreemed hair in place. His mind was on the girl who worked at Atterton's Cake Shop. He had caught her in the periphery of his vision for only a second when he walked past the cake shop a few days earlier, but could not erase her from his mind. He was determined to see her again.

Gabe entered the shop as a customer was leaving, carrying a couple of white boxes tied with string. The delicious aromas lingering in the shop made his mouth water, and he unintentionally licked his lips several times while looking around for the girl. Instead of the girl, he found an older woman meticulously wiping the bench. He lightly tapped on the counter to get her attention, startling the woman.

"Oh, sorry love," she said dropping the cloth she was using on the bench to wipe her hands on her apron. "I didn't see you there. I was off with the fairies," she laughed awkwardly. "What can I get you?"

"Are you closing?" he asked, displaying his best manners and masking his disappointment that the girl was not there, thinking she may have already left.

"Very soon, love. What would you like?"

To prolong his time in the shop, just in case the girl was in the kitchen, Gabe carefully perused the cakes left in the cabinet and eventually selected a half dozen.

"You can throw in a few pies with those, as well please."

"Are you having a party?" the woman asked.

"Nup," Gabe grinned mischievously. "Everything here's just too tempting to resist."

"We bake daily," she said proudly.

When Gabe did not respond, she glanced up from packing his order and found him looking through the small window on the kitchen door. The woman studied him a moment and wondered why his expression seemed so glum. What was he looking for?

Gabe caught her watching him and quickly turned his attention to the noticeboard on the wall near the kitchen door, hoping the girl would soon walk through.

'Ha!' The woman thought and put the patty cake she was about to pack on the bench. She casually strolled over to the kitchen door, pushed it open and called out.

"Bonnie, love, will you fetch me a couple of cake boxes from underneath the bench for this order, please?"

Gabe's expression brightened when he heard a faint reply. "OK, Mrs A, I'll just be a tick. I'm getting my things together."

A few minutes later a very pretty girl of about 18 walked through the door, carrying a couple of plain boxes. Her strawberry-blonde hair was tied back in a ponytail. She was wearing a pale lemon, cotton sleeveless top over lime green pedal pushers and sandals. "Are these the ones you want?"

Bonnie stopped talking when she noticed Gabe watching her. They stared at one another for several drawn-out seconds. Her legs felt like jelly and her heart thumped hard in her chest. She took a long deep breath to regain composure and smiled openly at Gabe. "Hello," she said to Gabe, with the confidence of the pretty girl she knew she was, then turned to Mrs A and handed her the boxes. "I'm leaving now, Mrs A."

As Bonnie lifted the end of the counter to exit, she snatched a fleeting peek at Gabe from under it and called out, "I'll see you in the morning, Mrs A."

The older woman nodded and watched her leave. "Alright love."

"G'day Bonnie!" Gabe said when she walked past. He quickly introduced himself. So sure she would want to meet him, just as other girls had.

Bonnie smiled and said, "G'day Gabe," and kept walking, hoping that he would follow her. Her mind was racing with wild thoughts. *'He is so cool and so, so handsome! Those eyes are gorgeous. I have never seen eyes as blue as his ... I love his smile ... he is beautiful ... and his hair is so black ... he's looking at me!'*

Gabe was gobsmacked by her peculiar behaviour. *'This isn't how it's supposed to play out. She should have stopped to chat. Girls always stop and chat!'*

"Aah, Mrs A, is my order ready?" Gabe asked, feeling panic mounting, afraid Bonnie would disappear before he had a chance to talk to her.

"Yeah love," she smiled, tying the string around the boxes in a bow. "There you are." She handed the boxes to him. He paid, thanked her, and then grabbed the boxes and dashed out of the shop and stood on the footpath a few yards from the shop entrance. He looked up and down the street only to discover that Bonnie was a fair distance ahead of him, walking towards Manly.

'I don't get it.' His shoulders drooped, with disappointment. *'I thought she'd wait for me. I thought she was interested.'*

When Gabe saw Bonnie stop and look over her shoulder, he made a dash to catch up to her.

"You took your time," she quipped when he caught up. "I don't usually wait for fellers. Another second and I would have gone home."

"You're a bit of a sassy chick. What do ya' mean ya' don't wait for fellars? How many fellars 'ave ya got?"

She turned back to the direction she was heading and started walking.

"Sassy, am I? Huh! Well if you say so. I've never been called sassy before. I rather like that." She grinned to herself. Looking back over her shoulder at him she asked, "What does it mean?"

Gabe was surprised at her honesty, which he liked. Girls her age usually acted sophisticated and worldly, even when they were not.

"Ya' honestly don't know what *sassy* means?"

Bonnie shook her head. "I wouldn't have asked if I had."

"Well, it means teasin' a bloke, which is uncool." He grinned with a twinkle in his eye. "It's sorta cruel."

She stopped walking and turned to face him – her features stern and full of fight as she placed her hands firmly on her hips.

"What do you mean by that? I am not a cruel person!"

"I don't know that ... if ya' a cruel person or if ya' not' 'cause I don't know ya. I'll have ta get ta know ya first, so I can see for meself if ya cruel or if ya ain't."

She laughed sarcastically and said, "Ha! Now, who is being sassy?" She dropped her eyes and tilted her head sideways and softened her voice. "You can take me to the pictures Saturday night ... so you can get to know me, to decide whether or not I'm a cruel person." She threw her head back and laughed out loud and walked away.

"Hey, wait up!" Gabe called, "Where ya goin' now?"

She raised her arm, waved to him, quickening her pace. "Home, see you tomorrow!"

Gabe stood forlorn on the footpath. The string bit into his fingers under the weight of the cake boxes, the discomfort adding to the disappointment of Bonnie sashaying off down the street. He cheered up when she turned and waved seconds before disappearing around the corner. He lifted his hand holding one of the boxes to wave back, but the heat from the pies caused the box to partially collapse. Gabe's juggling skills saved the pies from toppling on to the ground but he was unable to stop some of them from breaking open all over his tee-shirt and jeans. He smiled a wide smile, relieved that Bonnie was not there to see him covered in gravy and meat. She surely would have laughed at him scraping the mess from his clothes.

The tantalizing aroma of warm steak and gravy triggered Gabe's taste buds to salivate. He was tempted to immediately devour what was left of the pies but since the foreshore was just a few minutes away, he headed down to the beach to eat them in the fading light of the day. The moment he plonked himself down on the cool sand, several seagulls joined him, doing a merry dance, squawking, demanding any morsel of food he had. The scene was peaceful apart from being shattered at intervals by the gulls' piercing cries while they fought over the crumbs he threw to them.

It was dark by the time Gabe left Manly beach to walk back to Wynnum, to meet up with Daniel at Fisher's pub. As he came closer to the entrance, Gabe could hear the ruckus from the men inside, a crescendo of laughter and their loud razzing of one another. Daniel waved to Gabe when he appeared in the doorway.

On his way over to Daniel's table, some of the men in their inebriated state good-naturedly tussled Gabe's hair as he passed them. "How ya goin', kid?" they chorused in raspy voices racked from years of smoking. "Aaaw! You're a good bloke when ya wanna be!" There were echoes of agreement in the background, followed by more playful heckling.

Daniel stood inert, holding his beer and watching Gabe's reaction to the men jostling him. He was astonished that Gabe had not threatened to beat them to a pulp, given his irascible nature; on the contrary, he gave as good as he got.

"You're in a fine mood tonight." Daniel chimed, knowing he was testing Gabe's patience just by making that remark. "What's got ya walkin' on a cloud? What happened to your shirt?" he asked puzzled.

Gabe shrugged and half smiled. "I met a girl," he said. "She's a beauty too."

Daniel's jovial mood changed to sombre. "What girl?" He challenged.

"Bonnie. She works at the cake shop. I'm takin' her to the pictures Saturday night."

Daniel casually sat his beer down on the table and suddenly grabbed Gabe by his tee-shirt, pulling him in so close that their noses almost touched. The room froze as if someone had pressed a pause button. "Bonnie's a good girl," Daniel whispered into Gabe's face. "Her parents are close friends of mine, like family. I've known her since she bellowed her way into this world. Ya harm a hair on that little girl's head and ya 'ave me to deal with, understand?"

Gabe nodded and smiled, but not his usual confident smile. There was something in Daniel's eyes that told him he meant every word he had said. Daniel grinned with confidence, assured Gabe understood. When Daniel released his grip on Gabe and straightened his tee-shirt, the men released heavy sighs and mumbled a few words of disappointment, visions of a potential fight fizzling out quickly.

"Now lad, what are ya drinking?"

After having a couple of beers, Gabe went home. Daniel's response to him dating Bonnie alarmed him. He had never feared anyone since childhood, but was now cautious of Daniel.

Daniel sipped his beer, the liquid bitter in his mouth while churning things over in his mind, thinking about Bonnie and Gabe together. Gabe's peculiar behaviour stoked his suspicion. He envisioned disaster ahead. *'Huh!'* he shrugged, *'perhaps I should just harness me imagination and mind me own business.'* He sculled down the rest of his beer and headed home.

3

Bonnie fled to her bedroom in tears after telling her parents about Gabe. Her enthusiasm for a future with a perfect stranger put them in a state of piqued fear. They themselves had turned into strangers, quizzing Bonnie about Gabe's background, his family, where he worked, if he was a Catholic? Bonnie was forced to admit that she scarcely knew a thing about him.

The anger in her father's voice rattled around in her head long after their fiery exchange. *'I didn't work long hours to give you a good education, so you could marry the first bloke that comes along!'*

Bonnie adored her parents and was consciously aware of their approval or disapproval about the choices she made. Now she was totally confused by their outrage since they had repeatedly told her while growing up that all they wanted for her was that she be happy. She lay on her bed, her small delicate hands slowly curling into fists in a crescendo of outrage as she thought about their response to her plans.

'I'm old enough to make my own decision and I will marry Gabe Connor!'

Bonnie immediately saw the absurdity of that notion and had an inclination to laugh out loud. *'He has to ask me first.'*

She sat up and dried her eyes with the neatly folded handkerchief she pulled from her pocket and made herself comfortable on the edge of her bed. The room was in darkness except for a shard of light shining in under the door from the lounge room, where her parents watched television. She leaned over and switched on her record player. With a steady hand, she lifted the arm of the player and gently placed it on the rotating vinyl. Percy Faith's "Theme from a Summer Place" drowned out the muffled sounds of the television. Bonnie closed her eyes and the music carried her off to an imaginary world with Gabe.

Bonnie was totally dizzy at the thought of Gabe holding her as they danced in the bandstand by the foreshore. Her heart fluttered as though hundreds of butterflies were dancing deep within her chest. She imagined him drawing her closer and gently brushing his lips across hers as they twirled, round and around.

Joe and Beth Mason sat silently in their burgundy brocade lounge chairs, staring blankly at the images flickering across the television screen. Neither was paying attention to the show, both were thinking about Bonnie. The sudden change in her behaviour had them baffled. They were at a loss as to what to do.

Beth suddenly gasped, panic-stricken, recalling a memory as if history was repeating itself. Her eyes filled with tears when she told Joe they would have to let Bonnie go. He stared blankly at her.

"Why?" he asked, utterly confused.

"Because," Beth said, dabbing her eyes with a crisp white linen handkerchief, "I don't want to lose our only child. I was incensed when my parents forbade me to see you."

Joe looked at Beth as if she had physically struck him. "They did?"

She nodded.

"Really?"

"Joe, that was over twenty years ago. They didn't know how wonderful you were then – they do now, sweetheart and they love you."

"Well, well, your parents didn't approve of me?" Joe said with a benign smile. "All this time I thought they liked me." He then roared with laughter. "And you fought them for me? What I would've given to have seen that little piece of theatre!"

"Yes, I did and I don't want Bonnie to feel towards us the rage I felt towards Mum and Dad – it was horrible, Joe. I screamed at them, even said I hated them and then I ignored them for weeks afterwards."

Joe's eyes widened in disbelief and then immediately softened. "But you didn't mean it".

"That's just it, Joe, I did. I meant every word I said at the time. I honestly did, Joe. I loved you that much."

"What changed their minds?"

Beth shrugged." I don't really know for sure." She paused. "Perhaps my freezing them out of my life," Beth said reaching for Joe's hand. "I'm so glad I fought for you, otherwise," she laughed provocatively, teasing him as she often did, "You, my handsome husband, wouldn't be enjoying this blissful life with your wonderful wife."

Joe laughed out loud as he got up from his chair and kissed the top of her head, "Coffee?"

Beth's tantalizing smile in response to his question still made him tremble with excitement; his deep blue eyes sparkled at the sight of her. The magic was still there, even after twenty-two years of marriage. They were a rare and exceptional couple to outsiders, the envy of their friends. Their secret was simple – they truly loved each other and not a day passed without each of them showing just how much. They also kept the vows they made to each other on their wedding day; to honour, respect and to trust one another.

On his way to the kitchen, Joe called out, "By the way, darling," trying to harness his laughter, "Who was their first choice?"

Beth grinned to herself and called back, "Paul Jeffrey." She waited for a sarcastic retort, which he was entitled to.

"Ah huh," Joe said, thinking that name was familiar. "Hey, wait a minute," he said with a certain amount of satisfaction, "didn't he end up in Boys Town and then graduated to Boggo Road Prison?"

Bonnie left the house in the early morning light and headed straight for Wynnum Creek, hoping to see Gabe before she started work. Well before arriving at the creek, she could hear the commotion the mariners made maintaining their boats. She could visualise their cracked dry hands diligently mending nets and their weather-beaten faces roasting in the morning sun. She even imagined hearing Gabe's voice above them all.

The sun, which by mid-morning would be mercilessly biting into their backs, rose slowly, illuminating the creek crammed with boats. Squawking seagulls glided above, searching for food over fishing nets splayed for inspection by the old salts. Although Bonnie was awestruck by the beauty of the landscape, she could not stop thinking of how the pungent smell of fetid fish made her feel ill. She could never bring herself to consume fish or any animal for that matter.

Upon arriving at the creek, Bonnie lifted her hand to shield her eyes from the glare bouncing off the water that now resembled liquid silver. Looking in the direction of the Lusty Lady, she was surprised to find Gabe waving to attract her attention. She waved back and they hurried toward each other, instinctively knowing they were destined to be together even though they scarcely knew each other. Bonnie's smile sent a surge of love through him. Gabe reached for her hand and held it gently as the warm breeze ruffled her hair, fine as cobwebs.

"You knew I'd be here, didn't you?" she said, with the same certainty he had.

"Yep," he replied feeling a new hope for the future.

"Can you dance?"

Gabe looked at Bonnie as if she had asked a trick question with the wrong answer ending everything between them, but he decided not to lie.

"Not a step," he said and waited for the axe to fall.

She giggled playfully, rose on her tip-toes and kissed him lightly on the lips, then dashed away laughing, running straight into a hawker selling fish to a customer.

"Oh, excuse me", she said politely to the back of the bent-over local, then recoiled and discreetly covered her nose with her linen handkerchief. The man's tattered, bloodstained shirt and battered old hat had definitely seen better days.

He glanced over his shoulder and gave her a lopsided, gummy smile,

"Ya' right missy," he mumbled, through shrivelled lips clasping a roll-your-own.

"Rebecca!" Bonnie yelled with delight when she spotted her friend in the crowd. "It's been ages, how are you?"

"Hey girl, what are you doin' here so early, and on your own?"

Bonnie looked over her shoulder at Gabe walking back to the boat.

"Ah, gee Bonnie, that one's trouble ... heard lots of stories about him ... not good ones, either."

Contrary to Rebecca's ominous warning, it had resonated with Bonnie that every boy she had met in the past paled in comparison to Gabe. Even Oliver Walker, the best-looking boy in the area, according to him, who had tagged Bonnie as *his* from kindergarten.

"Enough about me, sweetie, what's the latest with you?"

Rebecca shrugged nonchalantly and said, "They're sending me up north to a home for girls. I'll have the kid there – dunno what I'll do after that."

Rebecca hated herself for lying to her dearest friend. She was forbidden to tell anyone she would be secretly working as a house-help for a wealthy local family until the baby was born at St Kilda hospital at Wynnum.

Bonnie reached for Rebecca's hand and squeezed it gently.

"You'll come back here, of course – won't you? We're going to art school together. You haven't forgotten our plans, our dreams – have you?"

"Nah," Rebecca replied flatly, "but all that'll have to be put on hold for a while." When her dark, tear filled-eyes overflowed, Bonnie quickly pulled a spare lace handkerchief from her pocket and handed it to her friend. Rebecca laughed as she dried her eyes. "Ya must have a million of these and ... and I bet I've at least half of 'em in me drawer at home".

"I'll miss you, Rebecca," Bonnie said, fighting back her own tears. "Keep them, so you won't forget me".

"That'll never happen, Bonnie. You're the best friend I got."

"Write to me, won't you?"

"Nah, won't be allowed. Maybe I'll see ya when I get back."

Critical eyes and furrowed brows observed Bonnie hugging Rebecca. She ignored their judgemental stares, feeling a tad sorry for the ignorant onlookers for not knowing her childhood friend as well as she did. Their prejudice and preconceived assumptions failed to recognised Rebecca's significance and her gentle nature. They were unaware of the talent that could one day propel her into the art world as a highly respected and much-admired indigenous artist. They only saw a half-caste Aboriginal girl.

As Bonnie ran to the cake shop, guilt tore at her heart for being ecstatic about having Gabe in her life when Rebecca was so unhappy. Paul, Rebecca's boyfriend, desperately wanted to marry her but neither of their parents would allow the interracial marriage to take place. Paul was forbidden to see Rebecca. Since he lacked the courage to stand up to his parents, he agreed to whatever they said, with the belief that it was best for everyone, especially for Rebecca. Six months later, Paul was fighting in Vietnam.

4

From the foreshore, Gabe watched the sun slowly rise and for a brief moment in time, night and day were the same, before the golden orb rose higher and brighter above the horizon, fetching a brand new day. He hated the darkness with its eerie sounds and shadows lurking in his dreams. He envied the freedom of the birds gliding above. For that moment he wished he could fly too, to escape the nightmares that haunted him in his sleep. The sounds of the lash tearing his healthy, young skin to pieces – the terror of having to lie naked in a bath while his father tipped buckets of ice cubes on top of him – the harshness in the voice of the person who was supposed to protect and love him, screaming at him not to cry.

"Only cowards cry!" the deranged father shrieked into the petrified face of his seven-year-old son. His mother stood by, watching her son's suffering with deadpan eyes. Then one night it was all over; both parents were found dead at the bottom of the stairs with severe head injuries and the child was taken into care. The report said: *Accidental death: slipped on an oil spill.*

Gulls squawked above, snapping Gabe away from the past to Bonnie and their first impending date. The image of her as his sweetheart and the idea of them spending the rest of their lives together lifted his spirits.

Joe answered the knock at the door. Although he was expecting Gabe, Joe openly gasped, unprepared for how striking the lad was. Gabe dropped his head to hide his smile. His looks were often an advantage, but sometimes a disadvantage; tonight he hoped it would be an advantage.

He had planned to turn on his genuine charm to disarm Bonnie's potentially hostile parents.

Beth came to the door and stood beside Joe. "Come in, Gabe, she said warmly, extending her small hand to him. "I'm Beth Mason and the statue beside me is my husband, Joe. She paused and looked at Gabe. "My, my, you're a handsome lad. Bonnie forgot to mention that," she said, honestly.

Gabe looked Beth squarely in the eyes and to his relief, saw a warm, friendly, attractive woman, welcoming a guest into her home. This was no provocative 'come on' as he had usually been offered from mothers of past girlfriends since he was a thirteen-year-old. Their overly made-up faces and heavily perfumed, sensual bodies repulsed him, yet he had never once resisted any of them. He took what they offered with vengeance, shooting the tall, muscular youngster into premature manhood. He embraced every temptation with gusto, allowing himself to be waylaid by women of all ages. They tenderly caressed his scars, murmuring promises of eternal love. Their vanity and ignorance led them to believe that their infatuation was reciprocated, which drove his passion to anger as his exquisite frame loomed above them, thrusting violently, possessing them. His beauty and his body were the instruments he used to survive whenever he needed to – everyone wanted a piece of him, even men. He knew what was behind their sly grins. No place was safe for him!

Gabe took Beth's hand briefly and said, just as Bonnie entered the room, "Nice to meet you, Mrs Mason and you too, Mr Mason."

"Looks like everyone has met," Bonnie said cheerfully, assessing the mood in the room as pleasant. "Well then, we had better choof off, otherwise we'll miss the newsreel."

Just as they were leaving, Gabe turned to Joe and Beth and said, "You won't ever have to worry about Bonnie. She's safe with me. I'll protect her with my life."

The young couple walked hand in hand along Kingsley Terrace to the Imperial Picture Theatre, occasionally glancing at one another just to make sure they were not dreaming.

"I like your parents; they seem really cool."

"I'm glad, so do I," said Bonnie, smiling mischievously. "They're the greatest!"

A dull roar in the distance from behind became louder. They stopped talking and turned around. Oliver Walker and four of his Bodgie mates, attired in black leather and greasy-looking hair plastered down with Brylcreem, pulled on to the shoulder of the road. The bikers parked in a row, revving their Harleys, whistling and hollering like menacing school boys. Gabe put a protective arm around Bonnie and told her to ignore them and to keep walking. The bikers followed slowly behind, heckling them.

"Whatcha doin' with me girl?" Oliver shouted to Gabe over the Harley's engine.

"Juicy ain't she?" he said, laughing and making disgusting sounds.

Gabe whispered to Bonnie to keep walking before he casually stepped off the footpath to walk alongside Oliver.

"Apologise to my lady," he said.

"Or what?" Oliver snarled.

"Or this." Gabe suddenly ripped Oliver from his bike. The engine roared and then fell silent. The Harley went crashing to the ground. Gabe's vice-like grip on Oliver tore his leather jacket from its seams when he lifted him high enough above the ground for his feet to dangle in mid-air.

"Apologise!" Gabe instructed. Oliver obeyed, but with attitude.

"Again," said Gabe, shaking him. "And mean it this time!"

The other misfits said nothing, inwardly jubilant that someone had finally gotten the better of Oliver Walker, the rich kid with the cool toys and jammy lifestyle – cricket set, football, Meccano set and board games. If he did not win the game, he would storm off and take his toys home. To appease Oliver, the kids let him win everything, just to keep the games going.

"I'm sorry, Bonnie." Oliver whimpered, shrivelling in fear. Disgusted, Gabe threw Oliver aside. He then moved over to Bonnie, took her by the hand, and they went on their way as if nothing had happened.

"Aah ha! He's pissed himself!" One of the Bodgies laughed hysterically, pointing to the wet patch on the ground.

"Not so tough now ... eh, Walker?" One of them yelled as they roared off down the street, disappearing in a cloud of dust.

Oliver Walker stood alone by the side of the road, humiliated to the core, vowing revenge on all of them.

When Bill Walker saw his son ride up the driveway, his facial features twisted in utter disgust.

"What happened to you?" he barked, devoid of any compassion.

After Oliver told his version of events, Bill Walker paled with fury. He turned around and stormed into the house, to his study. Oliver followed closely behind. He watched his father snatch the heavy black receiver from its cradle and dial a number he often called. Bill waited a moment before barking instruction down the mouthpiece. Just before he finished the call he said, "... you tell those bastards they won't see daylight if they ever utter one word to anyone about what happened tonight ... And, as for that bloody fisherman, I want him. "

"Dad, no Dad," Oliver interrupted. "He's mine."

Bill Walker looked up at his son and sneered. The closest he came to smiling. He nodded his approval then spoke to the person on the phone. "We've got the fisherman covered," then dropped the receiver in its cradle.

"Well son, I think it's time you took a long holiday."

5

The rest of the walk to the Imperial was made in silence. Gabe was concerned his behaviour had frightened Bonnie and she might not want to see him after tonight.

Bonnie was annoyed with Gabe, not about the way he handled Oliver, but for telling him to apologise to *his* lady.

Gabe bought their tickets, a box of Allen's Fantales, Jaffa's and two small bottles of Coca-Cola and then gently ushered Bonnie inside the theatre to seats in the back row. Once they were settled Gabe handed Bonnie the boxes of sweets.

She smiled at his thoughtfulness, and then asked intonation of surprise, "How did you know I like Fantales and Jaffa's?"

Gabe knew that confessing that every girl he had taken to the pictures in the past had loved Fantales and enjoyed reading about the movie stars careers that were written on the wrappers, this would surely be disastrous, so he shrugged and smiled, "Just guessed".

"I'm sorry about the way I acted with that drongo," Gabe said in earnest, wanting to put things right between them, "but he had it coming. No one gets away with insulting *my* lady."

'There, he said it again,' she thought, getting upset. "I didn't know I was *your* lady," she said with a twang of irritation. "You should have asked me first. I might not want to be *your* lady. You're taking me for granted, Gabe, and that's not cool!"

Although she knew they were destined to be together, Bonnie found it frustrating that Gabe was so sure of himself – and of her. *'There has to be some sense of mystery and intrigue in a relationship,'* she supposed, *not predictability or easy come, easy go.'*

Gabe turned to look at Bonnie with mild amusement to confirm whether or not she was serious. The way she was sitting, ridged and upright and looking straight ahead, indicated that she was indeed very serious. He made an attempt to apologise. Then the lights started to dim and the heavy, red velvet curtains slowly parted. Bonnie put her index finger to her lips, silencing him.

The newsreel burst onto the screen with a loud fanfare, but Gabe's mind was focused only on Bonnie. He repeatedly glanced in her direction throughout the first feature, hoping she would smile at him or give him a sign to indicate he was forgiven. She intrigued him like no other woman ever had, to the point that he willingly accepted responsibility for the awkward situation he had somehow created. Slumped in his seat, Gabe took solace in the images of Bonnie that ran through his mind – the way she flicked her fine, silky hair and the way it shone in the sunlight and floated in the wind. The way her hips swayed when she walked. He loved her eyes and how they softened when she looked at him. He loved her smile and the melody in her laughter. He desperately wanted to take her in his arms right there and then and tell how he felt about her.

At interval, he tried apologising again. Bonnie stopped him by saying that she would rather enjoy the evening than get into a debate about something that could wait. She passed him the box of Fantales.

Gabe reluctantly resigned himself miserably to defeat and took an interest in the main feature, 'To Sir with Love.' It surprised him how attuned he was with the film in view of the way in which he currently lived his life.

On the way home Gabe said sincerely, "You make me want to be a better man, Bonnie."

She gave him a questioning look. Gabe drew in a long breath, so Bonnie stopped walking and turned to face him.

"Alright," she said placing her hand firmly on her hips and giving him her full attention. "You've got something to say, now here's your chance to say it."

"OK," Gabe said, clearing his throat. "From the moment I saw you," he began, jittery as a love-sick first grader. "I've regretted my past and wished it didn't exist, but I can't wipe the slate clean. What you witnessed earlier between me and that galoot is just the tip of the iceberg, Bonnie. I'm a criminal by nature. I mean, was a criminal. You'd be horrified at some of the things I've done. I've spent my life lying and covering up things a girl like you shouldn't know, couldn't even imagine people doing."

"Why are you telling me this?" she asked, confused. She sighed heavily, realising the pent-up frustration she was feeling. She let her arms fall to her sides when Gabe said, "Because I love you. And for the first time in my life, I want to tell the truth. That's a big deal, Bonnie. You're a big deal and the first decent girl ... no, *lady*, I know!"

"Well Gabe, for the record Oliver has had that coming to him for as long as I can remember. He's a bully! His father has always cleaned up his mess when he should've given him a damn good hiding. He's a nasty piece of work. He strikes from behind and he'll seek revenge, so you'd better watch out!"

"I can take care of myself."

"Well, if you say so. All the same, be careful. As for the other ..."

"I haven't finished yet."

"Do I really need to know? Can't I judge for myself who you really are?"

"I've got a lot of baggage, Bonnie ... nightmares and stuff. I don't sleep so good."

"Why?" There was compassion in her voice.

"My old man was a cruel bastard..."

Bonnie's eyes filled with tears as she listened to Gabe describe his childhood. She fumbled with her purse to get out a handkerchief. Gabe took it from her and tenderly wiped her eyes. "Mind if I keep this?" he asked when he had finished. Bonnie nodded. Gabe tucked the handkerchief in his pocket. "I'll keep it close to my heart, always," he smiled then continued. "Honestly Bonnie, I didn't give a damn about anyone. Every speck of emotion was sucked out of me. I survived the best way I could. Being moved around from one foster home to another like discarded garbage wasn't fun and all that stuff my father did to me as a kid swirls around in my head every night."

He paused as he ran his fingers through his hair. "I'm trying to get a handle on it. Sometimes I can. Thinking about you helps."

Gabe dropped his head to hide his tears and then looked pleadingly at her. "I don't know what I'd do without you, now that I've found you."

They stood under the streetlight facing each other. Bonnie said nothing, contemplating everything Gabe had just disclosed. His sincerity was genuine; she could see it in his eyes. She could see they could have a future together. He had totally surrendered himself to her.

She reached out and took his hand, whispering, "You'll never have to find that out."

6

While Bonnie planned her wedding, Rebecca flashed into her mind, as she so often had. She wondered if Rebecca would come home from wherever she was, to be her bridesmaid. With that thought in mind, Bonnie dialled Rebecca's home number. Her mother answered saying after pleasantries exchanged, that she did not know where Rebecca was, just that she had left Brisbane, but added before ending the call, "Bonnie, I think it's best to leave sleeping dogs lie."

A full-figured young woman stood by the window, staring blankly through sheer curtains the hot Darwin breeze forced into a slow waltz. A strip of sunlight fell across her sad face. The sound of her infant son's cries was firmly fixed in her mind, refusing to budge. As always, the image of the junior nurse wheeling baby cribs into the ward and stopping by her bed would soon follow. In her naivety, the nurse carefully lifted a squawking baby wrapped in a blue, light-weight cotton blanket from the crib and passed him to her.

"I'll be back in a moment to help you with feeding," said the nurse, looking over her shoulder, hurrying from the ward.

"But nurse, I'm ..." Rebecca shouted.

"I won't be long." The nurse called back. Curiosity urged Rebecca to unwrap the blanket. Her melancholy eyes lit up at the sight of the perfect little human lying there in front of her, wriggling and stretching. She smiled when he jammed his tiny fist into his mouth. What she felt at that moment, while studying her tiny son's face, was beyond words. As naturally as any mother would, Rebecca slid her long, elegant fingers underneath the tiny bundle and tenderly scooped him up into her arms. She hugged him, smelt him and whispered in his tiny ear that she would always love him, that she was sorry she could not take him home; to forgive her.

Then Matron came rushing into the ward just as Rebecca was about to put her baby to her breast. He screamed when the eye-popping, scarlet-faced matron shouted, "Oh no!" lunging forward and snatching her son out of her arms with the determination of a Rugby player repossessing the ball for a touchdown.

"You can't do much about the past, Rebecca, but you sure can do a hell of a lot about the future. It's up to you now, love."

Rebecca did not verbally respond to her auntie's remark. She was looking straight ahead at nothing in particular, her expression forlorn. Her brow folded into several shallow creases, considering her aunt's comment, concluding that her auntie was right. The future was hopeful. This reasoning dispelled the gloom that lingered in the corners of her mind to consume her every thought if she allowed it.

'I will indeed, have a future. Not the one Bonnie and I planned, but a future all the same that I will determine, without marriage or children. I'll concentrate on my art. I'll be a great artist! Anyway, happily-ever-after is unrealistic and childish. It isn't part of my destiny.'

7

Time and tide wait for no man. Two years slipped by without much notice. Gabe and Bonnie were happily married, doting on their six-month-old son Gabriel Joseph Connor – the delight of the whole family.

Daniel quietly waited and watched for the monster that he knew lurked within Gabe to surface. To the contrary, by all appearances, marriage to Bonnie had transformed Gabe into a quiet man.

Then one day, during one of their fishing trips Gabe surprised Daniel by handing him a key. "What's this for?"

"The room at the boardin' house, there's stuff in there I keep to remind myself what I could've become. If anything happens to me, you'll know what to do with it. I trust ya, mate."

"What, are ya gonna do a runner?" Daniel barked, feeling his temper rise.

Gabe remained calm and looked Daniel squarely in the eyes for a long moment then shook his head. "Nah mate," he said as if he had had an ominous premonition. "Ya just dunno what's comin' round the bend."

The tension that had set Daniel's nerves on edge slowly dissipated and he nodded in agreement. Without another word, he slipped the key onto his key ring.

Before the wedding, Joe and Gabe worked tirelessly together for many weeks to turn the family garage into comfortable living quarters for the pending newlyweds. By the time they had finished, the place resembled a two-bedroom cottage.

"It's only temporary," Gabe promised, feeling that his wife was worthy of much more. Bonnie was unfazed. She adored her new home and would have happily lived in a tent with Gabe, just as long as they were together. Every time Bonnie looked at her husband, she found something else about him to love; the way his eyes crinkled up at the corners when he smiled, the way his whole face lit up whenever he looked at her. Their joy in each other was long-lasting. She took great comfort in how Gabe's love for her was reflected in his eyes.

Bonnie had no idea Gabe was concealing his insecurities at the thought of losing her. That he felt unworthy of her, fearing that his wonderful world would explode like a vulnerable bubble at any moment. On the surface, he remained confident and witty, in spite of his struggle with terrifying dreams and sleeplessness. Some nights were worse than others. Bonnie was always there to support and comfort him through the worst of it. What Gabe had suffered as a young child was so horrific and incomprehensible to ordinary people; Bonnie doubted the authorities would understand that his pouring oil on the steps, which caused his parents death, was the desperation of a young boy's self-defence. She also realised that Gabe would trust no one other than herself with his secrets.

The moon was full. It seemed brighter than usual that night, spilling shards of light through the sheer curtains onto Gabe's face while he slept. Tiny beads of perspiration played hopscotch, sliding down his face, freefalling onto the pillow when he tossed and turned, battling his demons. By the time Bonnie shook him gently awake he was drenched and momentarily disoriented. When fully aware of his surroundings, he rolled over and pulled Bonnie into his arms, clinging to her, apologising.

"Sssh ... it's OK, darling," Bonnie whispered.

She gently rocked him, humming a lullaby. Within minutes she could feel the tension in his body subside and then he came alive with a renewed urgency that neither could resist. She felt intoxicated, breathing in his salty scent, mingled with Sunlight soap and Old Spice aftershave.

She melted deeper into his embrace. They floated off to their paradise the moment their lips touched.

They lay together wrapped in each other's arms in the moonlight, utterly spent and completely satisfied physically and emotionally, until Gabe slid his arm from under Bonnie shoulders. She grabbed hold of him.

"Where are you going?" There was an unusual smattering of panic in her voice.

"I've got to clear my head, sweetheart. I'm going down to the foreshore."

Bonnie sat up to check the clock on the bedside table. It was two in the morning.

"It's so late and it'll be really cold outside by now," she said, feeling apprehensive even though he had often walked the foreshore at night.

"I know darling," he said, stepping into his pants. He moved slowly towards the bed as he did up the last button on his shirt. He bent down to kiss her on the cheek. "I won't be long," he said. "The walk will do me good."

"Now, you can do better than that," Bonnie said, in a sultry voice with outstretched arms, hoping to persuade him to stay. Gabe came back and stood beside the bed looking down at her. He smiled. Then knelt down and scooped her up into his arms. He kissed her long and hard and then gently laid her head back down on the pillow. He stood up and moved slowly towards the bedroom door. As he turned to leave, he looked back over his shoulder and said, "You're the joy of my life, Bonnie. I've never in my life loved anyone, but I love you, completely." And then he was gone.

Bonnie sat up quickly and threw back the bedcovers. She scurried out of the bedroom, grabbing her dressing gown on the way. She struggled while putting it on, slowing her down. She wanted to plead with him not to go, only to arrive at the door just in time to see him walking down the driveway. Her heart sank. She could not go after him; the baby was asleep in his cot.

The chilled air stung Gabe's nostrils as it flowed through the airways. He shivered, feeling colder than he had in a long while. He pulled the collar of his leather jacket up around his ears. '*Bonnie was right,*' he thought, '*It is bloody cold!*' He smiled to himself. '*But then, again she's right about most things!*'

He carried on walking in spite of the weather. The streets felt oddly eerie. Layers of mist hung in the air like a sheer, dirty curtain. The moonlight casting elongated shadows around the trees lining the street didn't help much either. A cat ran out from underneath bushes in one of the neighbour's gardens. It screamed as it crossed his path, startling him enough to cause every hair on his body to stand on end. He laughed out loud to settle his nerves.

At that moment, Gabe craved the cigarettes he had given up after he had met Bonnie, along with all his other vices – *booze, drugs and skirt!* He felt a smidgeon of pride when he thought about how easily he had changed for her. '*It's not too hard to be a good person for the one you love.* He thought. '*My lady deserves the best! I'm one lucky bastard.*' He shook his head in disbelief. '*Now, who would've ever thought a crook like me would ever end up scoring gold? Not me, that's for sure. Crikey, all that stuff I did in Sydney years ago seems surreal: like some other bloke did it. Anyway, I don't think I've got it in me now. All that rough shit's for losers. Bloody hell, I got away with murder. I should be in the lockup. But I'm not. I'm here, married and I have a kid. Never in my life did I ever think I'd be a dad – never! Gabriel's a great little mate and when he's old enough I'll take him fishing and do all the stuff that dads do with their kids. I have to get a handle on my bloody fear of holding him. Hell, it's a struggle! Bonnie keeps tellin' me I'm not my father. But what if I am? What if I lose it one day when Gabriel does something wrong? What if I beat the crap out of him the way my shit of a father did to me? Eh? What then?'* Gabe shook his head in shame for letting doubt creep in. *'Bonnie's right!'* He declared looking for something positive to cling to, *'I'm nothing like that bastard. She wouldn't have a bar of me if I was. I have to trust her judgement. I have to!'*

Gabe was feeling better by the time he had reached Wynnum Creek, even though he thought it odd how the mist had turned into a thick fog, distorting everything around him. The smell of fish and diesel fumes from the boat engines seemed repugnant to his senses. *'Strange,'* he thought, *'I've never noticed that stink before.'*

Wynnum Creek was peaceful. The gentle sound of water slapping the sides of the moored boats lulled him into a false sense of security. A loud splashing noise came from the concrete slab where the boats unloaded the fish. Gabe went to investigate. As he was about to look over the edge, he felt a sudden, excruciating, explosion of pain in his head that forced him to the ground. *'What happened? I can't move.'*

Someone was leaning over him. He could not make out who it was. The blow to his head had fuzzed his mind. Whoever it was had turned him over. They rifled through his clothing and took something from his jacket.

'Hey, you bastard, I'll get you for this!' he yelled, scrambling to his feet. Confused as to what had just happened, Gabe dusted himself off, shook his limbs and then ran his hands through his hair and down the back of his head. He expected to find some sort of injury. There was none. He was perfectly fine.

Gabe's eyes expanded as wide as dinner plates. He was shocked to discover a man's body lying at his feet. His skull was crushed and covered with a glossy liquid. He squinted, focusing to look through the fog to see if someone was still there. No one was in sight so he knelt down beside the body to feel for a pulse. He recoiled upwards from the sickly-sweet smell of blood and stumbled backwards in horror. Gabe's ghost was looking down at his own lifeless body.

8

Bonnie froze. Her heart filled with dread when she heard the sound of a car moving slowly up the driveway. She stared, with terror-filled eyes at the front door, reluctant to answer the determined knock. The commotion woke Gabriel. He began crying. She wanted to go to her son but knew she should answer the door before the person knocking disturbed the whole neighbourhood. Her hands trembled as she unlatched the lock. She was about to tell whoever it was that she had to attend to her baby, but her words dried up at the sight of two police constables. She simply stepped aside for them to enter her home.

The three of them stood in the middle of the lounge room in awkward silence until Constable Brady said, "Bonnie would you like to fix up the little fella first?" She nodded and then rushed to Gabriel's room. From there she heard the screen door bang and her father's voice. He was talking to the officers, then nothing, just an eerie silence.

Bonnie changed Gabriel's nappy at lightning speed. She gathered him up in her arms and hugged him tightly. She turned towards the door and then stopped. Joe was standing in the doorway. His expression confirmed her worst fears. The breath within her drained away, as though life was being sucked out of her body. Joe lunged forward and caught Gabriel before Bonnie fell to the floor sobbing.

9

The telephone rang for several minutes before Daniel and his wife Kay stirred. They were both sound sleepers and had often joked that it would take an earthquake to wake them in an emergency. Groggy from sleep, Daniel fumbled around in the dark for the light switch. He picked up the receiver and held it to his ear, but all he could hear was a distorted voice talking too fast to comprehend what the caller was saying.

"Hang on, hang on!" Daniel yelled down the mouthpiece, elbowing himself upright to lean against the headboard. He cleared his throat and then said, "OK. Now, who is it?"

"Daniel, it's me, Joe ..."

As Daniel listened, he was shocked, but lucid enough to realise he had to get to the boarding house in a mighty hurry, without being seen. As soon as the call ended, he dressed, quietly left his home and ran the two streets to the boarding house. Daniel knew Mrs Mac, the owner of the boarding house, was visiting her daughter who had just given birth to twin boys and would not be back for a few more days. He knew this as Kay usually kept him updated with the latest gossip and goings on around the area.

Kay was thrilled for Mrs Mac and for any new mother and their babies. Daniel and Kay's baby was stillborn. Kay accepted without question that she would never be a mother but was content to fuss over her friend's children and to love them as though they were her own, to be the willing babysitter for whoever needed her.

When Daniel arrived, he let himself into the boarding house. It was never locked due to the regular comings and goings of houseguests. He opened the door marked C, using the key that Gabe had given him several months prior. The blind was drawn when he entered the dark, musty smelling room so he raised it to let the streetlight shine in. Gabe had often complained about the brightness of the light keeping him awake at night. Daniel had thought about opening the window as well and then decided against it. It took a few moments for his eyes to get accustomed to the dim light. After a while, he regretted that he could see so well.

A number of photographs were pinned on the wall. The sight of a sadistic bastard's chronicle of brutal child torture had Daniel retching from shock. The face of the four or five-year-old was contorted in what must have been agonizing pain, judging by the scene in the photographs, but his beauty was clearly visible. The child was readily recognisable as Gabe.

Daniel held his head in his hands and cried shamelessly at his first encounter with such diabolical evil that he could never have imagined existed. Harnessing his anger, he pulled himself together and snatched the rest of the photographs from the wall without looking at them. The few he saw was all he could psychologically endure for one lifetime. That night Daniel had encountered horror beyond belief. He realised he had also encountered the power of extraordinary love recalling Gabe's cryptic words the day he said, *'What's in that room, I could've become.'* At the time of their conversation, Daniel had no idea what Gabe had meant. Now he understood. Gabe was telling him that Bonnie was his saving grace. He loved her enough to reinvent himself into the man she deserved. Daniel was determined to preserve the memory of the man Gabe had become. He destroyed all evidence of Gabe's tormented past.

10

The police were still at the house when Gabe returned home. He ran inside searching for Bonnie, calling her name, but there was no response. He followed the sound of voices coming from Gabriel's room. Joe was gently rocking young Gabriel back and forth to settle him while Constable Brady was lifting Bonnie from the floor.

He carried her to the room Joe indicated.

After Constable Brady laid Bonnie on the bed, he looked at Joe as he left the room. "A word, when you have a minute?"

Joe nodded.

Gabe crawled onto the bed beside Bonnie. She lifted her head from the pillow to look over her shoulder where Gabe was lying. "Gabe?"

Joe's eyes filled with tears when he heard Bonnie. He wiped his eyes.

"Gabe's dead, honey," he said softly, feeling utterly useless. He wished he had woken Beth before leaving the house. "Can I get you something, sweetheart?"

"No thanks, Dad. Where's Mum?"

"Right here, darling. Joe, Officer Brady would like to talk with you if you're up to it."

"Ok, but I'm not sure what I can tell him. I'm as dumbfounded about all of this as he is."

"He might be able to tell you something."

"Yeah, you could be right. Sorry sweetheart. I'm not thinking straight, Gabe going like that has thrown me. I was getting used to having him around. He seemed more like a son, I guess."

Beth reached for Joe. She wrapped her arms around him and hugged him tightly. She kissed him lightly on the cheek when she noticed tears in his eyes.

"I'm OK, love," he said, shaking himself. Beth released him. Joe slowly backed out of the room. "I'll see what I can find out."

"Poor Daddy," Bonnie said.

"Poor Daddy?" Beth responded in surprise.

"Darling, you've just lost your husband."

"I know, Mum, it's bizarre. I don't know how to explain it, except that when I first heard the news, it was as if the world had exploded in my face and there was nothing left for me to live for, but now ... I don't how, but that dread has gone. I know I should be beside myself with grief. I'm not, because it feels as though Gabe's here with me, even though I can't see him or touch him or even hear him. I certainly can sense his presence."

Beth sat at the foot of Bonnie's bed studying her face. There was no sign of grief reflected in her eyes. Beth thought it was extraordinary given that Bonnie loved Gabe so deeply.

Bonnie caught her mother watching her. She smiled and then said, "I know what you must be thinking, Mum. I'm not delusional. I am perfectly fine."

Bonnie turned her face towards the window. "Look, it's almost daylight, another new day. Daniel and Gabe won't be fishing today or ever again. I'm sad about that. I'm sad that I won't ever see Gabe or hold him in my arms again, but I am grateful to be able to sense his spirit around me. I am happy about that."

Beth was about to respond to Bonnie when Joe came back and stood in the doorway. He looked dazed. His voice trembled with emotion when he said, "Gabe was murdered!"

11

Gabe lingered at the entrance of the church, watching the mourners take their seats in the pews. He was impressed that so many people had come to pay their respects. He was surprised to hear that he was so well liked; *a changed man, loving husband, good bloke,* he heard people say, as he moved deftly among them. It also pleased him to know that Bonnie could hold her head high in the community since he was not considered a *bum* in their eyes. However, there are always the minority curiosity-seekers and gossip-mongers perched in the crowd, taking a morbid delight in people's misfortune. People such as the town's social climbers, Beryl Naed and her offsider, Gladys Lock.

Both women watched with greedy eyes, hungrily scrutinising Bonnie and her family in readiness to fire off whispers of any wrongdoing in all directions, should, heaven forbid, any of them happen to err.

As the grieved family walked up to the front pew, Beryl was quick to notice that Bonnie did not seem to be despairing. She knocked Gladys with her elbow. "Look," she whispered to her friend, "Bonnie looks as fresh as a daisy. Huh! One would have thought that that girl would've been sedated, or something. She could have at least pretended to be grieving."

"Look, look, Gladys, she's smiling," Beryl gasped.

"Huh," Gladys replied in a whisper, "the love of her life indeed! What was all that about? They're supposed to have been the perfect couple? Well, if you ask me there's nothing perfect about them. If she really loved her husband ..."

Gabe stood beside the two women, slowly simmering while listening to every word they uttered. Gladys' comment was the last straw so he slapped her. Hard! She yelped loudly on impact, loud enough to turn heads as her hand shot up to soothe the sting biting the side of her face. Shuffling in her seat, she was unsure of where to look as puzzled eyes stared at her. She smiled awkwardly at them and then hissed at Beryl, "Why the hell did you hit me?"

Beryl was horrified at her friend's accusation. She angrily spun sideways to face Gladys. "How dare you!" she whispered between clenched teeth. "Never in my life have I struck anybody."

Beryl was about to say more, but the sight of her friend's inflamed cheek silenced her. She leaned in closer for a better look. "Ha! The mark is on the other cheek so how could I've slapped you?" She then realised what she had said. "There *is* a red mark on your cheek ... oh, you poor darling! Who could have done such a dreadful thing?"

They both looked sideways and around them. No one was close enough to strike her. Beryl, who relished in melodramatics, said to Gladys, who was still rubbing the side of her face, "Do you suppose Gabe's ghost is here?"

"Oh, now that is ridiculous. If that were true, why would he hit me and not you as well?"

Beryl sat erect in a poised, regal position looking sideways at her friend, replied in her usual haughty intonation. "Well, my dear, dare I say it? But you can be very nasty at times."

Gladys' face turned crimson with rage. She was about to give Beryl a piece of her mind when the service started. The congregation stood at the Pastor's bidding, which gave Gladys the opportunity to shunt Beryl out of the pew. She fell flat on her face onto the floor. Gladys quickly assisted Beryl to her feet and back into the pew.

"Oh dear," Gladys cooed, saying loud enough for those within earshot to hear. "Not steady on our feet today, are we darling? Still, on the wine, I see. She moved closer and whispered in Beryl's ear, "Unlike you my dear," Gladys smirked, "I've thumped many a bully in the past."

The funeral service was short and simple at Bonnie's request, just as Gabe would have wanted it. He would have also wanted the wake to be at Fisher's Pub, where everyone headed afterwards.

Several people commented that they had noticed Bonnie was taking Gabe's death better than expected. Bonnie was quick to respond, saying that it did not feel as though Gabe was gone. She could feel his presence around her.

Beryl and Gladys overheard Bonnie. They looked wide-eyed at each other and shuddered.

"It was him!" Beryl muttered from the side of her mouth.

"Don't you utter one word to anyone either or people will think you're bonkers." Gladys cautioned.

12

Several weeks after the funeral, Constable Brady paid Bonnie an informal visit at her home with an update of the investigation into Gabe's death. He was very apologetic that the investigation was not gaining momentum. "It's actually stagnating," Brady said. "Homicide did not find anything substantial. They haven't found anything at all, to be honest, Bonnie."

Bonnie was pensive but alert, absorbing every word Brady said. There was something troubling her, so she asked him if all of Gabe's belongings had been returned to her? "Was anything kept for forensic testing?"

Brady looked puzzled. "No Bonnie, why do you ask?"

Shrugging her shoulders nonchalantly she said, "I was just wondering." She paused, considering whether or not to confide in him and then decided that she wouldn't. "Umm, it's nothing," she finally said, shaking her head. Don't worry about it."

"Look, Bonnie," Brady began with an edge of authority in his voice and then softened his tone. "If, if you know something, anything at all, that will help us catch the person who killed Gabe, you must tell me."

As Brady was speaking, Bonnie's attention had drifted; she was listening to what she imagined were her own thoughts. Gabe was standing behind her whispering in her ear. *'Don't say anything. Say you made a mistake. That your mind is still foggy with all that's happened.'*

When she failed to respond to Brady, he worried that perhaps his asking so many questions was upsetting for her. "Bonnie, are you OK?" he asked with a note of concern, gently touching her arm.

"Pardon? Yes, yes. I'm fine. I was just thinking that perhaps I've made a mistake. My mind is still a bit foggy."

"OK then," Brady said, with a twinge of doubt. "But if anything comes to mind, call me." Bonnie nodded.

Beth thought she would spend the morning with Bonnie while Gabriel had his nap. When she saw Constable Brady leaving, she waved to him. "Any news?" she asked, feeling hopeful. Brady just shook his head, waved back and continued on his way.

"Knock, knock," Beth said in a low voice. She opened the screen door and popped her head inside. "Is the little man asleep, love?"

Bonnie heard her mother as she came out of Gabriel's room. She put a finger to her lips waving her inside. "I've just put him down," Bonnie whispered back. "He should be asleep in a few minutes. Tea?"

Beth nodded and made herself comfortable on the couch and watched her daughter pour cold water from the tap into the electric jug and switch it on. She reached up, took two cups and two saucers from the cupboard and put them on a tray, and then grabbed a couple of Iced VoVos from the jar sitting on the bench. "What are your plans for the future, darling?"

Bonnie carried the tea-tray over to the lounge, to where her mother was sitting and handed her a cup and saucer in silence before she sat down. She then offered her the plate of biscuits. Beth took one, slipped it on the side of her saucer and left it untouched, waiting for Bonnie to say something.

Gabe was telling Bonnie that it was time she made plans and that she should listen to her mother.

With a heavy sigh, Bonnie picked up her cup and took a sip "You're right, Mum," she finally said, "I do have to think about the future. But of course, none of it can happen without your and Dad's help. Art school is at the top of my list, but I'll still need to get a part-time job."

When Bonnie outlined the plans she had in mind for herself and Gabriel, Beth's eyebrows shot up in surprise and in absolute delight. They continued discussing things for well over an hour.

Beth jumped up from the couch when she heard Gabriel crying. "C'mon love," she said, clapping her hands together, "We're going to Reedman's after you feed and change Gabriel. I want to buy you the prettiest fabric they have, to make you a couple of outfits to wear to art school. I bought some lovely patterns the other day ..."

As mother and daughter ambled along Bay Terrace, pushing Gabriel in his pram, a woman Beth knew only as an acquaintance hurried past, dragging her barefooted and bedraggled child behind her.

"C'mon!" the woman hissed at the little boy.

When Bonnie saw him, she caught her breath. Even through the dirty smudges on his face, she could easily recognise Rebecca's sad black eyes and thick ebony lashes. Beth turned towards Bonnie and placed a protective hand on her arm. "What is it, love? You look as if you've seen a ghost." Bonnie shook herself in disbelief.

"I might have, Mum. That child looks like Rebecca. But it can't be." She paused. "Rebecca had her baby somewhere up north." Confused and exhausted with past events, Bonnie released a heavy sigh. "Oh, I don't know Mum. I guess I'm just missing Rebecca. I wish I knew where she was, and if she is alright."

"Well love, the child is adopted. The Osborne's got him when he was just a few weeks old. Timmy is a dear little fella. Oh, but I do feel sorry for the poor little pet."

"Why?" Bonnie asked concerned.

"Mary, Mrs Osborne isn't well. Losing too many babies to miscarriages and not being able to have her own child has changed her. Sadly, she's taken to drinking."

"What about her husband? Is he helping her?"

"Ha!" Beth laughed sarcastically. "He's nothing like your father, love. Most men are hopeless when it comes to understanding their wives. Russ Osborne is just like the rest of them." Beth shook her head and then said in a kinder tone. "Oh, he means well, and he is kind enough. But really, he isn't much help to Mary. I shouldn't be too hard on the man, he is good to Timmy."

"Does Mrs Osborne have any friends?"

Beth shook her head. "She keeps to herself. You saw how she dropped her head and hurried past us without a word. That's how she is these days so we don't interfere in her business. It's rather sad ... especially for little Timmy."

Mary Osborne hurried along Bay Terrace, eager to put distance between her and the community, shrivelling in shame for ignoring Beth Mason the way she had. Mary chastised herself, *'You cannot be doing that to good people like her. But I cannot help it!'* she argued with herself. *'I'm not right in the head. I'm sick. I need a drink.'*

Timmy was struggling to keep his little legs at a steady pace with his mother's gait. "Mummy... Mummy stop!" he pleaded, but she only responded with a yank on his arm. "C'mon, we're almost home," she snapped back, increasing her stride.

The moment Mary reached her back door she pushed it open with such force that it slammed against the wall with a loud thud. The few groceries she carried were carelessly dropped at the entrance as she made a dash for the cupboard containing the alcohol that eased her heartache.

Timmy stood in the doorway in silence, watching his mother greedily drinking her medicine. When finished,

Mary sprawled herself across the table. Timmy bent down and picked up the groceries one at a time. He walked over to the sink, stood on tip-toes and slid each item, one at a time, onto the bench. He was very careful not to knock any of the dirty dishes into the sink, trying to avoid getting another thrashing from his mother.

Mary lifted her heavy head to speak to him. Although her words were incoherent, the four and a half-year-old's heart was filled with compassion. He went to his mother's side and gently patted her on the head, telling her that he loved her. Silent tears streamed down his sweet, forgiving, grubby face. Mary looked at Timmy through an alcoholic haze with resentment, wondering why she was given another woman's cast off, instead of being allowed to have her own child. She hated God. She hated the world for his unfairness directed at her. Mary felt Timmy's hand on her head. She wanted to push him away, but was too incapacitated to move. She resented being held captive to his tenderness.

Timmy left Mary where she had passed out, went outside as usual and plonked himself down on the top step of the back porch. He waited patiently for her to regain consciousness. His head was buried deep in his hands.

Jean Ryan looked out of her kitchen window and saw Timmy sitting there. She put down the knife she was using to peel the potatoes for the evening meal. Wiping her hands on her apron, she went out to her back fence.

"Timmy," she called softly. He looked up, his eyes lighting up with a sweet smile that always melted Jean Ryan's heart. She waved him over. Timmy jumped up and ran to the fence.

"Where's Mummy, darling?" Jean asked.

"Sleeping," he said.

"Well, how about you come inside and have one of my patty cakes. Perhaps two," she winked, when Timmy's dark eyes lit up like headlights. "C'mon," she smiled lovingly at him and pushed the two loose palings aside for him to climb through.

Timmy was familiar with Jean's rules. He asked to go to the bathroom to wash his hands. Jean nodded and he sprinted off farther into the house. As she opened the cake tin, Jean called out to him. "While you're at it, you might want to run the washer over that cheeky face of yours as well."

Seconds later Timmy bounced back beside her, with a damp shirt and wet hair standing on end. Jean smiled down at him, gently brushed his curly, blond hair into place and tidied his shirt. Timmy unexpectedly wrapped his thin arms around Jean and hugged her tight.

"Thank you, Mrs Ryan. I love you."

Jean's heart almost exploded. She desperately fought the urge to scoop the little fella up into her arms and tell him that he could stay with her for as long as he liked. She knew she could not say anything other than, "I love you too, Timmy. Now, eat up before Mummy wakes up and comes looking for you."

13

Gabe leaned up against the counter, smiling and shaking his head. He found it amusing watching Bonnie rummage through the many bolts of fabric Reedman's had in stock. Like most women who could not make up her mind, she had to go through a variety of materials. She rubbed the textiles between her fingers and up against her skin. She held them up to the light, looking for the one most suited for dresses. This exhausting task of selecting the perfect fabric warranted the pensive creasing of her brow. Bonnie held a bolt of lemon polished cotton up against herself and looked at her image in the mirror the store provided for customers, twisting one way and then turning the opposite way, to gauge what the finished garment could look like. She ended up wrapped in yards of cloth.

"You'd look beautiful in anything you choose," a voice from behind said with perfect diction.

Bonnie spun around, speechless. She let go of the fabric, and it slid from her body into a heap around her feet. The voice belonged to Oliver Walker, who looked as if he had just stepped out of a fashion magazine. He was decked out in a tailored tan suit with wide lapels and collars, a fitted lemon shirt and the brightest floral tie she had ever seen. She had to admit his clothes complemented his red hair and good looks. *'Carnaby Street, Soho had arrived in Wynnum,'* was her bemused opinion.

"Oh," she said, startled, stepping out and away from the cloth. She quickly gathered the fabric up off the floor and dumped the crumbled mess on the counter.

Patting her clothing and hair in place Bonnie said, "Hello Oliver," with a measure of cool politeness, slowly moving away to the other end of the counter to join her mother, who was quietly instructing Jilly, the shop assistant, to discreetly fetch the pile of crushed fabrics.

"Bonnie. Please, wait!"

"What for Oliver?" she responded indignantly, turning back to him. "I, of all people, have nothing to say to you after our last, memorable encounter. You really showed your true colours that evening, didn't you? And now you just walk in here, open slather, as if you own the world! You're still the same! Well, I think it would be very wise of you to just keep your distance from me from now on."

Oliver did not pursue Bonnie. He was surprised that she was still angry with him after all this time; four years obviously was not long enough for her to forgive and forget. He certainly was not ready to give up on her. Just more determined that one day she would be his wife. He hot-footed it to the local florist shop.

"G'day!" said Carla Benson, recognising Oliver; she had had a crush on him since her school days and thought this was her chance to get his attention. But Oliver nodded with indifference, brushing any pleasantries aside. He handed her a slip of paper with an address written on it.

Carla looked at it. Her brows shot up when she saw the name. She knew Bonnie Connor, but not well. Carla, Bonnie and Oliver were in the same class all through primary school. Carla was peeved that Oliver had not recognised her.

'Huh.' she thought. 'He's always had tickets on himself … thought he was better than everyone else.'

"Red roses will be a weekly order. I want them sent to that address." Oliver said officiously.

"Every week?" Carla repeated.

"Every week, without fail," Oliver instructed.

"Lucky girl," Carla purred, making direct eye contact with him.

"Send the account to my office," he said, ignoring the come-on and handing Carla his business card.

"What did that Walker lad want, love?" Beth asked as they headed home.

"I have no idea, Mum."

"Well, the bush telegraph says that he has been in London all this time. He has done very well for himself in commerce while he was over there. They say he has changed and isn't anything like the lout he used to be. He is now a gentleman, polite and charming, they say."

"Good for him," Bonnie said, sarcastically. "But that doesn't give him the right to just lob up, out of the blue and greet me, willy-nilly, as if we're the best of mates."

Gabe walked beside the women shouting that Walker was a *bloody moron! Idiot! Wanker!* ... and then suddenly without rhyme or reason, Bonnie yelled, "Wanker! "She stopped dead in her tracks and covered her mouth with her hand, horrified.

Beth's jaw dropped as she stared at her daughter in disbelief. They looked at each other bewildered and laughed hysterically.

"What made you say that?" asked Beth shaking her head, making an effort to regain composure.

"I've no idea, Mum," Bonnie giggled. "I've never sworn in my life. Well, not until now, that is," she said, smiling coyly. "I was just thinking what Gabe would say if he saw Oliver now," she added, glancing sideways at her mother.

The pair roared with laughter like dizzy school girls and continued walking.

Beth glanced at her daughter and said, "All jokes aside, love. You're young and have a full life ahead of you. I hope one day you'll fall in love again."

Bonnie looked straight ahead at nothing in particular and then sighed impatiently.

"Mum, I will never fall in love again. Gabe was it for me. No one could ever take his place."

Gabe was grinning from ear-to-ear, swollen with pride as he listened to Bonnie. But that smile and pride soon deflated.

"Darling, I said one day. I know it has only been eighteen months. It's too soon for you to decide about that just yet. One day. Remember, you have Gabriel to consider as well, now."

To change the subject Bonnie said, "Oh, damn."

Beth looked alarmed. "What it is, love?"

"I was so distracted rushing out of Reedman's that I forgot to buy any fabric."

Beth quickly pulled a parcel from her shopping basket. It was wrapped in brown paper and tied together with string. She handed it to Bonnie. "I hope you like what I have chosen. I noticed the way you arced up when you saw Oliver Walker. It looked like you were about to give him a ripe ear-bashing, so I hustled Jilly along to cut the fabric for you."

As the months rolled by, Gabe lingered in the background as an observer to the life of which he was robbed. He had no idea as to why or which one of his many enemies had killed him. He repeatedly went over names and faces, coming to the conclusion that it had to be someone from Sydney. After more serious consideration he realised that none of them knew where he had gone and no one around Wynnum or Manly knew anything of his past, drawing another blank. For now, he had to be content just being the audience.

Gabe marvelled at Bonnie's drive and endurance. She could feel his presence and his love for her, the sustenance of her strength. Without it, she would have simply died of a broken heart. Whenever she was melancholy at night, Gabe would wrap his arms around her; during moments of doubt, he whispered words of encouragement.

Bonnie made a schedule to manage her time between taking care of Gabriel, their home, her studies and her casual job at the bakery. She found solace in sensing Gabe's spirit around her, but her mother's words had ear-wormed into her mind, *'You have Gabriel to consider.'*

She was annoyed with Oliver for sending her flowers. Every week! They began arriving the day after their chance meeting at Reedman's Department Store. She dare not call and thank him, which would certainly open Pandora's Box. Instead, she ignored him.

'He's persistent. I have to give him that,' Bonnie thought as a winsome smile brightened her pensive mood. She visualised her mother eagerly opening the door to the florist's delivery man Monday evenings and, the next morning, placing the beautiful bouquet on display for her craft group friends to enviously admire.

Her father complained that the lounge room resembled a funeral parlour, which made him question his mortality.

"Darling," Joe said in jest. "You have to end this affair."

"I can't, sweetheart," Beth teased. "I'm only having the affair for the flowers. I'd have an affair with you if you sent me flowers every week," she cooed.

"Oh, I can't do that. My wife would definitely not approve," he winked.

"Ooh, good answer!" Beth replied, clapping her hands and laughing.

"Coffee?" Joe nodded.

The flowers were forgotten until the next bunch arrived.

14

During the time he spent working in London, Oliver Walker had observed his colleagues with great interest. He marvelled at the way they shrewdly manipulated their clients with persuasive charm and flattery, convincing them that they must have the mediocre product on offer, which would undoubtedly be an amazing life-changing experience for them.

He also learnt that if he wanted something, he had to offer something in return. His most important lesson of all was to be patient or fail. So, therefore, with that in mind, Oliver was content to wait, for however long he had to until Bonnie succumbed to his charm. His Uncle Bart, while taking Oliver under his wing, cautioned his nephew to never trust anyone one completely with anything he wanted to keep private.

"We're all fallible beings, my boy," said Bart seriously, during their farewell dinner the evening before Oliver returned to Australia. "Trust or the lack thereof, is often one's downfall. Putting too much trust in business colleagues is the biggest mistake a man can make."

It was this piece of advice that contributed to Oliver's success in business. He was in complete control of everything ... until Bonnie. *'But that was about to change,'* he had decided.

Prudently, Oliver set about ingratiating himself within the community. He donated money to various sporting groups and charities in the area, requesting that his sizable contribution be kept anonymous. He was fully aware that the news of his generosity would be broadcast around the town like wildfire and hopefully, reach Bonnie.

When invitations to dinners and community functions started arriving in the post, Oliver smiled with contented satisfaction. Of course, he willingly endured all the pomp, ceremony and puffery in the hope it would attract Bonnie's attention.

As the weeks passed without a word of thanks from Bonnie for the flowers, Oliver was by no means discouraged. Her silence only fuelled his ambition to win her at any cost. He kept a dossier and a vigilant eye on her – what she did, where she went, who her friends were, etc., so he could 'coincidentally' be at the same places as she, without causing suspicion.

Oliver was always in the company of a mate or business colleague, never a woman. He would keep a reasonable distance from Bonnie and cordially wave when she noticed him. At first, she nodded and then turned her back. Over time, she smiled politely and then eventually returned his wave.

Every move Oliver made was manipulated, except for the day they literally bumped into one another. Bonnie was leaving the chemist as he was about to enter the shop. Oliver caught Bonnie and prevented her from falling when she tripped on the doormat. Blushing and laughing awkwardly, she fumbled with her hair and blouse, apologising, looking in every direction other than at him.

Oliver laughed with genuine pleasure for having held her for the first time, asking if she was okay.

"Thank you. I'm fine," she said, a tad frostily, and then checked herself. She finally looked at him and smiled. He could not help but wonder if he had imagined her eyes had softened. Then something he had read, but could not recall when or where flashed into his mind. *'Love is a universal headache that blurs a man's vision and distorts all logic.'*

Once Oliver was sure Bonnie was steady, he turned to leave but she called to him.

"Wait, Oliver! I want to thank you for the flowers ... they're lovely. But please, don't send anymore."

'Ha! Step one. She's finally talking to me!' he wanted to shout to the world.

"I'm trying to apologise to you, Bonnie," he said, hoping she would not reject him and quickly added, "for, for my juvenile crass behaviour, way back when I was nothing but a spoilt punk kid."

During Oliver's supplication, Gabe folded his arms in a huff and leaned against the wall, pulling faces and mumbling obscenities under his breath.

Bonnie laughed. "Yes. You were. And then some," she said. "But I have to give you credit for admitting it. You were really an awful kid, Oliver."

He slammed his hand against his head and moaned, "Oh God, I was, wasn't I ... I've changed though. I hope you've noticed that."

He hated feeling vulnerable, standing there in front of this woman. Since kindergarten, he had desperately wanted to have her like him. He also hated that he was invisible to her, that all his malarkey to gain her attention had only alienated her from all he thought was good about him.

"You certainly look different in those fancy clothes you wear these days," she said in earnest.

"I'm a businessman now," Oliver said, said a little defensively. "I have to look the part."

"Oh, I wasn't criticising you, Oliver," she said apologetically. "You look great ... like a model in the Women's Weekly magazine!"

"Will you join me for lunch?" he said on impulse and immediately wished he had not. He braced himself for the knockback.

"I can't. I have to hurry home. Mum's looking after Gabriel."

'There it is,' he thought disappointed, but could he not believe his ears when she said, "Perhaps another day." She

only said that after she saw how disappointed he seemed. "I do appreciate the invitation though. I'm sorry, Oliver. I have to go. Bye for now."

All the way home, Gabe angrily ranted to Bonnie about Oliver being a loser and a good for nothing. By the time she had reached her mother's backdoor, she was in tears and racked with guilt.

The squeaking of the screen door distracted Beth from her embroidery.

"Is that you love?" Beth called from the lounge room. She carefully folded the cushion cover she was working on and left it on the chair. "Gabriel's still at Robbie's house. Mary will bring him home soon. I'll put the jug on for a cuppa."

Beth fell silent when she found Bonnie leaning against the kitchen sink crying.

"Aww, what is it, love?" she cooed, wrapping her arms around her daughter. She had been expecting that someday the realisation of Gabe's death would finally hit her. By the look of things, this was that day.

Bonnie pulled a linen hankie from her pocket and dried her eyes. "Oliver asked me out to lunch. I literally bumped into him at the chemist," she said, laughing awkwardly between sniffles. "He stopped me from falling on my face … anyway, now I feel awful. But I don't understand why I feel this way, Mum."

Beth realised that Bonnie's desire to start living again was wrestling with her desire to keep grieving.

"It's not unusual, love. A handsome young man is paying you some attention and you probably feel guilty about that. You probably even feel as though you've betrayed Gabe."

"Yes! That's exactly how I feel. I didn't know how to put it into words. How did you know that?" Bonnie asked.

Beth laughed and hugged her daughter again.

"Mothers are all-knowing, darling. It's called intuition. Just you wait until Gabriel grows up. You'll soon know what I mean. Seriously, love, accepting Oliver's invitation won't in any way dishonour the love you still feel for Gabe. Just don't be in bondage to that love. Gabe wouldn't want you to be his grieving widow for the rest of your life. He'd want you to be happy, to have all the things that permit you to have a wonderful life. Real love is like a phantom, darling. Everyone talks about it, but only a few have experienced it. You and Gabe were two of the *few*. So whatever awaits you won't be anything like you and Gabe has had. But it can still be beautiful. It's time you started living again. The next time Oliver Walker asks you to lunch, say yes."

As Gabe listened, he knew Beth was right. He moved closer to Bonnie and wrapped his arms around her and kissed softly on her cheek.

'I don't want you to be in bondage to my love, Bonnie. I want you to be happy. So go for it! But I'll be here if you ever need me.'

Later that evening, Beth answered the door to the delivery man once again. She was surprised to see him holding a dozen of the most magnificent long-stem velvet roses she had ever seen.

"Your husband will definitely be in your good books for a very long time for these beauties. They're the best money can buy." the delivery man winked.

"Oh, the roses aren't for me," Beth said. "They're for my daughter." Just before she closed the door she smiled sweetly and said. "For the record, my husband is always in my good books! Good night."

Beth bustled around the house, giddy with excitement. Instead of putting the roses on the table to show off to the craft ladies as she usually did with the other flowers, she rushed them over to Bonnie.

"Oh my, they are stunning!" Bonnie gasped when her mother placed the roses on the table. "That man is incorrigible."

"You must call him now to thank him. Go on." Beth urged. "I'll stay here with Gabriel. Go on ... shoo!"

Gabe was sitting on the couch like some spectator, watching everything going on around him, utterly helpless to do anything other than to let the pieces fall where they may.

Bonnie could not bring herself to embrace the possibility of a relationship with Oliver. She thanked him for the roses and graciously declined his lunch invitation.

That night, she cried for Gabe for the second time since his passing. She lay in her bed clinging to one of his shirts, holding it close to her heart, weeping softly, suddenly awakened to the raw reality of his death. She could no longer hold him in her arms or feel his tender caress, or breathe in his scent.

The sadness came in waves, hammering at her resilience to believe that having Gabe's spirit around her was enough to keep her going. The stark realisation of that not being enough was slowly suffocating her and she kept revisiting their last night together in her dreams, depleting her will to live without him.

"I should've stopped him from leaving, somehow," she chided herself, sobbing and thumping the pillow. "Oh, my dear heart ... why, why did you have to go out that night ... why? Why did you go? I miss you so, my darling. I don't want to live without you!"

'Shhh, sweetheart,' Gabe whispered as he lay down beside her to lull her to sleep, where he could visit her in her dreams. 'I was a jerk for being so cocksure of myself. I'm sorry.'

Bonnie forced her swollen eyes apart when she heard Gabriel calling her. He was standing in the doorway holding his 'comfort' blanket. "Are you talking to daddy?" he asked, making his way over to the vacant side of the bed. "Daddy talks to me all the time, Mummy, but I can't tell anyone 'cept you. Can I sleep here tonight?"

Bonnie lifted the bedcover, "Of course you can, darling," she said, not taking in what he had said. Gabriel climbed in and curled up into a little ball. "Good night. I love you, Mummy."

Bonnie leaned over and kissed him gently on the forehead. "I love you too, darling." He was sound asleep before she had finished the sentence.

'There's your reason to keep living, Bonnie, and to have a full and happy life.

I don't like it. But if you can find happiness with Walker, then go for it! If he isn't good to you or to Gabriel, he won't know what hit him. I still don't know who killed me or why. You might stumble across something by mixing with the community.'

"Yes," she mumbled, half asleep. "I have Gabriel to consider ... and I must find the killer."

The following morning, Bonnie felt a shift in her mood and with it came the feeling of optimism and a sense of purpose.

15

The phone call from Bonnie had infuriated Oliver. All his expectations after his efforts to gain her attention instantly evaporated with just a few words. *'Thank you for the lovely flowers Oliver, but I can't ...'*

At the end of the call, he stood in silence gripping the phone so hard that his knuckles turned white. The rage that churned deep within his gut surfaced with an angry roar. The phone went flying across the room and crashed against the wall, falling onto the floor. He stormed out of the house to his car.

The Holden's engine came to life at the turn of the key and rumbled under the pressure of his foot on the accelerator. He released the brake and dropped the clutch, then sped off down the street at neck-breaking speed to disappear in a cloud of dust.

Constable Eric Samuels was on his Triumph, about to make a left turn when the Holden flew past him. Every nerve in the constable's body wanted to give chase. He didn't because he recognised the car. He had been informed that that family was off limits. He was seething as he watched the sparkling green vehicle fade into the distance. If it had been anybody else, the siren's banshee wail would have been echoing through the sleepy streets of Manly.

Samuels was a huge hairy man with a kind heart. Because of his size, the kids around the town nick-named him, Samson, The Walkers were a thorn in Samson's side. He loathed the power Oliver's father had and that Oliver was never held accountable for any wrong-doing. He vowed that one day he would get that thug and his old man before he retired from the police force. *'But for now, 'I'll go with the flow. One day he'll slip up. His type always does at some point,'* he reasoned.

Oliver parked in front of the florist shop. Still feeling the pangs of rejection, he fished around in his jacket pocket for his cigarettes. He needed one to calm down. He snatched a cigarette from the packet with one hand and pushed in the car cigarette lighter with the other. It took several short draws on the cigarette before it came alive and then one long, hard, satisfying drag, taking in a lung full of tar and toxic alkaloid, then expelling a thick white cloud of smoke.

Fifteen minutes later, Carla Benson appeared in the doorway. She waved to him when she saw him sitting in his car. He did not wave back. He ogled her, conjuring up explicit images of the two of them together in bed.

Carla could feel his eyes on her. Smiling with smug satisfaction, *'At last,'* she relished, *'he's taking an interest in me'*. Ignoring him, she carried on nonchalantly locking up. She slipped the shop keys into the side pocket of her handbag and began walking, in a somewhat thespian manner, up Bay Terrace. She stopped and turned around. Oliver was calling her.

"Hey there," she smiled provocatively as she sashayed over to the car. "Are you lost?"

He opened the passenger's door. "Get in."

"Why should I, Oliver Walker? You ignored me the other day."

Oliver dropped his head and then looked up at her. He was smiling broadly. "Hi Carla," he said, "How are you? It's been a while … would you like to join me for dinner tonight?"

"I'm fine, thank you, Oliver," she said in a sing-song manner. "Thank you for asking. I would love to join you for dinner tonight."

The next morning, Carla watched from her upstairs bedroom window as Oliver walked to his car. He waved to her just before he climbed in and drove away. Although she once had a schoolgirl crush on Oliver, she no longer had any romantic illusions about him since it was clear to her, he was pursuing Bonnie Connor. Carla wanted his lifestyle and would do just about anything to have it. *'If I play my cards right,'* she thought, *'I could be Mrs Oliver Walker someday.'*

Oliver's evening with Carla had softened his disappointment at Bonnie's rejection. As he arrived home, the phone was ringing. He made a quick dash for it and caught it just in time.

"Oh, hello Oliver," Bonnie said, "I was about to hang up. I thought I'd already missed you."

"Bonnie!" Oliver's voice raised an octave as he struggled to catch his breath. He had to clear his throat to continue speaking. "You're the last person I expected to call me."

She tittered awkwardly. "Yes. I imagine I would be. I want to apologise for that ... ah, um ... I wasn't feeling well when we last spoke." She paused. "If your invitation to lunch is still open, I'd like to accept."

Oliver rubbed his forehead, unsure of what to say. "Ah well ... could we make that dinner ... tonight, instead? I have an appointment that I can't put off". Once the arrangements for dinner were sorted out, he showered, changed and bolted back to the florist shop.

Carla was gob-smacked with absolute pleasure when Oliver entered the shop, so soon after their liaison. Seeing him there, looking so handsome in his trendy clothes sent a quiver of excitement through her. She drew in a long, silent breath to steady herself as she carried on serving the last of her customers.

As soon as the customers had left, she relaxed and welcomed Oliver with a fetching smile that lit up her pretty but heavily made-up face. Feeling a sense of comfort, she raised her arms to embrace him, but to her surprise, Oliver took a step backwards out of reach. Her eyes instantly welled up with tears.

"Why did you do that?" she asked.

"I can't see you again," Oliver said sternly. "I'm sorry, but last night didn't happen." He turned around and strutted out of the shop without turning back, leaving Carla devastated and hurt. He was feeling smug, thinking how easy it was giving Carla the brush-off.

'Tonight, I'll be spending the evening with Bonnie,' he smirked. 'Life's pretty darn near perfect at the moment,' he was thinking as he marched in the direction of his car. His ego was soaring and remained elevated all afternoon.

While Oliver was anticipating a future with the girl he had claimed in kindergarten, Bonnie was at home feeling apprehensive about accepting his dinner invitation. The knock at the door confirmed that it was too late to cancel. She could not help but smile when she opened the door. Oliver was grinning like an awkward schoolboy peering through another bouquet of roses. A large box of chocolates was tucked under his arm.

"You never do anything by halves, do you?" she giggled.

Gabe was perched on the arm of the couch, watching the scene play out like a B grade movie – *the dashing, unscrupulous suitor and the shy beauty.*

"Thank you," she said warmly, accepting the roses and chocolates. "Now, where on earth do you expect me to put these?" she quipped, looking around the lounge room. "My home resembles a floral exhibition."

Gabe nodded in agreement but he was not laughing. He was mumbling under his breath, '*Ya better take good care of Bonnie or else.*'

Oliver was smiling, then suddenly he felt uncomfortable and wanted to leave quickly but Bonnie insisted she put the roses in a vase. "They're too beautiful to neglect," she said, lifting a rose to her nose. "It'll only take a minute."

The longer Oliver remained in the room, the more agitated he became. Although the evening was warm outside, the room temperature felt chilly to him. He folded his arms to keep warm.

"I hope you've got good heating because it's like a refrigerator in here," he called to Bonnie in the kitchen.

"Pardon?" she replied, walking back into the lounge room carrying a vase and stopped in the middle of the room for a moment to give him a quizzical look, before sitting the vase on a side table? "Now why would I need heating in the middle of summer?"

Oliver shrugged. "Are you ready?"

Gabe was puzzled as to why Oliver was acting so weird. *'What's up his nose?'* he shouted out aloud. *'You're sure acting odd, mate. Got a guilty conscience, eh?'*

"I'm almost ready," Bonnie said, "I want to say goodnight to Gabriel first. He's with Mum and Dad. Come in and say hello."

That was the last thing Oliver wanted to do, but he forced a smile. "Sure, why not? It's as good a time as any to meet the little fella."

When Gabriel heard the back door bang, he dropped the toy he was playing with and went charging through the house shouting, "Mummyee!" with outstretched arms ready to clasp hold and squeeze her tight.

The striking resemblance between Gabriel and his father shocked Oliver. Joe caught a fleeting glimpse of Oliver's loathing for Gabriel before he regained his composure. Oliver's reaction to Gabriel reminded Joe of a conversation he had had with Constable Brady during Gabe's murder investigation. That particular day, they were standing in the middle of Joe's driveway. Brady seemed distracted. He scratched his head slowly and said, just as old bushies do when they have something on their minds, thinking out loud more than actually making a statement. "There's something missing. I can't quite put my finger on it. Things don't add up here."

When Joe asked what he meant, Brady cleared his throat and said, "Ahh, nothing, Joe. Just trying to put the pieces of the puzzle together, but nothing is fitting in the right places." He paused and then continued. "Did Gabe have any enemies? Someone he had a run-in with ... anyone you can think of?"

Joe told Brady about the incident between Gabe and Oliver the evening Bonnie and Gabe went to the pictures on their first date. "But they were all just kids then, and that was a few years ago now. Besides that, Oliver was living in the UK when the murder took place," Joe said.

The constable shook his head and thinking out loud said, "That family is ..." Brady stopped himself from saying more when he heard the sound of his own voice, which left Joe feeling uneasy. But he did not press Brady for more information. Joe had forgotten about that conversation until now.

Bonnie was saying goodnight when Joe was still deep in thought, and he missed what she had said.

"Goodnight, Dad," she said louder giving him a questioning look, "Are you alright?"

"Yes, yes I'm fine, sweetheart," Joe replied, brushing her concern aside, as well as trying to shake off the uneasy feeling he had about Oliver Walker.

"Goodnight, love. Enjoy the evening!"

Beth knew by the tone of Joe's voice that something was bothering him. She suspected that it had something to do with Oliver. She was beginning to have her own reservation about Bonnie keeping company with him, but if Oliver Walker was Bonnie's choice, then so be it as far as she was concerned.

16

The restaurant in Manly village Oliver had chosen for their first date was within walking distance of Bonnie's home. Since rain was forecast he decided to drive instead. He parked in Cambridge Parade, opposite the hotel. The sounds of angry, jeering voices coming from the hotel attracted their attention. A little boy about six years old was struggling to lift a drunken, bedraggled woman to her feet. Bonnie thought he looked familiar, but could not recall who he was.

The child's desperate pleas and cries for the woman to get up rose above the laughter and taunting from the menacing crowd, prompting Bonnie to go to his aid. Oliver caught her by the arm to stop her. She shook him free and dashed to the child.

"Get away from me!" Bonnie heard the woman yell, as she approached them.

"Go on, get! I don't want ya, ya nothing but a little black bastard!"

"I love you, Mama. I love you! Stop saying that. You don't mean it. You're sick, Mama."

The child was sobbing, frantically brushing away tears that blurred his vision. He was hell-bent on getting his mother up out of the gutter. He pleaded again, tugging on her arm but she refused to budge. He knelt down and wrapped his skinny little arms around her. She squirmed at his touch.

"Yeah, I'm sick, sick of you. Get away!" she shrieked, cursing him. She shoved him with such force that he fell backwards. Bonnie arrived just in time to break his fall. She hugged him for a brief moment then released him.

"Are you alright, sweetheart?" she inquired. He nodded.

Oliver came up behind Bonnie. He took hold of her arm and guided her away from the scene. "You can't interfere with people like that, Bonnie."

"Like what?" she snapped.

Oliver quickly apologised for his off-handed comment and added that he had not meant to sound heartless. "Kay Osborne is a chronic alcoholic," he said. "For years she has emphatically refused help from everyone who has offered it to her." Pausing, he drew in a long, deep breath in an effort to hide his frustration, as if his life depended on it. "My mother occupies her time with all kinds of women's groups in the Wynnum and Manly area. One of those groups involves helping people like Osborne. She constantly talks about that woman and her tragic existence. Her concern for that boy is touching. It's ironic," Oliver laughed with an edge of envy, "how so many people can feel empathy for that wretched kid, and yet no one gives a damn about a poor, spoilt rich kid who has to cause mayhem to get his parents attention. Getting a *dressing down* is better than being ignored."

Bonnie green eyes widened. "Oh Oliver," she said, briefly touching his arm. "I had no idea. We all thought you were just a selfish brat!" When she realised what she had said, she laughed, pulling a face and said without apology, "Well you were … you were a monster but now I understand why."

Oliver laughed too. "There's no denying that I was a monster."

Bonnie smiled in agreement.

"I didn't mean to disclose my dark secret like that. It's unmanly. I'm the tough kid who cares about nobody, remember?"

"Oh, you're a better man than that, Oliver ... if you choose to be. But that's up to you. Come on," she said, taking him by the hand. "I'm starving!"

He smiled and playfully bowed. "Lead the way, Mademoiselle."

Harbour Lights was one of the most prestigious restaurants, not just in the area, but the whole of Brisbane. Bonnie was flattered that Oliver had chosen to take her there. When they entered the restaurant she smiled with appreciation, inhaling the delicious aromas coming from the kitchen.

The head waiter greeted them at the door. "This way, please," he said, bowing slightly, "if you would like to follow me."

He led them to a corner table, covered with a crisp, white tablecloth. The cutlery and wine glasses sparkled in the candlelight. A fusion of expensive perfume, cologne and cigarette smoke wafted around the room. To Bonnie, all this seemed chic and sophisticated.

There were no specific vegetarian dishes listed so Bonnie settled for roast vegetables and greens rather than make any comment. Noting that Bonnie had selected only vegetables, Oliver assumed that she was a vegetarian, so he asked if she would mind if he ordered the steak. His sensitivity to her choice, let alone him noticing that she was not eating meat, had totally surprised her. She pondered that there could be far more to Oliver Walker the adult, than Oliver Walker the infamous teenager of Wynnum and Manly.

They ate their meal in comfortable silence. Bonnie could not dismiss the oddity of socialising with Oliver. Never in her life had she ever imagined herself speaking to him after the way he had treated her in the past, let alone dine with him.

Oliver was also reflecting, counting his blessings that Bonnie was actually sitting opposite him, looking utterly beautiful and enjoying a meal with him. His silence was not from the oddity of the situation, but from the euphoria of it.

Catching sight of their empty wine glasses, the waiter appeared at their table and filled them then quietly faded into the background. Bonnie's cheeks were flushed after her second glass of wine, liberating her enough to feel confident that she had indeed made the right decision to accept Oliver's dinner invitation. Should he ask her out again, she might accept.

Out of the blue, the child on the street flashed into her thoughts. Through a searing wave of emotion, she said, "Oh, I do hope that dear little boy and his mother will be alright."

Oliver looked up from his meal. He was moved and surprised to see tears welling up in her eyes. He reached for her hand and gave it a squeeze. "I'll check on them in the morning."

Bonnie smiled her thanks with genuine warmth.

The following morning, Beth sensed a change in Bonnie when she popped in on her way to the gallery; she exuded an aura of peace. Beth had not seen her daughter look that relaxed in a very long time.

Beth studied Bonnie. "Do I detect love in the air?"

Bonnie gasped. "No Mum! No. I did enjoy the evening though," she laughed out loud adding, "Oliver was surprisingly *nothing* like the horror he used to be. He was so sweet, being very attentive and thoughtful. It made my head spin a little. But love? No – there's no room in my heart for another love; it's already full to capacity. My life is so enriched with memories of Gabe and that's more than enough for me."

"Does Oliver know that?"

Bonnie shrugged. "The subject never came up." She paused, realising what her mother was hinting at. "Oh dear! Yes, I see what you mean. When Oliver calls again, I'll tell him ..."

"Hello Mummy," Gabriel said sleepily, rubbing his eyes as he wandered up to Bonnie. She lifted his 'rag doll' body up onto her lap and hugged him.

"Did you like your special dinner last night?" he mumbled, half asleep.

"I did sweetheart, it was delicious," she said, smiling. That smile quickly vanished when Gabriel said frankly, "Mr Walker doesn't like me, Mummy. His eyes went funny when he looked at me."

Beth's mouth fell open and Bonnie's eyes widened, but her voice remained calm and steady as she spoke.

"Oh darling, who wouldn't like you?" she said, tickling him. "You're one of the sweetest little boys in the whole wide world."

"Grandpa and Uncle Daniel are taking me fishing today," Gabriel yelled and squealed with laughter.

"Well then," Bonnie said, "you'd better have brekky and get ready or they will leave without you. The fish won't wait you know!" chasing him around the kitchen, puckering her lips together, opening and closing them imitating a fish.

Gabriel screeched with delight, laughing hysterically. "I will, Mummy if you stop chasing me," he said, running off to his room.

"OK," she said breathlessly, flopping down at the kitchen table. She called to him, "No dilly-dallying, you little scallywag, and getting distracted with your toys."

Bonnie and Beth smiled at each other when they heard Gabriel's faint giggle.

Beth's smile faded as she remarked, "Gabriel's comment was surprising, don't you think? What will you do now, love?"

"Absolutely nothing, Mum. I can't see any point in saying anything to Oliver. Our future isn't with him, even if he had responded well to Gabriel. My son will always be my first priority."

Beth nodded, feeling secretly relieved.

17

During her last year of Art College, Bonnie literally bumped into a woman with flaming red hair, sending the armful of books she was carrying flying. Although Bonnie was already late for class, she stopped to help the woman pick up the books, apologising profusely. She had no idea that her fateful decision would dramatically affect her future or that this woman would become her closest friend and business partner. Bonnie felt so embarrassed that she offered to buy the woman lunch.

"Luvvy, luvvy. It's alright! No harm was done!" she said, laughing loud enough for heads to turn. "I like the idea of lunch though," she grinned, revealing a row of perfect teeth, "My treat. No arguments."

Shaking her head Bonnie chuckled saying, "That's very thoughtful of you. Ahh?" She paused a moment. "I don't know your name."

"Sandy Brewer," she replied, bending a little and poking out a hand from under the heavy load, "Nice to meet you, ahh?"

"Bonnie, Bonnie Connor," Bonnie replied with a gentle shake of Sandy's hand.

"Let's meet up at the café, say 12.30? That suits you Bonnie?" Sandy said, looking back over her shoulder as she flitted off before Bonnie could reply.

The difference between the women was as stark as night and day. Bonnie was petite, with the poise and elegance of the movie star, Grace Kelly, while Sandy's 'wild child' sign shone as brightly as a lighthouse beacon. The outlandish clothes she wore had people doing double-takes – psychedelic caftans covered in multi-coloured whirls and swirls had a hallucinating effect if people stared at the fabric too long. They would end up feeling a little dizzy. The four-inch peep-toe platform shoes Sandy wore exaggerated her height of five-feet-seven-inches. Sandy's theatrical habit of flicking her hennaed tresses away with the back of her hand when they fell across her heavily made-up eyes had people smiling.

Bonnie instantly liked Sandy. They became great friends and each other's confidants. Both, on several occasions, had mentioned they would like to someday open a studio cum art gallery.

"Let's do it then!" Sandy said one day, after discussing the plan for the umpteenth time. "We can pool our money and ideas."

Some months later they achieved their dream and opened the studio and gallery. It was a huge success.

As Bonnie drove to the gallery, she grappled with how to tell Oliver she would never be interested in him, or any man, beyond a friendship. She was so distracted thinking about what she should say to him that she did not see the oncoming car, but she definitely heard Gabe shout, "*Veer left Bonnie!*" She reacted immediately and ended up on the shoulder of the road. She remained there until she had regained composure. The incident shocked Bonnie into realising that the concern with Oliver was not worth risking her life. That she must pay attention while driving. "I shall ring him as soon as I arrive at the gallery and settle this with him once and for all," she said out loud, pushing her left foot down on the clutch. She then slipped the little white Morris Minor into first gear. She faltered, stalling the car. "That was Gabe's voice I heard. I'm sure of it," she whispered, astonished. "He saved my life!"

The disbelief of almost having an accident had suddenly overwhelmed her. She was about to break down weeping until Gabe wrapped his arms around her and spoke softly, "Focus on Gabriel ..." Bonnie nodded, acknowledging that notion. She inhaled deeply and then slowly exhaled, started the car and carefully drove away, eager to get to the gallery to make that call.

When she arrived at the studio, Bonnie prickled at the sight of Oliver's car in the parking lot. *'What's he doing here? He's taking far too much for granted'.* Her nervousness had transformed into frustration, igniting the fire of independence within her feisty spirit. "He has to stop this nonsense," she muttered, her anger rising while she gathered her things together from the back seat.

Gabe managed to calm Bonnie with a gentle touch on the back of her hand. He was concerned that she might say something to Oliver which she would later regret. Instantly, she relaxed and smiled with some satisfaction. 'I don't know why I'm getting all worked up, he has saved me a phone call,' she thought.

Bonnie entered the building through the gallery door and found Sandy and Oliver deeply engaged in conversation. It appeared they were discussing the students' work hanging along the gallery's wall. One of Bonnie's seascapes had caught Oliver's attention. He was enquiring about the price of the painting when Bonnie called to them, "Hello you two!" ending their conversation abruptly.

They exchanged pleasantries, pecking each other lightly on the cheek, then came a moment of awkward silence as Sandy's mind worked overtime, trying to think of a way to distract Bonnie so Oliver could discreetly purchase the painting.

The phone rang but neither Bonnie nor Sandy moved to answer the call. When it became obvious Sandy was not about to budge Bonnie said, a tad irritated, "I suppose I should answer that!" Sandy and Oliver nodded.

As soon as Bonnie was out of earshot, Oliver whispered, "I definitely want the seascape. Mind you, this transaction and future transactions must be confidential. Agreed?"

"Yes, you have my word. Confidential it is!" Sandy said.

They both stopped talking when they overheard Bonnie say in a surprised tone, "Oh, you mean Oliver Walker," Bonnie laughed. "Sorry about that. I thought you were referring to his father."

"Could I please speak to him?" replied the chilly female voice.

Bonnie immediately stood taller and replied in her professional manner, "Yes, certainly." Turning to face Oliver, Bonnie held out the receiver to him, grinning. "Mr Walker!"

Oliver's brows knitted together as he took the phone. "Hello?" He did not say another word after that. His shoulders drooped the longer he listened to the caller. A few minutes later he replaced the receiver in its cradle. He stood motionlessly staring at the phone, as Carla's voice replayed in his head. *'Well, Oliver,'* she laughed sarcastically. *'It looks like our liaison hasn't finished after all. It's just beginning. You're going to be a daddy!'*

As he began to focus, Oliver heard Bonnie asking what was wrong.

"Pardon?" he said, "Oh nothing. Something has come up at work. I've got to go, but I'll call you later," he said dashing out of the gallery, leaving Sandy and Bonnie wide-eye and puzzled.

Oliver burst through the door of the florist shop. He gave the place a quick visual sweep before he bellowed.

"How can I be sure the kid's mine?"

"Hello, Carla! Nice to see you again after that lovely night we spent together," she said sarcastically, feeling very confident of her position with him now.

"Cut the bullshit! I asked you a question!"

77

She glared at him for a moment. "I might be ambitious and calculating, but I am NO slut! This baby is YOURS!"

They both stood in lethal silence, on opposite sides of the room, facing each other. Carla changed her posture by relaxing her shoulders and Oliver mirrored her. She spoke first.

"I didn't plan this but I'm not sorry it's happened either. I'll be honest with you, Oliver. I want your lifestyle. I believe we could be good together. I know a lot about the people in this town; who's sleeping with whom and who has a mistress. Your father has a couple. Who beats his wife ... Oh ... I have a lot of useful information."

Oliver was dumbfounded listening to Carla. His future with Bonnie was swirling round and round, going down the drain right before his eyes. The temptation to put his hands around Carla's throat and squeeze the life out of her was strong. His imagination was running wild. He felt the pressure of his fingers on the skin of her neck; her eyes bulged as he squeezed tighter and tighter. She gasped for air, squirming desperately to break free. He stopped and released the pressure on her throat. The idea of her carrying his child had stopped him. He cleared his throat.

"I will marry you, but if you are lying to me. I will kill you!"

Carla's smile was confident, as she sauntered over to Oliver and reached out to embrace him.

"Ah no, you don't," he said, moving backwards away from her. "You can live in a big house and buy expensive clothes, whatever you want. But we'll be married in name only. Since we are being honest with each other, I don't want to marry you. It's for the child's sake that I'll marry you. My kid won't wear the brunt of my actions, you hear me? We'll do the family things and keep up the appearance of a happy union for all to see, but you're not to discuss this relationship with anyone, understand? ... Nobody!"

Carla nodded. Her confidence abruptly sapped. She was close to tears.

Oliver continued talking in a calm and deliberately hard tone. "If I hear even a whisper of our *deal*, I'll divorce you and take my kid away from you. Your name will be mud by the time I'm finished. Do you understand me?"

"Yes!" Carla bellowed at him.

"Don't shout at me. You're getting what you want. Nothing is ever free, Carla. Everything comes with a price tag. Now, I'll make an appointment with a specialist in the city to confirm your dates, etc. If they add up, we'll have a civil ceremony at the end of the month."

"I want a big wedding and ..."

Oliver cut Carla off midsentence. "There'll be no big wedding. As I said, everything has a price ... I have a business to take care of, so I'll call you tomorrow."

Oliver's first call was to Bonnie, asking if she would meet him down at the foreshore. "I'll tell you when I see you," he replied when she asked if something serious had happened.

18

It was mid-morning by the time Bonnie arrived at the foreshore. The sun was high and shone brightly in the clear cornflower sky, with the exception of a cluster of thick clouds hovering to the east of the bay. The water was flat, like a huge plate of glass reflecting a mirror image of the sky; the warm breeze that caressed Bonnie's bare arms carried a subtle scent of jasmine. A smile creased her pretty face as she recalled the days when she and Gabe playfully teased and chased each other along the beach. The memory of their laughter sang in her head like a beautiful melody. She captured him in her mind's eye; strong and perfect standing by the water's edge, waving and beckoning her to join him.

'Everything around here's still the same as it was back then, during our time together,' she mused. *'People strolling along the waterfront, kids tearing about laughing and calling to each other, fishermen a mile or two from shore, sitting motionlessly in their tinnies, hoping to catch the 'big one'. Babies are born, people die and life just rolls along without missing a beat.'*

"Sorry Bonnie," Oliver said, breathlessly, rushing towards her and breaking into her reverie. "I didn't mean to keep you waiting."

Bonnie turned suddenly and caught her breath. "What's wrong, Ollie. You look positively awful!" She paused and immediately apologised. "Oh dear, I didn't mean it to sound like that. What's going on?" she said, brushing aside the pleasantries.

"I'm getting married!" he blurted out.

Bonnie could hardly believe her ears.

"You're what?"

"Getting married. Have to, is more like it."

Although Oliver's news took Bonnie by surprise she wanted to jump for joy. By his mood, it was not the right time.

"I hadn't realised you were seeing someone," she said. Her intonation was even and without judgement.

"I'm not! I wasn't." Burying his head in his hands he cried, "Aaah, hell Bonnie, I've really come a cropper this time."

Oliver sat down on the seat beside Bonnie. They were silent. She faced the bay, watching the gulls gliding above and then swooping and landing on the grass, as the sun danced on the water, waiting patiently for him to calm down.

"I could blame you for this," he growled.

"Me?!"

"Yes," he said, and then gave her a full account of the time she rejected his lunch invitation.

"I had no idea just how that night with Carla would change my life, until now," he said, bogged down with regret.

"I know it wasn't really your fault. I take full responsibility for my actions. Even after that night to this day, Bonnie. I feel a different person when I'm with you; relaxed and light-hearted."

Bonnie was uncomfortable. "Oh, I think you give me far too much credit, Ollie." She paused. "I mean, Oliver."

"I remember the first time you called me Ollie. I'd fallen off the swing. You ran over calling out to me, "Ollie, are you alright?" he laughed ... "Always 'Ollie' to you, he said, looking directly at her. "You know Bonnie," he said seriously. "I saw Carla as an albatross around my neck. I wanted to kill her. To squeeze the life out of her because I want to marry you, not her!"

"Ollie! Oliver! Stop! You couldn't possibly mean it. That's so much wasted emotion. Honestly, it's not worth it. I couldn't marry you or anyone else. My heart belongs to Gabe. It always will. He is here," she said, resting a hand over her heart.

As Bonnie was speaking, Gabe sat down next to her and wrapped his arm around her shoulders. "I could never love anyone else," she said.

Oliver shook his head when he finally realised Bonnie's love for her husband was incandescent, and would never fade. Her face glowed at the mere mentioning of his name. No one could compete with that.

"Oh my God," he whispered very close to tears. "It was all for nothing. I am so sorry, Bonnie. You have no idea how sorry I am."

Bonnie's brows knitted together in confusion. "What are talking about? Sending me all those beautiful roses?" She half smiled and said, "It was rather sweet, in a way."

He looked at her momentarily puzzled then shouted, "Yes! Yes!" somewhat relieved that Bonnie had accepted his apology.

"You must have thought me a fool - overcompensating for my 'bad boy' years, with the arrival of so many rose bouquets ... and so often!" Oliver groaned. "I failed miserably in my quest to woo you,' he said, smiling awkwardly. "I honestly thought if I display my romantic side you'd eventually swoon into my arms."

Oliver dropped his head in mock shame. "When a man is utterly besotted, he can do some pretty foolish things to gain the attention of his heart's desire, as you have witnessed firsthand." He laughed heartily this time, releasing the tension he had bottled up.

"Oh, plan B was a doozy. It would have had me standing on my hands or jumping off a tall building. Anything, and I mean anything, to get your attention. But you crushed my big fat manly ego before I could embarrass myself further by declining my invitation to lunch."

Bonnie was giggling almost hysterically. "Well ... Oh ... let's forget about all of that. It's in the past now."

She looked directly at him. Her laughter had vanished. "I'm going to give you some unsolicited advice though," she said in earnest, "and I hope you'll take it and imprint it on your brain."

"What's that my dear friend?" Oliver grinned mischievously.

Bonnie took in a deep breath and then let it go. "OK, since you've asked," she said. "The decision you made to visit Carla that fateful night could be your redemption, your chance to be a good husband, a wonderful father and a better man. Although Carla and I were in the same class at school as children, I didn't know her well. But I do know she's had a crush on you for years. Who's to know," Bonnie shrugged, "perhaps you and Carla will be good together. You should at least give the marriage a good try for the baby's sake, keeping in mind that it's cruel and destructive to be careless with someone's feelings, so be kind to her."

Oliver admired the hope that glowed in Bonnie's eyes for him. But he had his doubts about the success of the marriage. He knew himself and Carla's type, too well ... and he still wanted Bonnie.

19

After leaving Bonnie, Oliver headed straight for his father's office in Brisbane. The sparkling green Holden travelled along the single-lane road passing Hargraves Factory, bushland, a public housing estate and the army camp at Cannon Hill, the fish works and abattoir.

The journey seemed long, travelling at a snail's pace when caught behind sedate drivers. Oliver followed along patiently, surveying the road for a chance to overtake staid motorists. While waiting, a thought had crossed his mind that perhaps the consensus of many Brisbane residents about the Wynnum/Manly area being 'out in the sticks' could be valid. Perhaps he and Carla should reside in the city after they marry. But then again, he reasoned on second thought, *'even with the stigma of being 'out in the sticks', this did not dissuade the posh nor the poor from travelling from the city, and as far away as Toowoomba to enjoy the bay's pristine beach and camping grounds. Nor did it deter The Royal Yacht Club from relocating to the Manly Boat Harbor from Kangaroo Point.'*

"Bloody hell," Oliver said, after calculating the time lapse, *"that was way back in nineteen sixty-four, almost ten years ago!"* He shook his head in amazement, thinking, *'so much has changed in that time and Clem Jones was still rapidly improving infrastructure all over Brisbane.'* So Oliver came to the conclusion that there was no other place he would rather live than Manly.

When Oliver finally arrived at the office, Bill greeted him with a gruff, "What do you want? Can't you see I'm busy?" and quickly closed the desk drawer that housed the whisky bottle and glass.

By the ruddiness of his father's complexion, Oliver knew any conversation they had would probably end up badly. Oliver ignored the rebuff.   "I thought you should know I'm getting married."

The old man's eyes lit up. "Bonnie Connor?"

"No, unfortunately, I didn't make the grade. The lucky lady," Oliver announced with a tad of sarcasm, "is Carla Benson."

"What, that little trollop managing the florist shop? I won't have the likes of her in this family. I'll cut you out of my will. You'll get nothing from me!"

Bill Walker's rage penetrated the office walls and his panic-stricken secretary came barging into the office without knocking. Bill waved her away.

"It's alright. It's alright, June," Bill growled. "It's just another bloody family dispute."

June backed away hesitantly, apologising as she closed the door behind her.

"Cut me out of your will!" Oliver laughed bitterly in his father's face. "That won't cut the mustard anymore. You old fool, I'm no longer the gutless teenager you use to scare shitless. I've grown up."

Oliver stood in front of his father's desk, staring contemptuously down at him and said in a mean, low voice, "I could buy and sell you twice over, you pompous, arrogant bastard!" and then he heckled him with the truth. "Unlike yours, my wealth was gained through hard work and wise investments. I didn't sell my soul to corrupt politicians and crooked cops the way you have."

Oliver turned his back on his speechless father and strolled over to the window. He stood in silence looking over the city and then he turned around abruptly. "I guess I owe you a major debt for sending me to Uncle Bart in the UK. If it weren't for him teaching me life and business ethics, I'd probably be like you, screwing half the whores around town and doing underhanded deals with criminals.

Great role model, you were!" he scoffed. Smiling, Oliver added. "Uncle Bart assured me that I'm not cut from the same cloth as you. I hope to bloody hell he's right about that!"

Bill was about to protest, but Oliver shut him down. "Rumours of your gambling, whoring and your unscrupulous business dealings are rampant around the town. You and your cronies' boating jaunts to Stradbroke Island for boozy weekends with your whores ... and beating up your mistress! Hell Dad!" Oliver shouted. "Since when do the men in this family beat women? You're a disgrace! You respect nothing. And no one! Not even yourself! You seem to have this belief that nothing is beyond your reach. You're untouchable! Everything is for sale! Have you looked in the mirror lately? You're disgusting. A drunk! I don't blame Mum for abandoning you. I just wish she had the courage to divorce you. She won't. Like you, she loves the prestige that comes with wealth, being known as *someone of significance,* flitting here and flitting there, involving herself with one committee after another. Her need to be valued and being 'a pillar of society' was so great that she ignored her own child's welfare."

Bill was slumped back in his large, leather Chesterfield chair, lethargic from the effects of alcohol. Listening to his son spruik the truth about his failings angered him enough to cause him to muster a surge of energy. He rose up like the phoenix from the ashes to sit rigidly and upright, ready to challenge him.

"Who are you to judge me, you with your high and mighty ways and uppity accent and fancy clothes?"

Oliver cut him off before he could utter another word. "Carla is pregnant! Oliver paused a moment to give his father time to absorb what he said. "You may not like the idea of Carla as a daughter-in-law," Oliver declared. "However, I expect you to treat her with the utmost respect since she will be the mother of my child, your grandchild.

We'll do the monthly 'family' Sunday lunches and play happy families. Should you step out of line just once, all contact will cease. Understand?"

Bill nodded, content with the arrangement, he slouched back in the chair.

The wedding was a quick, understated civil ceremony, much to Carla's disappointment. She did, however, get some satisfaction from donning the title of Mrs Oliver Walker, regardless of having to endure spiteful gossip that she had 'trapped' poor Oliver. Fortunately for Carla, she had the fortitude of an elephant and was wise enough not to react to the gossip. She was determined to win over her enemies. *'I'll eventually have them eating out of my hand,'* she thought smugly.

Anita Walker, Oliver's mother, became Carla's strongest ally. Initially, she was sceptical of Carla's sincerity towards her son, seeing her only as a social climber, but as time passed Anita came to realise that she had misjudged Carla, who did indeed, genuinely love her son. It was he who was not reciprocating that love. *'To be ignored is one thing, but to be ignored by someone you love is soul destroying,'* Anita reasoned. *'I should know. The shame was that Bill abandoned me in order to be accepted into the 'cheating husbands club' to further his business opportunities. Cronyism served Bill well.'* Anita believed her husband sold his soul to the devil in exchange for success and power. She can remember overhearing one of Bill's phone conversations.

"Buy the bloody building then!" he barked down the mouthpiece. "And close down that bastard's business. Do it today!"

The context of that conversation came to light much later through the wife of the mechanic whose business was next door to one of Bill's buildings. She told her friends that her husband had complained many times to his landlord about his clients having nowhere to park. This was occurring because visitors to Bill Walker's building were using the car park reserved for her husband's customers. Bill Walker's tenant refused to inform his visitors that the area was not available to them.

Anita knew there would be no come back on her. She did, however, feel embarrassed about the horrid situation but carried on regardless, proudly wearing her humanitarian heart on her sleeve for all to see, lest they judge her harshly, too.

Observing Carla's interaction with the local women's groups, Anita wondered just how resilient her daughter-in-law was. *'Would this façade relationship with Oliver crush Carla's spirit or would she adapt and create a splendid life for herself, as I had?'* Anita smiled, sensing that the latter would be more of a reality. *'Anyway,'* she mused, sporting a cunning grin. *'Carla's holding the 'trump card'. If she's a wonderful mother to Oliver's child, as I suspect she will be, Carla could end up attracting Oliver's attention and his love.'*

It was at that moment that Anita had an insight into her own mothering skills and regretted that she had not been a better mother to Oliver. "Ah well," she shrugged with an air of indifference, "I shall be a wonderful grandmother!"

Before Carla accompanied Anita to one fundraiser after another, she took great care to simplify her hair, make-up and outfits. The first thing to go was her long, painted 'flame red' nails. They were cut to a respectable length and coated with a pearl nail polish. Two coats of black mascara replaced the long false eyelashes she had always worn, revealing dark brown, intelligent eyes. She coloured her bleached hair light brown, had a few highlights added around her face and styled her hair into a soft 'page boy'.

The purpose of the change was to blend in, to be accepted into all of the women's groups, and to not alienate the women. Anita applauded Carla's efforts but chuckled to herself. *'Those old busybodies will feel even more threatened since Carla's transformation was positively stunning.'* She cautioned Carla.

"Please don't be seduced by the pretentiousness of it all. Only a few in the association are genuinely kind and considerate, Carla. Most of the women there are living a lie, pretending their lifestyles are the envy of others, when in fact, they are at times miserable. Their lives would have been unfulfilled and without purpose if it were not for them being involved with the women's association."

Carla gave her mother-in-law a rueful smile and replied, "Well then, I should fit in perfectly."

"Circumstances can make us less than we can be, my dear, but only if we embrace that notion," Anita replied. "Ha! I certainly don't!" she laughed, "and neither should you. Why walk meekly among the crowd when you can be outstanding? Be yourself, Carla. Be brave! Be daring! That's how one *gets on* in this superficial world."

During a committee luncheon the president, who was dressed to the nines, was on stage in full swing, thanking all her partisans for a job well done. Of course, it was her photograph featured on the front page of the local 'rag', receiving the accolade for the success of the recent fundraiser. And of course, she failed to mention the names of the women who did all the work that made that success possible.

"Look at Sue," Carla whispered to Anita, "all puffed up and full of herself. She didn't lift a finger to help anyone. All she did was *bully* everyone."

"That's right. But do you see anyone confronting her about it?" Anita shook her head in disgust. "And you won't, either. That's what power is all about. These women's husbands have business around the area. Sue's husband could disrupt their businesses if he felt inclined. Understand?"

Carla was about to respond when she heard a pop. She was drenched. Her water had broken, setting off a vortex of confusion and panic. A gabble of high-pitched voices swirled around the room, drowning out the president's instructions to call an ambulance and to bring Carla a glass of water.

Anita, who seemed to be the only calm person in the room, clasped hold of Carla's hand.   "Well, my dear," she said, smiling and feeling inwardly excited, more than she had thought possible. "You are about to become a mother."

20

Oliver rushed to the hospital as soon as he heard the news. Anita was there waiting for him. She realised how anxious he was and assured him that Carla and the baby would be fine. "It's a waiting game from here on," she told him, "so make yourself comfortable, Oliver. We could be here for a while."

Oliver paced the floor for hours. He had a lot of time to reflect and guilt finally penetrated the wall he had built around himself. He thought about how he had wilfully ignored Carla, punishing her for getting pregnant. Now, he regretted doing that. *'It was as much my fault as hers. She has done everything right ... has gone to such lengths to fit in. I should've told her how marvellous she looked after all the trouble she went to transforming her image.'*

Although Oliver did not love Carla, he liked her and vowed to treat her with the respect she deserved. He recalled his Uncle Bart saying on numerous occasions, "One can't go through life avoiding mistakes. That's how one learns. Therefore, you shouldn't hold onto regrets. But if you do something terrible, fix it right away!"

Oliver knew Carla wanted her own home. He deliberately ignored her wishes, insisting that they live in his parents' Oceana Terrace house for the time being, as it suited his purpose. She did not complain when he told her where they would be living. The Oceana Terrace, as his parents referred to their home, was large enough for everyone living there, and to come and go as they pleased without being seen.

Oliver looked over at his mother. The change in her since his marriage to Carla was remarkable. *'She is warmer towards me and seems much happier within herself,'* he thought. *'She obviously likes Carla. The bond they have has done them both a lot of good.'*

Oliver was still pacing the corridors when the nurse appeared in the doorway, holding a squawking infant wrapped in a pink blanket. Oliver spun around. He froze on the spot, unsure of what to do.

"Would you like to meet your daughter, Mr Walker?"

Anita jumped up and stood beside her chair. Smiling broadly, she waited for Oliver to respond. "Go on, son," she coaxed gently.

Oliver looked at his mother. She was smiling in a way he had not seen before this moment. He reached out to her, she took his hand, and they moved towards the baby together.

"Would you care to hold your daughter, Mr Walker?" Asked the nurse, and Oliver opened his arms awkwardly.

"She is perfect!" Anita declared.

"Yes. She is," Oliver answered, mesmerised.

"She is beautiful! Poor little tyke has my red hair. I'm sure she'll wear it better than me, though."

"What name have you chosen? You can't keep referring to the child as 'she'." Anita said frankly.

Oliver looked puzzled. A child did not seem real until now.

"I have no idea, Mum. I'll have to discuss that with Carla."

Anita raised her brow in surprise. "Yes. I should think so, too."

"How is Mrs Walker, nurse?"

"Mrs Walker is fine, just a little tired, as expected."

"May we see her?"

"Of course, I believe Mrs Walker is anxious to see you." said the nurse.

Oliver eyed his mother. "Coming?"

"You go ahead, son, I'll come later. Give Carla my love."

Oliver glanced astonished at his mother. He had not heard her say that before. Ever! She would usually say, give them my best wishes. Tell them that I'm thinking of them or they are in my thoughts. Never, 'Give them/her my love'.

The nurse knocked gently on Carla's door and popped her head inside.

"Are we ready to receive a special visitor, Mrs Walker?" she asked as she entered.

Carla beamed. "I am. Thank you, nurse."

Oliver followed the nurse into the room and watched in silence as she placed his daughter in the cot. He smiled his thanks as she left.

"Well," Oliver said, drawing in a deep breath as he moved closer to the bed. "You certainly have presented me with a very beautiful daughter, for which I'm most grateful." He leaned forward and kissed her on the forehead and then settled himself on the bed facing her. A comfortable silence fell upon them.

"And what name have you chosen for our little imp?"

"All through my pregnancy, I've been reading up on names, suitable for redheads, just in case," she smiled

"And?"

"Grace?"

Oliver considered the name, repeating it again and again, rolling the sound around on his tongue, like he would a fine wine. "Hmm, Grace Walker ... Grace Walker ... Grace Walker. Yes, I like the sound of that."

Carla said, "How does Grace Anita Walker sound?"

"Even better," he smiled warmly and squeezed her hand.

"Can I get you something?" Oliver asked, surveying the room. He was still holding Carla's hand as he continued talking. "I have to apologise to you for not bringing flowers. I simply rushed to the hospital without much thought of anything other than being here to meet my daughter."

Oliver stopped and corrected himself. "Umm, I mean, our daughter, and of course," he added, "to check on you."

Carla was cautious. She did not know how to respond to Oliver. He had not been this tender towards her before. She had seemed invisible to him, or so she thought.

A knock on the door came just at the right time. It was Anita.

"Forgive me for intruding," she said sheepishly. "I just couldn't wait any longer. How are you, my dear?"

"You're not intruding, Mum. Come in." They both said in unison and they laughed together. "In sync at last," Carla teased.

Oliver nodded, smiling at her, "Yes, I think we are," he said.

He stood up and gave Carla a light peck on the cheek.

"Well, Mum, you've got the next shift. I have work to do, so I'll see you, ladies, later."

Before leaving, Oliver went to the cot. "Our little Grace is magnificent! She won't want for a thing. I'll make sure of that!"

By the end of the day, Carla's room was filled with flowers from friends and from all the women's group, she was involved in. But none had arrived from her husband. Carla had thought, by Oliver's reaction this morning, a spark had ignited between them.

'Perhaps, I've misjudged him. Perhaps he was just being polite for the baby's sake.' She thought with a heavy heart, sinking into depression. Tears silently flowed. 'I'll never be good enough. Oliver will never love me!'

"Knock! Knock! Mind if I come in."

Carla sat up and dried her eyes on the corner of the sheet.

"Who is it?" she called, tidying herself.

"Bonnie Connor. I'll go if you don't feel up to a visitor."

Carla was shocked that Bonnie Connor would visit her, particularly since Oliver had for years fallen over himself chasing after her. Out of curiosity, Carla invited her in.

"Bonnie smiled. "I'm sure I'd be the last person you'd expect to visit you, Carla."

"You are," Carla said frankly. "Why are you here, Bonnie?"

"For several reasons Carla. First of all, to congratulate you and Ollie, I mean Oliver, on the birth of your daughter. You both must be feeling pretty chuffed, but most importantly, to tell you that I'm not a threat to your marriage."

Carla's jaw dropped.

"You're rather candid," she said a little indignantly.

"Yes. I am. I think for your peace of mind, I have to be. I know you're aware of the rumours and talk about Oliver having pursued me. He has gotten over that. I told him that I was not interested in any man. That I am and always will be in love with Gabe."

Carla's demeanour towards Bonnie softened.

"Gabe has gone, Bonnie. You'll be alone for the rest of your life if you don't marry again."

Bonnie smiled. "That's just it, Carla. I don't feel alone. It feels as if Gabe is still with me. My love for him is incandescent in my heart, the eternal flame that gives me the will to live."

For a moment, Bonnie seemed to have drifted off into her own world. She smiled and said as if she was talking to someone else in the room. "Gabe used to leave me symbol messages for example ... a leaf, a feather, a piece of string, a button on my pillow, in my drawer, in my coat pocket, on the fridge. She laughed. I'd find them everywhere. There would also be a note explaining its meaning. For example; this feather means, with you by my side I can fly. You are the wind beneath my wings."

Carla was lost for words. She was thinking how could she have misjudged her? Bonnie was the 'kind' girl at school. Everyone liked her. Carla silently cursed. *'I was blinded by jealousy.'*

The baby stirred.

"Oh!" Bonnie grinned shyly. "May I sneak a peek at the baby?"

"You can pick her up if you like. She's due for a feed."

"Oh, you darling, little cherub, what is your name?" Bonnie cooed, as she scooped the baby from her cot.

"Grace," Carla proudly announced.

"That's a beautiful name for a beautiful, baby girl!"

As Bonnie was leaving the hospital, she passed Anita in the corridor.

"Hello, Bonnie! What brings you here?" Anita had always liked Bonnie and her family.

"Congratulations, Mrs Walker." Bonnie beamed. "Your granddaughter is absolutely beautiful."

"You've been to see Carla?" Anita asked. Her brows rose, *'I would have liked to have been the fly on the wall during that meeting.'*

"I did. We had a good chat. It was a lovely visit. Carla looks wonderful for just having had a baby. She will be a wonderful mum. I just hope she and Oliver will be happy together."

"As do I my dear," Anita replied. "Please do pass on my best wishes to your dear mother."

21

"I've so much to do before Carla and Grace come home," Oliver mumbled as he made a mental list.

"Grace," he repeated several times. Speaking the baby's name out loud sent a pleasant feeling through him, a feeling he had not experienced before.

"Grace. Grace. Grace!" He recited, over and over again until it became embedded in his brain. "My daughter. My little girl with curly, red hair!" he shouted with a proud, joyful heart. "And I'm her father!" he declared in his office.

Oliver shook himself and laughed. "Steady on mate, you've got work to do." He left his office with a spring in his step, heading towards the real estate agent down the street. He intended to negotiate a deal with the person handling the sale of the three-bedroom house he had seen, nestled into the side of the hill on Benalla Street. The bay views from the front veranda were amazing. *'A perfect home for my new family',* he thought, feeling chuffed that he discovered a house by chance. It was within walking distance from his parents' home in Oceana Terrace.

'Walk!' He laughed out loud. *'No one in this family walks. OK, drive then,'* he grinned to himself.

The house had been vacant for some time, which gave Oliver leverage for a quick sale at the right price. By the end of the day, he had hired a house maintenance company to clean and fumigate the place from floor to ceiling. The following day he drove into the city, and with the guidance of an interior decorator, purchased furnishings, rugs, bed linen and a few kitchen items.

"My wife," he said hesitantly, thinking the words, 'my wife' sounded odd to his ears, "will come in later on to choose the other items we need." He explained that she had just given birth to their daughter, "and we're moving into a new place in the middle of it all."

Oliver was about to drive from the city back to Manly when he realised he had not sent Carla flowers. He got out of the car where he had parked in George Street and dashed down to Queen Street, looking for a florist.

"The best bouquet you have, please. I don't care what it costs," Oliver said. "It's urgent!"

"I'll deliver the flowers myself, sir," replied the sales assistant.

"Thank you," Oliver nodded, handing the man a wad of dollar notes.

Meanwhile, at the hospital, Anita had no idea where Oliver was or of the surprise, he was planning. She was at her wits end trying to comfort Carla, doing her best to reassure her daughter-in-law that Oliver had not abandoned her and Grace.

"But what if he has? What if he's changed his mind and has decided he doesn't want all this responsibility? Look around you, Mum. Where are the flowers from him?"

A loud, "rat, tat, tat" silenced Carla. Both women turned towards the door. They watched with great curiosity as it opened. A woman, cheerful as sunshine, burst into the room carrying a huge crystal vase full of the most exquisite flowers they had ever seen.

"Well, someone is very special," the woman proclaimed, carefully placing the vase on the locker beside the bed. She plucked the card from the bouquet and handed it to Carla and then promptly left the room.

"Oh, these are from Oliver," Carla smiled through her tears. "Oh, they're so beautiful! My mind is so out of whack. Was that caused by the birth?" Carla was almost hysterical again. "I heard that some women go crazy after having a baby. Is that what's happening to me, Mum? Is it?"

"Of course not, dear. It's natural for you to feel insecure in the circumstances," Anita said, keeping her voice calm. "You mustn't let the past cloud your judgement, dear. Otherwise, the walls will come crashing down on top of you. Trust your husband, Carla, and trust yourself," Anita said in earnest. That's the best advice I can offer you."

The Benalla Street house was a huge hit. When Carla was strong enough, she set about putting her stamp on the place, adding modern art pieces, mirrors and a few more vases. "We'll need several of these, I expect," she smiled provocatively at Oliver, "to accommodate all the lovely flowers you will send me each week."

"Of course," he replied, with a peck on her cheek as he left for the office.

And so began their life as a family. As the months passed, they were seen out and about together, attending social and business functions, presenting every bit the image of the happy couple, dousing rumours that their marriage was one of convenience due to Carla's pregnancy.

Grace was the delight of her grandparents. The child's winning smile melted the heart of whoever was fortunate to have crossed her path. Her intelligent, dark brown eyes seem to study people as if she had a sixth sense about them and knew what they were thinking. It unnerved some and delighted others. Time passed quickly and although on the surface, her world seemed perfect to onlookers, Carla struggled emotionally. She equated her marriage to shallow breathing, like gasping to get a full breath – that one long, deep breath of reassurance she so desperately needed to believe that her husband could love her. To achieve that, Carla seriously considered leaving *symbol messages* for Oliver to find, like the ones Bonnie mentioned Gabe had left for her. But then, with a despondent heart, she realised they shared nothing memorable to speak of, apart from Grace.

'I could start there, I suppose,' she shrugged. *'It's as good a place as any.'* The flowers she saved from the

beautiful bouquet Oliver sent the day after Grace's birth flashed into her mind. *'Hmm,'* she pondered, *'how will I phrase the note? This flower means: Thank you, Oliver, for our beautiful daughter, your loving wife? Or this flower represents how my life has changed in so many ways since the birth of our beautiful daughter. Thank you, from the bottom of my heart, your loving wife? This flower is a symbol ...* she wrote over and over again, until a pile of expensive, crumbled note paper eventually ended up on the floor.

"I'm useless!" she declared, frustrated. "I can't even write a silly little note!"

The pitter-patter of little feet from behind instantly brightened her mood.

"Mama!" Grace, now two years old, called from the doorway.

"Hello, my angel," Carla cooed sweetly. Grace ran in a wobbly fashion towards her mother and scrambled up onto her lap.

"Play in the park?" Carla asked.

Grace's curls bounced wildly about her head when she nodded and clapped her hands as she yelled, "Park! Park!"

Playtime in the park had become a daily ritual, especially on glorious spring mornings. The five-minute walk from home was pleasant. People strolling past nodded and said, "Good morning!" Some stopped and chatted a while. Somehow Grace, with her engaging smile, always managed to attract the attention of whoever was talking to her mother. She squealed with delight when people took an interest in her.

That morning, Carla noticed Bonnie sitting on one of the seats, facing the bay. She was staring out at the water, oblivious to the world around her.

"Good morning Bonnie!" Carla chimed. "Lovely day, isn't it?"

Bonnie did not respond. She looked as if she was in a trance.

"Are you alright?"

Silence.

"Bonnie!" Carla called again, touching her shoulder. She jumped.

Bonnie looked dazed. "Oh, I'm sorry, I didn't hear you," she said when she realised Carla was talking to her.

"Are you alright?"

"Yes," she said, a little confused. "What are you doing here, Carla? Oh yes, Grace. Of course, you're going for a walk," she laughed awkwardly. "I was day-dreaming. I'm sorry if I sound vague."

"I assume you were thinking about Gabe?" Carla said ruefully, sitting down beside her.

"You assumed correctly. He's always in my thoughts," Bonnie said, leaning in closer to the stroller to touch Grace's cheek.

"Hello, sweetheart. I wonder how many hearts you'll break when you're all grown up?" she said. Grace beamed at the attention. "You're beautiful and you know it."

Bonnie then turned her attention back to Carla. "How are you? Her interest was genuine.

"Oh, I'm fine," Carla lied.

"Do you see much of your family?"

"They have disowned me," Carla replied.

"Why?" Bonnie was clearly shocked.

"For shaming the family... I committed the biggest sin of all ... pregnancy out of wedlock. Primitive, I know. They obviously missed Germaine Greer's 'women's liberation' speech," she grinned.

"That would be hilarious if it weren't so horribly cruel. I'm so sorry."

"I'll survive," Carla said, brushing the conversation aside, "I hear you have a studio and an art gallery? How's that going?"

They moved from the seat over to the sandy area, where Carla took Grace from her pram and popped her down. Both women sat down beside Grace. As they began building sandcastles for Grace, Bonnie explained the day to day workings of the studio. She told Carla that the gallery was an outlet for the work of the students that she and Sandy tutored, as well as for their own. Bonnie even mentioned that she had an anonymous benefactor interested in her paintings.

"Don't ask," Bonnie said, shaking her head when Carla's eye swelled with curiosity. "I've no idea who it is ... just that it's one of Sandy's clients." Bonnie paused and in the spur of the moment she blurted out, "You must come to the studio for a visit!" In her excitement, Bonnie inadvertently placed her hand on Carla's arm. Although Carla noticed, she did not pull away.

"Oh," Bonnie said sheepishly, making a twisted face. "I shouldn't think you'd want to, would you?"

"I think I'd like to do that," Carla said, surprising herself as well as Bonnie.

While Grace entertained herself, Carla and Bonnie carried on talking like old friends. "I see Gabriel has started kindergarten ... his resemblance to his father is remarkable."

"Yes," agreed Bonnie. "It is, in an odd way," she said, forgetting that Carla would have no idea what she meant. "It's as if Gabe was getting another chance at life ... a happier one this time around. Gabriel is quite the 'big boy' these days," she said, smiling proudly.

"I'm glad for you, Bonnie," Carla replied, scooping up handfuls of sand and then letting it run through her fingers. "I'll have a lot to look forward to when Grace grows up. I had no idea that being a mother would bring so much joy to my life."

As they talked, Bonnie noticed the sun was higher in the sky. She glanced at her watch. "I have to go!" she exclaimed, jumping up and shaking remnants of the beach from her clothing. "I've well and truly overstayed my time here ... I shall see you at the gallery? Next week? Bonnie said, before hurrying away.

Carla waved. "I'll call and make a time."

That evening, Carla was feeling happy within herself. She decided to hide the dried flowers and note in among Oliver's underwear. She carefully placed them in an envelope and then lifted up one of his vests. She was about to slide the envelope under it when she discovered a bloodstained, white linen handkerchief with the initials B.M.1967 embroidered on a corner, crammed in the side of the drawer. Her hands trembled as she picked up the handkerchief. *'He still has feelings for Bonnie.'*

Although her heart felt as though it had been torn to shreds, Carla could never have imagined the consequences of discovering that handkerchief. Tears welled up in her eyes and spilled onto her dress. She was absolutely shattered. She collapsed onto the floor weeping. Questions ran through her mind.

'Do I confront him? Do I ignore this and go on as if nothing has happened and hope he will eventually love me?' Question after question she asked herself throughout the morning. Failing to come up with a satisfactory answer, her dilemma remained unresolved. *'I'll know what to do when I face Oliver later this evening.'*

Carla tried not to think about the situation while she got on with her daily routine. Since it was Friday, she packed Grace's clothes for her overnight stay with the grandparents and took her to Oceana Terrace earlier than usual.

"Oh, that doesn't matter, my dear," Anita said jubilantly, crouching down to speak to Grace's face to face when Carla apologised for their early arrival. "The earlier the better, I say." She clasped her perfectly manicured fingers together and then flung them open. "That way Granny and Pa can spend more time with our darling little Grace."

The child threw back her head laughing and ran to Anita, yelling, "Ullo Gwenny!"

22

Still overwhelmed with hurt and anger, Carla shot all sorts of accusations at Oliver the moment he set foot in the door. The wine she had consumed after arriving home from dropping Grace off at her in-laws was supposed to calm her nerves and put her in a better mood. It had the opposite effect.

"When are you going to realise, Bonnie isn't interested in you?" she shrieked. "Why can't you appreciate what you have? I've done all I can to please you. But oh, no, Mr Oliver Walker isn't satisfied. He has to have exactly what he wants, and bugger everyone else!"

"Have you gone mad?" Oliver shouted, taken aback. He stared at his wife, puzzled. She stumbled. "Ha! You're drunk!" he declared venomously.

"I have to be to exist with you!" she cried. "I found this in your drawer," she said between sobs, waving the linen handkerchief in the air. "I was going to put a love note in there for you to find. A LOVE NOTE!" she screeched at him.

Oliver snapped at the sight of Bonnie's handkerchief, the precious trophy he took from Gabe the night he murdered him. He angrily snatched it from her hand and hit her with such force that she heard the sound of her jaw breaking before she passed out. An eerie silence hung in the air. Carla moaned in pain as she regained consciousness. Oliver knelt down beside her and she could see the hate in his eyes. He relished her fear as he wrapped his hands around her throat and slowly squeezed, tighter and tighter. Her blue eyes bulged just as he had imagined. She did not struggle for long but went limp. He stood up and looked down at Carla's lifeless body. *'It just a matter of cleaning up now,'* he thought, devoid of any remorse.

A plan formed in Oliver's mind. He realised that if the body washed up somewhere around the bay, Carla would be recognised. He recalled that workmen had left a saw and hammer behind in the garage when they did some work on the house a few weeks ago and went to fetch them.

Oliver disposed of Carla's dismembered and mangled remains, which took far more time and effort than he anticipated. He however, did not mind as he was sure she would never be found. He glanced at his watch. *'I better call Mum, now,'* he thought as a devious plan to cover his tracks manifested in his brain, *'to ask if she knows where Carla is'.*

"I have no idea, Oliver." Anita gave an account of Carla dropping off Grace earlier that day. "Other than that, she hadn't mentioned anything about going elsewhere. Why?" Anita was concerned, "has something happened?"

"I'm not sure, Mum. She wasn't here when I got home this afternoon. We had dinner plans so I showered and dressed. I fell asleep in the chair waiting for her. I've just woken," he said, so convincingly that he was beginning to believe his own lie.

"Do you think you should notify the police?" said Anita. "It's two a.m."

"To be honest, Mum, I'm not sure what I should do."

"Were you two having trouble?"

"No, not really," Oliver said, laying the foundation to the possibility of Carla having had enough of a loveless marriage and taking off. "Our situation was sorting itself out, or so I thought. Were you aware that Carla had started drinking?"

"Not at all!" Anita exclaimed, horrified. "She was doing her utmost to fit in. I was aware that she was a little anxious because you didn't love her, but as for her drinking, absolutely not!"

'Ha!' Oliver thought. *'There's my explanation ... she was anxious about my not loving her...'*

"Are you listening, Oliver?" Anita said.

"Sorry, Mum. I'm out of my mind with worry. I'm trying to think where she could be. What did you say?"

"I think you should inform the police, straight away."

"Yes, I think you're right," Oliver said, thinking, *'Step one, all good so far!* 'He paused a moment. "I'll keep you informed," he said, pausing again, then said, "How's my little girl? Can she stay with you until things are sorted, or until Carla comes to her senses and returns home? I have no idea what possessed her to go off like this. Without a word! I'm worried sick, Mum. What if she's ill, or worse?"

"For heaven's sake Oliver, Carla could be out with friends," Anita said, surprised that her son was so emotional. *'Perhaps,'* she thought, *'he cares for her more than he realised, until now.'*

Oliver changed into a suit, messed up his hair and made himself look dishevelled before going to the police station. He was told to go home and wait to see if his wife returned. It had been less than twenty-four hours since she had been gone.

Oliver went back to the local police station later that morning to officially report Carla missing. He was distraught and convincing enough to arouse sympathy from everyone, even from the tough police Sergeant.

Bonnie called him the instant she heard the news. "Oh Oliver," she said, "Carla wouldn't have run away without telling anyone."

"How do you know that for certain?" he responded sharply, which made her jump. "You didn't know her well. You told me that yourself." He realised he had spoken too harshly and quickly apologised. "I'm so worried Bonnie. I just want Carla to come home."

"Yes, I did say that, Oliver. That was before Carla and I became friends. We caught up at the foreshore during the mornings she took Grace to the park. She was happy and was hopeful about your marriage."

Oliver's anger was mounting as Bonnie told him about the symbol message. He was thinking that all this was her fault. *'If only she had just minded her own business, I wouldn't have had to kill Carla.'*

Gabe, who was standing beside Bonnie, could sense that something was amiss. Oliver's energy had changed towards her. Gabe was sensing that Bonnie was somehow in danger.

"I had no idea you two had become friends," Oliver said, feigning warmth. "I'm glad of that. Perhaps Carla might have mentioned a place she liked, that she would have gone to?"

"No. I can't recall any. You and Grace were the main topics of our conversation. Oh, and that she would like to come and see the gallery. She was supposed to pay us a visit one day this week," Bonnie said, feeling oddly uneasy. "If there's anything I can do, just let me know," she said, ending the call.

'Now, that's strange. Why was Oliver angry with me one minute then completely changed his tune the next?' she thought. *'I get the feeling he really wasn't too pleased about Carla and I being friendly. Hmm, something is very wrong here. Carla didn't seem upset enough to me or appear to want to leave Oliver. She certainly wouldn't leave without Grace.'*

As weeks passed, all sorts of ridiculous rumours about Carla circulated around the area; she had run off with another man, or that she had a secret life. Bonnie vehemently defended Carla whenever those rumours came up in conversation. Beth and Anita did the same at the Women's Association meetings.

Oliver played the deserted husband well. He refused dinner and social function invitations. "Not up to it," was his response. "Thank you, all the same, I couldn't attend without my wife being by my side," became his mantra. He had even kept a discreet distance from Bonnie. He conducted his business as always but without his usual playful manner. Carefully staging every move he made, his manner of dress was not as immaculate as before, nor was he as well-groomed; all part of his plan of masquerading as the sad and dejected husband.

One other person in the town was not completely convinced Carla Walker had run away. Constable Eric "Samson" Samuels was now Detective Samuels. For years, he had been quietly investigating Gabe Connor's murder in his own time. He and Brady believed Oliver Walker was the killer but could not prove it yet. Now Walker's wife had conveniently left town without a trace.

The week before Brady left for his new posting up to North Queensland, he had handed Detective Samuels the case file on Gabe Connor. "It's up to you now Eric, to get this bastard," were Brady's parting words. They shook hands and went their separate ways.

Detective Samuels was reading through the case file when he saw several accentuated question marks after a notation Brady had made regarding Bonnie Connor: *I think she knows something. She asked some odd questions. Did we hold something for forensics? What was missing from her husband's belongings???'*

'Hmm', Samuels thought, feeling he had struck gold, *'I think I'll pay Bonnie Connor a visit.'*

23

Sandy was sitting at the reception desk, speaking to a client on the phone. "Yes, yeess," she was saying patiently. "That'll be fine Mrs Anderson. I'll personally see to it that the painting is delivered first thing in the morning. Yes. Thank you once again. I shall pass on your compliments to the artist. Good-bye, Mrs Anderson."

She put the phone down with a heavy sigh and thought, '*I should pay myself more money as compensation for mental bloody torture!*'

As she was about to jot down a few more things on her to-do-list, a car she did not recognise drove into the car park. Two official-looking men with blank faces got out. They were dressed in almost identical dark grey suits, white shirts and narrow black ties. Both also wore dark felt hats. Their heavy footsteps walking up the pathway scattered the constellation of fine pebbles.

'*Heavy footed galahs,*' she thought, feeling somewhat annoyed and watched them come inside. '*Trying to be big macho-men, bet they're hen-pecked at home.*'

"Good morning, gentlemen," Sandy beamed in a cheerful manner as her large blue eyes surveyed their hands.

"How may I help you?" '*Hmm, the big fella is kind of cute. He's not wearing a wedding ring.*' She directed all her charm to him.

Samuels and Allen, Brady's replacement, introduced themselves and showed identification. Sandy immediately stood up and thrust her clasped hands towards Samson.

"OK!" she cried, batting her false lashes at him. "You've found me. I surrender! Here, take me!"

Both men were thrown off kilter. They both took a step backwards, puzzled as to what to do. They glanced at each other and shrugged.

"You should see your faces." Sandy laughed outrageously.

The detectives were unsure in which direction to look. Bonnie, working in the studio, heard the laughter and headed towards reception to see what was going on.

"OK," said Samson, shaking his head and trying to harness a smile. "I get it."

"Get what?" Detective Allen grunted, looking baffled.

"Miss ... ahh?"

"Sandy Brewer. But you, Detective Samuels, can call me Sandy," she said provocatively.

"Sandy," Samson said, quickly sizing her up in one glace and liking what he saw, "was taking the piss ... Ah, pardon the language, Sandy ... sorry about that ... was taking the *mickey* out of us for being so *official*."

The three of them turned towards the sound of footsteps heading their way. "It would seem that I'm missing all the fun out here, being cooped up in the studio," Bonnie teased. "Oh, hello, Constable Samuels."

"It's Detective Samuels these days, Mrs Connor."

"Congratulations, Detective," Bonnie said, genuinely pleased for him while thinking, *'But you'll always be affectionately known as Samson to all of us in the area.'* Pausing briefly, she asked, "Are you gentleman here to admire the artwork, or is this an official visit?"

"An official visit, Mrs Connor," Detective Samuels said, clearing his throat and standing taller. "Can we talk in private?"

Bonnie glanced at Sandy and raised her brow. "I won't be long," she said and directed Samuels to her office. Detective Allen followed a discreet distance behind.

"Now," Bonnie said, pointing to seats, "What's going on, Detective?"

"We're working on two cases, Mrs Connor, the disappearance of Mrs Carla Walker and your husband's murder. I think you could have some information that might help me with your husband's case."

"Go on," said Bonnie.

"I have to give credit to Brady for the detailed case file he kept on your husband. He worked on it for years, in his spare time, going over different scenarios and possibilities of how, when, why and who. Of course, I can't disclose any of this to you, yet. When reading through your husband's file, I came across a note Brady made about your query regarding your husband's personal effects. Did you notice something missing from his belongings, when they were returned to you?"

Samuels studied Bonnie as he addressed her. He thought he saw a flicker of relief reflect in her eyes. He certainly saw hope there.

'You can trust him, Bonnie,' Gabe whispered.

"Yes Detective, Brady was correct. There was something missing."

"Will you tell me what it was?"

"A white linen handkerchief with my initials B.M. embroidered in one corner, between two pink roses. My Grandmother gives me a box of linen handkerchiefs every year for my birthday." Bonnie took a handkerchief from her pocket. "It looks like this one, but the one I gave Gabe had 1967 embroidered on it as well – the year I turned eighteen. It was also the year we were married."

Samuels made a quick calculation in his head and calculated Bonnie's age to be twenty-six, ten years his junior. "Can you tell me when you last saw Mrs Walker?"

He wrote rapidly as Bonnie told him the details of her association with Carla, from when she had first known her to the last time they had spoken.

"Carla's disappearance is completely out of character from what I know of her, Detective. She was planning to visit our gallery ... a person who makes plans doesn't just run away without leaving a note to at least one friend or a family member," Bonnie said candidly. "I can't help feeling she's in trouble or something worse."

"What can you tell me about Oliver Walker? I hear you two were an item for a while."

"Ha! Well, Detective," Bonnie retorted, "whoever told you that little gem of information was very much mistaken."

"You were seen in Oliver Walker's company on several occasions," Samson said.

"That's correct," she sighed in frustration. "But just as friends. When I realised Oliver's intention, I told him I wasn't interested in him or any man that I was still in love with my husband."

"And how did he deal with the rejection?

Bonnie's expression was blank. "OK, I think." she shrugged absentmindedly. "I didn't analyse his reaction. As far as I was concerned, it was no longer an issue. Soon after that Carla told Oliver she was pregnant."

"How did he react to the pregnancy? Was he angry?"

"What are you getting at, Detective? You're not suggesting that Oliver had anything to do with Carla's disappearance?"

"I'm looking at all angles and possibilities, Mrs Connor ... leaving no stone unturned." His tone reflected absolute determination.

Samson noticed Bonnie's expression falter as if she remembered something. He was familiar with that look. "What is it, Mrs Connor? You've recollected something, haven't you?"

"Yes, yes I have – but," she hesitated. "It could be nothing ... just Oliver being Oliver."

"What do you mean?"

"When we were kids, Oliver threw the most frightful tantrums whenever he couldn't get his own way. The day he told me about the pregnancy, he admitted to me that he wanted to kill Carla."

"Did he say why?" Samson asked, keeping the excitement of finally getting somewhere from his voice.

"Yes, Detective, he did." Bonnie was clearly uncomfortable, so he waited until she was ready to continue. "I'm sorry to say that Oliver had aspirations of marrying me. He felt that Carla had ruined his chances of doing that but," she quickly added, "as I've already told you, Detective, I made it very clear to Oliver that I was still, and would always be in love with Gabe. He appeared to accept that and seemed happy for us to remain friends. He gave me no reason to think otherwise."

"Then why do I sense that you don't like Oliver Walker?"

"Ha!" she quipped. "I detested Ollie while growing up. He was a horrible kid and a worse teenager. The man he is today is far different from the person he once was, I can tell you that."

"Please do, Mrs Connor. I'd like to hear your perception of him," he said, even though he was already well briefed on Oliver's infamous history.

"Gosh!" Bonnie said, taking in a long breath, "Where do I start?"

"How about you start from the beginning?"

"Well ..." she began. Detective Samuels picked up his pen. He wrote pages and pages of notes, being vigilant not to miss a word Bonnie said.

Detective Allen sat quietly in the background during the whole interview. As an observer, he was impressed with the easy manner with which Samson had conducted himself, and could see why his colleague had graduated with honours.

When Bonnie had finished talking, Samson closed his notebook and slipped his pen inside the pocket of his jacket. Satisfied that he had more than enough to move forward with the case, he was eager to get back to Roma Street to call Brady. *'He would want to know about this,'* being true to his promise to keep him up-to-date with the case. Samuels thanked Bonnie for her time and the detectives made their way out.

"Oh, Detective Samuels," Sandy called, "a message for you," she said, offering him a folded slip of paper. He looked puzzled as he took it from her. He unfolded the note and read it. Although his expression was blank, she noticed the corners of his mouth turned up slightly.

"Thank you, Sandy," he said as he waved good-bye.

After the detectives had gone, Bonnie said to Sandy, "Did you do what I think you did?"

"That depends on what you think I did," she said archly, admitting to nothing. "I shall inform you of the outcome when I know myself."

Detective Samuels and Sergeant Brady discussed both cases at great length over the phone, concluding that they were connected. Also, they were willing to wager their careers on the fact that Oliver Walker was involved, up to his neck in both cases – they just had to prove it.

"I'll do whatever I can from this end. One way or another, we'll get this bastard! I hear his old man is losing it … too much booze, they say. I was hoping we'd lock him up too. He might cark it before that happens though. Anyway," Brady sighed, "Poetic justice is better than no justice at all."

"It's going to be difficult; you know that don't you, mate?" Samuels said. "The family's off limits, orders from the top. I'll have to work on this in my own time. I've been told to tidy things up and close the case, a.s.a.p."

24

Anita usually read the morning paper from cover to cover while eating her breakfast. Since Carla's unexplained disappearance she had only glanced over it, avoiding the wild accusations written about her family. As weeks turned into months, the articles about Carla's disappearance had moved from the front page to a few lines in the middle of the paper.

It was beyond her understanding as to why Carla would leave, just out of the blue. She began to suspect foul play and seriously considered that Oliver might be involved, somehow. She was also disgusted with her husband, who had promised to keep his philandering private. To his shame, Bill Walker flaunted his womanising, drinking and gambling openly, as if his days were numbered, thumbing his nose up at the media, doing more harm than good to the family.

Then came the morning when Bill had not joined Anita for breakfast. They had an agreement that if he stayed anywhere overnight, he would let her know. She knew he was home as she had heard him drive in the night before.

Anita was feeling frustrated due to the mounting pressure of the past few months and Bill's erratic behaviour. She furiously dabbed the corners of her mouth with her napkin and then dropped it beside her plate, pushed the chair away from the table and stormed off to Bill's room. She knocked. No answer. She opened the door and discovered that his bed had not been slept in. *'That's strange,'* she thought, and then hurried down to the garage to make sure she had not been mistaken, that she had heard him come home. His car was there and so was Bill. He was slumped up against the car window. She caught her breath and froze for a moment then rushed back upstairs to call an ambulance.

As the paramedics went through the procedure of lifting Bill out of the car and laying him carefully on the stretcher, Anita stood in the background watching in silence, assessing her feelings for him - she had none, just a sense of relief that she would no longer have to bear the brunt of his behaviour.

The coroner's report said the cause of death was heart failure. There was no mention of the drugs and alcohol she knew would have been present in his system, which surprised her. *'Bless him,'* she thought of the coroner, *'I just couldn't have survived the scrutiny about that from reporters wanting a story.'* Anita made up her mind there and then to leave the country. *'London will be a nice change for Grace and me, until this mess settles down,'* she reasoned.

The funeral was a low-key affair. Anita was not surprised that so few attended. Now that Bill could no longer assist them, there was nothing for anyone to gain by going, other than gossip-mongers like Beryl Naed and Gladys Lock, who delighted in all kinds of tittle-tattle. Their hungry eyes scanned their surroundings.

Anita walked towards the front of the chapel. When she saw Beryl and Gladys perched up the front smirking, she cringed. To her relief she noticed the Masons sitting on the opposite side. She acknowledged them and a few others whom she considered genuine friends and ignored everyone else.

After the service, Joe and Beth approached Anita. "I won't be a hypocrite, Mrs Walker," said Joe frankly, "I didn't like your husband, but Beth tells me you're a good egg." Anita smiled.

"So, if you need help with anything, you just let Beth know and we'll be there, OK?"

"Thank you, Joe," Anita said, and then turned to Beth. "So the gossip about Joe is true," she winked.

Joe's ears immediately pricked up, "Gossip? What gossip?"

"That you are an open and honest, generous man and a wonderful husband. That you and Beth are the happiest married couple in this town."

"Aaah," Joe said, bashfully. "I do the best I can, Mrs Walker."

"Anita," she said.

"Anita. Yep", he said, hugging Beth to him. "We sure are happy. I've had a few highlights in my lifetime but the best decision I've made was marrying this amazing woman." Joe beamed with pride.

The trio chatted a little longer and during the conversation, Anita mentioned that she intended to live in London for a while.

"Of course, I shall take little Grace with me. I can't have her growing up in this quagmire of tragedy. So, yes Joe, there is something you can do for me."

Joe nodded.

"Will you take care of my house while I'm away? That will save me the rigmarole of interviewing potential caretakers. I shall employ you instead. I will feel more comfortable with you in charge."

"I'd be happy to, Anita," Joe said. "I can check on the house on my way home from work."

Before going their separate ways, Anita invited Joe and Beth to her home the following day to finalise details regarding the house. A few days later, Anita and her granddaughter departed for London. Oliver was grateful that his mother took Grace with her.

'I wouldn't have been able to look after her on my own,' he reasoned. Although Oliver had agreed Grace should go with his mother, he really wanted her with him.

On the evening of Anita and Grace's departure, Oliver began to have night terrors. Over and over again he relived the horrific murder he had committed in the house. Odd things began happening. Doors opened and slammed shut for no apparent reason.

Away from his home, Oliver functioned normally. He was clear-headed when managing his business affairs and dealing with clients. At home, it was a different situation. His mind was addled. After repeatedly and very convincingly telling the story about Carla running off and leaving him and Grace, his lie became his truth.

"Damn you to hell Carla, for leaving like that!" he bellowed, walking from room to room. "It's your fault that my little Grace isn't here with me…"

During one of his relentless rantings, the house suddenly turned icy cold and eerie. The frightening chill that ran through Oliver made every hair on his body stand on end. He imagined the walls pressing in on him. His heart rate quickened and perspiration oozed from his pores, soaking his clothes. Overcome with fear, he ran to the front door. The handle would not turn. The door was jammed shut. He dashed to the back door and tried to open it, frantically yanking on its knob. It too would not budge.

'What the hell's going on?' Oliver thought as panic took over. Sweat dripped from his face. He could smell gas. He looked at the stove and just caught sight of a flash seconds before it exploded. He managed to escape the flames and the thick smoke billowing out of the side of the house. He ran to his bedroom, to the drawer that hid Bonnie's handkerchief, his trophy. He grabbed hold of it and clutched it tight. With arms outstretched, he blindly fumbled his way to the veranda through choking smoke, flames now licking the roof and walls. Burning timbers began falling around him as the fire rapidly consumed the oxygen in the room. Oliver covered his mouth with the sleeve of his shirt as he made his way through the inferno. The veranda door was just visible. As he reached for the handle, Carla's bloodied and disfigured body appeared in front of him. Oliver froze, disbelieving his eyes. They had not deceived him. When

Carla moved towards him, he screamed in sheer terror then collapsed in a heap on the floor.

A neighbour had phoned the fire brigade. When they arrived, one of them called out, "Is anyone inside?"

"I think so," said the distressed neighbour, "I thought I heard screaming a while ago."

Samson was sitting at his desk, going over reports of a recent robbery, when the phone rang.

"Detective Samuels."

"G'day, mate. It's Jono," the forensic pathologist said.

"Hey, Jono," the detective responded blithely, leaning back in his chair. "How's it hangin' mate?"

Jono laughed. "I've got something very interesting here you just might want to have a gander at. How fast can you get over here?"

"I'm on my way."

A short time later, Detective Samuels was standing beside his long-time friend John Gibson, staring at a charred corpse laid out on a stainless steel slab.

"I don't know how you can cope with this, day in and day out," said the detective, cringing, "this place gives me the bloody willies."

"Ah, you get used to it," said Jono nonchalantly. "Now tell me, do you see anything unusual?"

"Mate," the detective squirmed. "All I see is a lump of blistered, stinking flesh."

"Look again, carefully. Take your time."

The detective forced himself to run his eyes over the charred carcass. At first, he did not see anything significant, but once he had accommodated to the fact that the sight before him was human, he saw it.

"The hand!" he shouted, pleased with himself, "It's not burnt."

"Right," Jono said.

"It's closed. Was this … this … person clutching something? Who is this? Who was this?" asked the detective holding a handkerchief over his nose.

Jono walked over to a nearby table and picked up a small plastic bag and held it up – inside was a white linen handkerchief, with B.M 1967 embroidered in one corner between two roses.

"Will this answer your questions?"

Detective Samuel's eyes were as large as saucers. He shook his head saying, "I don't fucking believe it!" He paused dumbfounded, scratching his head. "Are you telling me that this piece of garbage is Oliver Walker?"

"Yep!"

"You bloody beauty!" Samuels laughed.

"Brady and I can finally put this baby to bed. Well, well, how about that? Poetic justice got him in the end."

NEXT GENERATION

25

"Granny, I need help closing my bag!" Grace called from her bedroom as she struggled to jam in the last of her clothes.

"Darling," Anita said, shaking her head in amusement when she came into the bedroom and eyed the swollen suitcase. "Little wonder it won't close. It's full to capacity. How about we start again?" She smiled warmly, scooping up a hand full of clothes and placing them on the bed. "I really wasn't thinking when I agreed to Edward going on holidays before we left. He would have had your things packed in a jiffy. Ah well," she sighed heavily, "we'll just have to manage without him. Thankfully, he has promised to be in Brisbane in time to unpack the boxes I have already shipped to Australia"

Edward had come into their lives soon after Anita first arrived in the UK when she realised that she needed help. She placed an ad in the local paper. Hours later, a tall, fit-looking man, in his late fifties, with a ruddy complexion and warm smile, knocked on her front door. "Hello Mrs Walker!" he said confidently in a cheerful Irish accent. "My name is Edward O'Malley."

Anita checked out all his glowing references, and then Edward moved into the downstairs annex and quickly became their 'go-to-man' whenever disaster struck or things needed fixing or fetching. 'Edward, will you drive me to the shops?' 'Edward, will you fix my shoe, please.' 'Edward, I need …'

Edward happily obliged. *'As long as they need me,'* he thought, *'I have a job.'* He had no idea that neither Grace nor Anita considered him as an employee. He was family, as far as they were concerned. It was the Australian way to eventually 'adopt' people into the family they liked and trusted.

Over the years, little by little, Edward revealed things about himself to Anita. He was born in Derrylin, a small town in Northern Ireland, an only child, and did not have any family that he knew about. "I've travelled alone all my life. Fewer complications that way," he told Anita with honest frankness. "I've been all over the world – did odd jobs here and there when I needed money."

"Why did you stop travelling?"

"Just got tired," he said, without clarification. "This is the longest I've stayed put at any one place. I guess this is where I'll remain ... if that's OK with you, Mrs Walker."

"Edward, you have been with us long enough now. I think it's high time you called me Anita."

He smiled awkwardly. "Ok," he shrugged. "Mrs, ah ... Anita."

One day when Edward came into the kitchen to replace a leaky tap washer, Anita casually said, "Grace and I are moving back to Queensland."

He froze, thinking he was being abandoned. His heart sank as his eyes clouded in shock.

"Would you like to come with us?" she added.

Edward smiled broadly with relief. "I would indeed, Anita. Thank you for including me."

"Oh Edward, Grace and I couldn't function without you," she said, sincerely. "Of course," Anita added thoughtfully, "there will be a matter of immigration, etc. You will have to take care of all that first. At least you have employment."

Edward smiled confidently. He was very familiar with what was entailed having travelled extensively and lived in many countries, including Australia.

"I can hardly wait to get to Brisbane," Grace would say, full of enthusiasm every time her grandmother mentioned how beautiful the bay was or how glorious the weather. "I loathe the cold!" she said, melodramatically. "I never want to feel this cold again, ever! I couldn't bear it."

Anita smiled and listened attentively to Grace. She adored her and took great delight in Grace's nattering, how she was looking forward to making new friends, and how thrilled she was being allowed to enrol in the local state high school instead of a private college, as she had in the UK.

"Oh, I shall miss Jill and Casper, of course." Grace expressed, with downcast eyes while holding her hands to her heart. She then brightened, suddenly. "Perhaps," Grace said, "they could visit me in Brisbane, eh Granny?"

"That depends on their parents."

"Oh, they will be allowed to come," Grace said, confidently.

"Let's just get settled into our new home first, before you start inviting everyone to Brisbane," Anita said kindly. "After that, you can have as many guests as you like."

"Our new life will be wonderful, Granny! I can feel it. It's our destiny. We shall be very happy living in Australia. I'm going home!" Grace said, oozing with pride.

The bubbly teenager's motive for wanting to return to Australia was far more involved than just escaping the cold weather. She intended to find out what happened to her parents.

Grace was six years old when, quite unexpectedly, at breakfast one morning, she asked Anita, "Where's my Mummy and Daddy?"

Anita coughed, spilling tea from the cup she was about to sip from all over the tablecloth.

"What made you ask that, sweetheart?"

"Casper's mummy and daddy are getting a divorce. Where are my mummy and daddy?"

"Oh darling, they are in heaven," Anita said, keeping her voice steady. "The angels came and took them when you were just a little tot. God needed them to be with him. He knew I loved you so very much and that you would be safe with me. He also knew that you would be alright without a mummy and daddy because you're a very brave little girl."

That was the day Anita gave Grace a photo album full of photographs of her parents. Over the years, Grace had often perused that album and thought that she would have been proud to have introduced her friends to her parents. She also recognised herself in both of them, which gave her a sense of identity. She had inherited her father's flaming red hair and her mother's large brown eyes and full mouth. As Grace matured, she noticed that in every photograph there was a gap between her parents, never with arms around each other. *'What were their smiles hiding?'* she wondered. Grace sensed that her grandmother was uncomfortable talking about them. She decided that she would quietly investigate the matter herself when she arrived in Brisbane.

As the aircraft landed Anita was apprehensive. *'We're home. But I wonder what awaits us.'*

Gabriel was at the airport to welcome Anita and Grace. He waved when he saw them coming out of customs.

"Oh, how lovely of you to meet us, Gabriel," Anita said warmly. "I was expecting your grandfather. I hope he isn't ill?"

"G'day, Mrs Walker!" Gabriel said, winking at Grace. "Nah, pa's giving the house a last minute check over. He's a perfectionist."

"Well, according to our correspondence over the years, I can only imagine that my home is the best-kept house in the street," she laughed genially and then stood back and studied the lad a moment. "I'm sure you must have grown a foot taller since the last photograph I saw of you." Anita went quiet a moment and then said. "I do believe, Gabriel, you are the image of your father, he certainly was the most handsome man I'd ever set eyes upon."

"So people say, Mrs Walker," he replied, smiling at Grace, ignoring the 'handsome' compliment. "I've grown just as fast as Grace, the pretty toddler who to use to play in the sandpit all those years ago."

"Well then, Gabriel," Grace replied quickly in playful banter, "You would've been about four years old at the time, a bit of a toddler yourself, eh?"

"Yep, I guess you could say that," he said passively, recalling the advice his grandfather once gave him: *'If you want a peaceful life, never argue with a woman'.* Gabriel reasoned, *'Judging by her red hair, Grace would be one hell of a force to reckon with.'*

Grace discreetly observed Gabriel as he collected their luggage and loaded it onto the trolley. *'Yeah, he's very handsome,'* she thought, *'with those big broad shoulders. He's too cocky for my liking. I imagine we'll be best friends.'* Then something he said suddenly struck a chord with her.

As they walked to the car, Grace spoke to Gabriel in a voice low enough so that Anita could not hear. "You mentioned my playing in the sand when I was a baby. So you were there too?"

"Yep, I was sometimes," he grinned, giving her a sideways glance, about to start joshing her again. The expression on her face stopped him.

"Hey, are you alright? You looked sorta weird."

"Shhh, don't let Granny hear you. I'll explain later. It's about my mother."

"Righto," he shrugged.

"So much has changed in the years we've been gone," Anita said, wistfully peering through the car window. "This bridge wasn't here when we left." Anita sighed, "It was such an ordeal to get to the airport. We had to drive through the city, taking precious time and now, here we are, just minutes from home. How marvellous that is!"

"It's called the Gateway Arterial, Mrs Walker." Gabriel announced, proudly "Prince Philip opened it May 14th, 1986." He grinned mischievously, "It was really unofficially opened before that – January 11th from my recollection, for people to walk across it on that day. Brisbane sure is changing since the announcement of World Expo 88, there's been a lot of road works and construction going on around the city for a few years now."

"I love what I'm seeing, Granny," Grace said, looking every which way. "And it's so warm! We'd be freezing our bottoms off by now if we were back in the UK. This is the place for me. I shall never leave. It's heaven on earth!" she said, taking a deep breath and then chimed, "Gabriel?" Her voice trailed off.

"Hmm?" He responded, glancing at her in the rear-view mirror. She went silent, looking pensive. He looked at her again when her silence lengthened.

"You have an interesting name," she finally said.

"Your point is?" he asked nonchalantly.

"Gabriel is the name of the Guardian Angel," she said and went silent once again. She was looking out of the car window. As an afterthought, she quipped, "I think you can be my guardian angel. You're big and strong enough."

"If you keep dishing out cheek to other people, the way you're giving it to me, you'll surely need more than a guardian angel," he grinned.

"You can also introduce me to your friends," she said, unperturbed.

"Ah, I think they might be a bit too old for you."

"I'm sixteen!" Grace declared indignantly.

"That's what I mean. But some of my mates have little sisters your age."

"What! I'm not a little ..."

Anita sat back in her seat, quietly watching and listening to the pair bantering back and forth like sibling rivals. She had no doubt Grace would settle into her new life with ease. By the looks of things, she had already made her first friend.

Gabriel liked Grace. He felt comfortable around her. *'She's the only female I've met that didn't ogle me,'* he thought, *'she hasn't done the 'flirty thing' girls do with their eyes. She obviously doesn't take herself too seriously,'* he reasoned and glanced at her again. *'It appears that she has no idea just how beautiful she is, either'.*

Gabe was travelling with them too; he often kept an eye on his son. When they arrived at the house he got out of the car and was leaning up against the wall, watching as Gabriel unloaded the car. *'Well, well,'* he was shaking his head. *'Who would have thought ... the daughter of my killer has caught my boy's attention.'*

"That's the last of the luggage, Mrs Walker," Gabriel said. He turned to leave and then stopped. "Oh, I almost forgot. Dinner's at our house this evening. Mum thought you wouldn't be up to cooking after your long flight."

"Great!" Grace replied, looking at her grandmother. "Granny?"

"That's very thoughtful of your mother. I shall look forward to seeing everyone again," she lied. She was terrified at the thought of seeing everyone again.

"OK. See you both at six."

Addressing Grace, Gabriel said, sporting a mischievous grin, knowing full well Grace would bite. "I'll invite one of my friends' little cousins over for you to play with ... if it isn't past her bedtime."

"Go home Gabriel Connor, your mother's calling you!" Grace shouted at him as he ran down the stairs, laughing.

26

Grace and Anita looked at each other in surprise when the taxi pulled up.

"Wow, there are so many cars parked in the street, Granny," said Grace with mounting excitement. "I can hear music coming from the house." There was a twinkle in her eyes when she smiled. "It looks like a party. C'mon, Granny!"

Anita hesitated, unsure of what to expect. *'I did leave under awkward circumstances.'*

Grace took hold of her Grandmother's hand and half pulled her up the pathway. "C'mon," she repeated, unaware of the reason for Anita's wavering.

"Hello, Anita!" Beth called, hurrying towards her with outstretched arms. "It's wonderful to see you again," she said, embracing her warmly.

Beth turned to Grace and hugged her too. "Aaah," she remarked, casually as if she were talking about the weather. "Gabriel was right. You are beautiful!"

Anita beamed with pride at her granddaughter, who brushed off the compliment. Grace would rather be praised for her intelligence than her looks.

'Beauty will fade, but intelligence is evergreen ... that's if age or illness doesn't screw up my brain,' was her mantra.

"Thank you, Mrs Mason," Grace responded politely. "It's nice to finally meet you. Granny has mentioned you many times over the years. She holds you in high regard."

Beth smiled and glanced at Anita with raised brows. "Well, the feeling is mutual, Grace. Your Grandmother is certainly esteemed around here."

"Yeah, Granny's pretty cool!" Grace said, pulling Anita close to her and then releasing her. "If you don't mind, Mrs Mason, I'll go and look for Gabriel. Where will I find him?"

"Just follow the sound of the music, love. He's in the backyard chatting to his friends."

Beth and Anita ambled up the path arm in arm. "Grace is very mature for her age," Beth remarked admiringly. "You've done an excellent job with her, Anita. She certainly minds her Ps and Qs."

"Like an old woman at times," came Anita's reply. She added, "I hope I have redeemed myself with the good Lord by being an engaged grandparent to Grace. He knows I wasn't much of a mother to Oliver," she confessed remorsefully.

"Oh, don't be too hard on yourself, Anita. Children don't come with a *how-to* manual. We try to do the best we can and hope for a good outcome."

The chatter over the music became more distinctive as Grace walked up the path. She could easily distinguish Gabriel's voice above the other guests and heard him say, "Gracie should be here by now. I'll go and see what's keeping her."

A moment later, he came face to face with an irate redhead. "I heard that!" she said, through pursed lips, both hands placed firmly on her hips in a declaration of war. "It's Grace! Not EVER GRACIE!"

"So you eavesdrop, too!" Gabriel replied, rebuffing her fury. "C'mon. Come and meet my mates."

Grace faltered; she was thrown off kilter when she had not received an apology from Gabriel. *'He has no respect. Moron!'* She was warming up to have a good, silent rant when she heard Gabriel's passive voice say, "Are you coming?" Grace nodded and followed him.

"Here they are." A tall, well built, olive-skinned lad with broad shoulders and unruly blonde hair called out, spurring the small group to cheer Gabriel and Grace, as they walked towards them.

"This is Tim Osborne," Gabriel told Grace, punching his friend lightly on the arm. We've been mates since the day he rescued Bobby and me from a gang of 'rough-heads.' "

Grace gave him a questioning look.

"Yeah, I know. It doesn't seem like it now, but Bobby and I were squirts when we were kids. Fodder for tough kids to cut their teeth on when they needed to be initiated into a gang if you get my drift?"

Grace nodded.

"We were travelling home on the train from the footy, full of grand final fever, and thrilled that our team had kicked arse when a gang of punks boarded our carriage. They took one look at us 'weeds' and it was on. Unbeknown to us, Tim was on the train too, sitting behind us." (*So was Gabe, ready to intervene if he needed to.*) "When the five of them sauntered over to us, acting like tough dudes, Tim stood up and challenged them. Those kids nearly crapped their duds ... he towered over all of them." The boys laughed. "We can laugh about it now. But we sure as hell weren't laughing at the time. We've been mates ever since."

"You and Bobby are the same height and size as Tim, now," said Grace amazed. "How did you both grow so big and tall so fast?"

"Vegemite on Weet-Bix that's how," Bobby Taylor chipped in, winking at his mates.

The lads grinned cheekily at each other when Grace asked, "What's Vegemite Weet-Bix?"

"C'mon," Gabriel said, 'I'll show you."

They all trailed into his grandmother's kitchen. Grace grimaced at the sight of the thick black 'stuff' in the jar Gabriel took from the cupboard. "It looks and smells weird," she said, leaning in to study the contents when Tim removed the lid. She was almost convinced it was some sort of prank they were about to play on her. "OK. What about the Weet-Bix?"

"I'm getting it now. Keep cool!" Gabriel said, with his back to her.

"Here, take a bite," he said, swinging around on his heels, offering Grace a small, thick, rectangular, wheat biscuit he had covered with the thick, black paste. She accepted it with hesitation and bit into the biscuit anyway.

"Yuck!" she yelled, spitting it out. That's gross!" she shouted wiping her tongue with the back of her hand.

"Water, water, please!" Grace cried.

"Now you're a true blue Aussie kid!" the boys declared, laughing good-naturedly.

Beth came rushing into the kitchen when she heard the commotion, Bonnie and Anita following. They sighed with relief when they realised nothing grave had happened.

"What are you boys up to now?" Beth challenged with mocked seriousness. Beth and Bonnie harnessed their laughter at the sight of the opened Vegemite jar and Weet-Bix packet on the bench, guessing what must have had taken place. Anita was totally confused.

"Granny," Grace said, between wiping her tongue with a paper towel Gabriel handed her. "I've just been tricked into eating Vegemite on a Weet-Bix. "So now I'm officially an Aussie kid!" she chuckled.

The laughter subsided and everyone turned around when they heard knocking on the screen door. "May I come in?" came a female voice. The light behind the visitor made it difficult to see her face. Beth took a step closer to the door to see who it was.

"Oh, hello, Lilly," said Beth, surprised to see her. "Of course, you can come in. Is Max with you?"

"Thank you, Mrs Mason. No, he's on a skiing holiday in Switzerland. Gabriel asked if I'd like to come over to meet Grace."

"That's me," Grace chimed before anyone could introduce her. Glancing over at Gabriel, she said in jest, "So, you're the *little cousin*?"

"Yeah," Lilly nodded, pulling a face, and looked over at Bobby. He winked at her. "It's a drag being considered *little*. They treat me like a child."

Grace instantly liked Lilly Dixon. She liked her warm smile and her lovely long, dead-straight, raven hair, the way it shone like glass. Grace sensed that they would be life-long friends.

The girls forgot about the others as they quickly engaged in easy conversation. They left the kitchen and wandered outside to sit beside the swimming pool.

"It's lovely sitting out here," Grace stated, with sincere appreciation. "The weather wasn't anything like this in the UK. I hate the cold. I couldn't get warm even with all the heating we had in our lovely home. Now, this climate is more to my liking."

A warm breeze swept across the yard as Grace was speaking. The lights in the paper bags placed around the yard flickered, catching Graces' attention. Her curiosity got the better of her.

"Those bag things around the yard look amazing the way they light up the garden," Grace remarked, pointing at them. "I haven't seen anything like those before. Obviously, they are some sort of lanterns?"

"They're candles in paper bags," replied Lilly casually, as she lounged in the deck chair. "They're filled with sand to secure the candle sitting inside. They look great, but I think they're better during the winter. They make cold nights feel warm and cosy," Lilly paused. She leaned closer to Grace and whispered.

"What's really cool is that pool. It looks so inviting. I'd love to jump in," she grinned.

"It sure does," Grace beamed. "We could ask."

"Nah, I can't stay that long," said Lilly.

As the girls talked, Grace learned that she and Lilly had much in common.

"What's Wynnum High like?" she asked, with wide-eyed interest.

"You're going there?"

Grace nodded.

"That's great!" exclaimed Lilly, adding, "You'll love it. We have so much fun. Our group is the 'cool' group," she said, smiling mischievously. "We, there's about twenty of us, sit on the hill at recess ..."

They also discovered that neither of them took high school too seriously and they both adamantly agreed that school was the best place to socialise.

Gabriel was observing Grace and Lilly from across the yard while his mates bantered among themselves. He was pleased they had hit it off so well. Sue, the girl he had been casually dating for the past few weeks, sidled up to him.

"I'm feeling neglected," she purred. When Gabriel did not respond, she followed his gaze to where the girls were sitting.

"Cradle snatching now, are we?" she joked, but there was malice in her tone as she slid her arms around his waist.

"What? No!" he exclaimed, pulling away from her.

"Ouch!" she shrieked. "You almost broke my arms."

In a flash, everyone there was buzzing around Sue like flies on a corpse and she milked it for all it was worth. Gabriel quickly apologised. But her remark revealed to him her true personality. Feigning concern he said, "You're hurt. I'd better take you home."

As the party came to an end and Lilly had already left, Grace offered to help Bonnie clean up.

"You knew my mother, didn't you Mrs Connor?" Grace casually enquired while tossing paper plates and plastic cups into the bin. Bonnie baulked at the question. She was reluctant to say anything. She had no idea what Anita had already told Grace – if anything at all. Grace waited patiently for her to respond. She followed Bonnie into the kitchen. Bonnie cleared her throat and took her time replying. "I did, Grace. Why do you ask?"

I want to find out what happened to her," Grace said adamantly, refusing to be dissuaded, as she put the dirty dishes she had carried inside onto the benchtop. There was a determination in the look she gave Bonnie.

"Granny avoids the subject whenever I ask her. I was six years old when she told me my parents had gone to heaven. That's won't wash anymore, Mrs Connor. I need to know what happened to my mother. I know my father died in the fire that burnt our home to the ground. But, I know nothing about my mother."

"It's not my place to say anything," Bonnie said. She paused and studied Grace. It was evident to Bonnie that Grace was not about to let the matter drop. She sighed heavily and said, "How about you leave it with me. I shall have a chat to your grandmother ... now that you're older perhaps she is ready to tell you herself."

"Thank you, Mrs Connor. I'd appreciate that." Grace said, feeling hopeful.

A week later, Anita and Grace were having breakfast. "Mrs Connor," Anita began, "mentioned you had asked her for information about your mother."

"Yes, that's right. I did."

"Well, I imagine you are old enough to know the truth. It's not a pretty story, sweetheart." Anita waited for Grace to respond but she simply sat still, bracing herself for whatever she was about to hear.

"Your mother vanished one day, without a trace. No one knows what actually happened to her."

Grace's eyes widened. "Then Granny, doesn't that mean there's a chance she's still alive?"

"Oh darling, I wish that were true, but I doubt it."

"How can you say that if no one knows for sure?"

Anita hung her head weighing up the pros and cons of how much she should tell Grace. "Perhaps now isn't the right time for discussing this, Grace. Perhaps you're not mature enough to grasp what happened …"

"I am, Granny!" Grace interrupted. "I am. So please, please tell me the whole truth. Please, Granny!"

"Darling, this is disturbing even for me to think about it. How can I be sure it won't affect you in some negative way later on? That's why I have avoided telling you."

Grace became impatient and interrupted again. "Please, Granny, just tell me."

"Alright," Anita agreed, pouring herself another cup of tea.

Graces' emotions rode like a roller coaster throughout the course of Anita's narrative. She had to repeatedly assure herself that she was an adult and could handle hearing that her father was narcissistic and that more than likely he had murdered her mother. What puzzled Grace was that there was not a skerrick of evidence to substantiate a probable murder, one way or another. It was all assumption.

"My father was insane," Grace said, devoid of all emotion.

"No, Grace. Your father was without restraint. Which, I have to admit is where your grandfather and I were at fault. I certainly wouldn't have ever won the mother of the year award. I was busy doing charity work when I should have been looking after my own child. I forgot that charity begins at home."

"Oh, Granny, I could never fault you. You've been both mother and father to me. I would easily give you that award. You're the best!" Grace said, jumping up from the table to hug her. "What was my mother like?"

"She was very pretty. You have her beautiful dark eyes and her lovely full mouth." Anita smiled and continued. "She was smart and kind. I know she loved your father."

"Was mother unstable?"

"OH NO!" Anita declared unwaveringly, "Whatever gave you that idea?"

"You mentioned that she thought father didn't love her."

"Your mother didn't feel secure. There's a difference, Grace. She hoped with all her heart that he would come to love her. But sadly, he was besotted with someone else."

"Mrs Connor?"

"Yes Grace, as I told you." Anita looked at her granddaughter. Her brow creased. "You do realise none of what happened was Mrs Connor's fault."

"Yes, of course," replied Grace. "I was just thinking that I couldn't blame my father for being in love with her. She is beautiful. She reminds me of Grace Kelly, the movie star."

"I hope I have put your curiosity to rest now?"

"I've just one question, Granny. I want to know what happened to mother. I'll keep investigating her disappearance, even if it takes me the rest of my life to find the answer."

27

Edward arrived in Brisbane a few days before the many boxes of Anita and Graces' precious possessions were delivered from the UK, as he had promised. Soon everything was unpacked and in its place.

Anita marvelled at the many changes that had taken place during her absence. Newspapers and television stations were full of news about World Expo 88, overshadowing the infamous Fitzgerald Inquiry into police corruption, which already had been in session for over a year.

'Oh, my Lord,' Anita thought, rubbing her forehead as she followed the inquiry in *The Australian,* the only newspaper she trusted to accurately report the facts. *'After all this time, the dirt is finally coming out in the wash. If Bill were alive today, no doubt the family would have been embroiled in a horrid scandal.'* Anita exhaled heavily with gratitude for being spared all of that. She turned the page.

The excitement was mounting as the days drew nearer to the opening of Expo 88. Channel Seven's slogan, 'Love you, Brisbane' that Kim Durant sang from the early eighties until 1988, became the city's anthem. The song was so addictive that many people were prone to belting out, *'Love You, Brisbane!'* every time they heard the song.

'Together We Shall See the World', written by Frank Millard and Carol Lloyd was Expo's theme song. The commercial promoting the major event was aired non-stop on the radio and television, the way 'Love you, Brisbane' had. This tune was just as catchy. Anita could not get the melody out of her head. She began humming the song without even realising it and when she did, she thought, *'I'm brain-washed already and the show hasn't even opened yet.'* She chuckled to herself, *'I wouldn't have thought I would be looking forward to visiting Expo, loathing crowds the way I do. But I have to admit that I am.'*

Anita was familiar with the area of largely abandoned industrial land on the southern side of the Brisbane River, opposite the city's central business district, the chosen location for Expo 88. The daily news reports of the site's transformation were astonishing. Old derelict buildings that had littered the grounds for years were replaced with spectacular pavilions which the thirty-five participating countries would call home for six months.

An enthusiastic TV reporter walked around the grounds at South Bank with a camera crew, giving the people of Brisbane a glimpse of what to expect when they visit Expo. As the cameraman panned the area, huge white sails came into view, the reporter then gave a robust commentary about the sails having been erected to protect visitors from Queensland's searing heat. As he continued, the cameraman scanned the grounds, catching snapshots of restaurants that represented one country or another and of the overhead monorail that would carry passengers from one end of the park to the other.

Even before Expo was opened, it was a dazzling sight to see South Bank nightly on the news, awash with colourful flags of countries from around the world, dancing gracefully in the wind in readiness for the big day.

On Saturday, April 30th, 1988 Anita made herself comfortable in front of the television, and turned on to channel Ten, the host broadcaster of Expo 88. She watched Queen Elizabeth II and Prince Philip sail up the Brisbane River on the royal barge from HMS Britannia to officially open Expo. During the Queen's speech, as she addressed the audience of VIPs and government dignitaries, Queen Elizabeth said: "While Queensland is known as the 'Sunshine State', I much prefer its original name – Queen's land". Anita smiled and the crowd applauded. The Queen then declared World Expo 88 open.

Television cameras scanned the crowd. A record number of one hundred thousand people came through the gates that day, after queuing for four hours.

"Well," Anita muttered to herself, as she switched off the television, "I won't be rushing off to see Expo anytime soon. I'll wait 'til the interest wanes."

"Pardon, Anita?" Edward said, standing in the doorway holding a small ladder. "Did you say something?"

"Oh, Edward," she said, looking up at him. "I didn't hear you come in. What are you up to with that ladder?"

"You mentioned that the curtain in Grace's room wasn't hanging straight."

"Of course," Anita broke in. "The thingummybob holding the rod is broken. I had a look at it this morning."

"OK," he said.

"I was just watching the opening of Expo on television," she said.

"I was watching downstairs," Edward replied. "Big crowds, I see. Much bigger than anticipated, I believe."

"I hate crowds," Anita said, squirming. "I would like to go sooner if it weren't for all those people I would have to contend with. I might not even go at all."

"Oh, you have to go, Anita," Edward said with enthusiasm. "It's a once in a lifetime thing. We could go together – on Monday evening. The crowds would have thinned out by then."

"Now that's a good idea," she chuckled playfully. "You could walk in front of me, shooing people out of my way."

"So, it's a date then?" said Edward leaving the room.

"It's a date!" she called out, chuffed as a teenager going to her school formal.

A loud knock on the front door caused Anita to jump. Grace came running out of her bedroom shouting, "It's OK

Granny, I'll get it. It's probably Jerry, my friend from school. You've met him. We're going to South Bank."

"Oh," Anita said, surprised. "I thought you were going with Lilly".

"I am. We're meeting her and the other kids from school at Manly station." Grace said, hurrying to greet the lanky lad with blond shoulder-length hair.

"G'day, Grace! Ready?" Jerry chirped, sporting a wide smile.

Anita went to the door to say hello to him. Jerry did look vaguely familiar; she could not say for certain. The front entrance was more like a revolving door, with one friend or another of Grace's arriving or leaving. *'At least he had the good manners to look me in the eyes when he spoke,'* she thought. "Have a marvellous time!" Anita said as Grace and Jerry descended the steps. She stood on the veranda and watched them walk in the direction of the train station. The phone rang.

"Hello?" It was her old friend, Wendy Bradshore. Wendy had recently separated from her husband of thirty years.

"Anita, you'll never guess what has happened? I'm shocked to the core." Wendy prattled on without allowing Anita to respond to anything she said. "As you know, William and I have parted ways. But I never in all my days expected to hear this." Wendy drew a long breath and Anita waited in silence for her to continue, aware that Wendy would not have listened to her anyway.

"I'm sure you remember my best friend, Jilly James? Well, she called me this morning to tell me William was dead and I had to identify his body. Of course, I was stunned." Wendy paused a second. *'DEAD? "How do you know that?'* I asked her."

"Jilly had the hide to shout at me saying, *'Wendy, please. Just come to my house. William is in my bed. The police are here. They need you to identify his body because he is still your husband.'*

My best friend and William had been having an affair for years. I knew he was a womaniser, that's why I tossed him out. But, my BEST FRIEND for heaven's sake!" Wendy shouted into Anita's ear. "I don't know if I should laugh or if I should cry," she said, in earnest.

'Ha!' Anita was thinking as Wendy jabbered on. *'Karma has come to kick you in the teeth, as subtly as you had done to me when you had an affair with Bill.'*

Wendy finally ceased talking and waited patiently for the outpouring of sympathy from Anita. "Never mind, my dear," said Anita with an edge of sarcasm. "Jilly and so many *other* women in this town have slept with my dear departed, Bill." Anita thought she sensed Wendy squirm.

"I'll never trust another man again!" Wendy barked, indignantly.

"Oh, Wendy, you can't blame the whole male gender for the shortcomings of a few rotters. I still have hope in my heart that one day I'll meet a man who will love me regardless of my shortcomings, a man who will ..." Anita stopped midsentence when Edward interrupted her.

"Good," he said, seriously. "I'm glad you said that because he's standing right in front of you."

"I'll call you back, Wendy," Anita said, dropping the phone when Edward took her gently by the hand. Mesmerised, she took a step closer towards him. He cupped her face with his hands and looked into her eyes. Then he slowly drew her closer to his face and lightly brushed his lips across hers. She quivered with delight. "My, my," she said breathlessly, "please do that again."

Edward held her in his arms, pressed his mouth to her lips and kissed her in a way she had never been kissed before. He then scooped her up into his arms and carried her to the bedroom where he kissed her from the tip of her lips to the tip of her toes.

Sometime later as they lay in each other's arms Anita said, utterly contented, "Never in my life have I felt so, so alive and as free or as uninhibited, as I was while we were making love. Never!" she said. "Silly as this may seem, Edward. I hadn't noticed until now, just how attractive you are."

"That's because I was always dressed," he teased.

Anita laughed and playfully slapped him. "Being here together like this reminds me of a poem by Yeats that I read some years ago. While I was reading it, I dearly wished I had someone that I cared enough about to share it with. Would you like to hear it?" she asked. Edward nodded.

"Wine comes in at the mouth and love comes in at the eye; that's all we know for truth before we grow old and die. I lift my glass to my mouth, I look at you, and I sigh," Anita quoted.

"A few years ago, you asked me why I stopped travelling," Edward said, as he gently stroked her arm.

"I remember."

"Well, you were the reason."

"Really?"

"You took my breath away, the day you opened the door to me. I hoped with all my being that you'd hire me. I think I fell in love with you that day. You're a beautiful woman, Anita Walker. God only knows how patiently I've waited for this moment." Edward confessed as he basked in the pleasure of his dream finally has become a reality. "Oh, and by the way, my darling, I'm a wealthy man. I've made some very good investments and have bought profitable shares over the years," he said, kissing the top of her head. "I actually felt a fraud taking your money. But I had to or I wouldn't have been able to remain here with you and Grace."

Anita sat up and looked at him. "You've got it all worked out, by the sound of things, haven't you, Edward?"

"I've had plenty of time to think about the future – our future. Do you mind?"

"Not at all," she said, snuggling in closer to him. "Never in my wildest dreams did I see this coming. But, on the other hand, I couldn't have imagined life without you. I got used to you being around," she smiled and was about to kiss him when a frenzied knocking on the front door echoed through the house. The pounding felt strong enough to shake its foundations. Worried that something could have happened to Grace. Anita threw on her dressing gown and ran to see who it was.

"Wendy!" Anita said, loud enough for Edward to hear. "What on earth are you doing here?!"

"I came to see if you were alright," she said, looking anxious. "Are you, alright?" Wendy asked, examining Anita, her brow creased. "Why are you wearing your dressing gown at this time of day? Are you ill?"

"We were making passionate love, that's why," said Edward, coming out of Anita's bedroom, tucking his shirt into his jeans.

Anita threw back her head and laughed heartedly at the flustered look on Wendy's face. "That's right," she said, boldly.

"Good for you!" Wendy said when she finally grasped the situation. "I shall leave you to it then. Carry on!" she tittered to herself on her way out.

"I guess you'll have to marry me now," said Edward nonchalantly, slipping an arm around Anita and pulling her closer to him. They stood on the veranda, watching Wendy walk to her car. "She won't be able to control herself; you know that don't you? We don't want to have to deal with a scandal."

"Oh, no," Anita said, pretending to be shocked. "We certainly don't want that! Ahh well," she sighed, "I guess I'll just have to marry you then. A small wedding in November will be nice."

28

Brisbane's coming of age was the talk of the town. "Brisbane will never be the same after Expo 88," people said. "The city has been exposed to the world, and the world has been exposed to Brisbane."

Although the big country town was blossoming into a beautiful, cultured, stylish city, it was not about to surrender its laid-back charm.

In December 1987 Queensland's illustrious Premier, Joh Bjelke-Petersen, had been ousted by his successor, Mike Ahern. Before that, Joh had an apparent fascination with Romania's dictator, Nicolae Ceausescu, and had invited him and his wife Elena to come to Expo 88. The controversy caused by the invitation was casually discussed with unsophisticated amusement at backyard barbeques, pubs and clubs. There would always be someone among them who would pipe up and repeat Joh's famous catchphrase used to avoid interrogation from journalists, "Now don't you worry about that!" This would send ripples of laughter through the group. The subject of the Ceausescu's came up again when it was reported that the dictator and his wife were executed – machine-gunned to death – on Christmas Day, 1989 for unimaginable atrocities committed on the people of Romania. "Well," came a voice from the crowd in the pub, "Joh sure can pick 'em!" and immediately, the back-slapping men chorused, "Don't you worry about that!" laughing heartily.

As the seasons rolled by, Grace and her friends were coming to the end of their school education. Graduation was just a few weeks away and they now faced the major decision of what to do in the future.

Grace found her solace down at the foreshore, sitting under a tree. She had often seen Bonnie there too. She did not know Gabe was also there. Grace would have said 'hello' on several occasions if Bonnie had not seemed so deeply meditative. Grace wondered why a woman as lovely as Bonnie had not married again. She had heard titbits of Bonnie and Gabe's love story, which hardly satisfied her curiosity. *'One day,'* she thought,' *I shall ask her'*.

Grace was so distracted with her own thoughts that she did not see Bonnie walking towards her.

"Hello, Grace!" Bonnie called, waving.

"Hi, Bonn ..." Grace paused and dropped her head embarrassed. "Sorry. I mean Mrs Connor."

Bonnie smiled. "That's alright Grace, Bonnie is my name. How are you? All ready for graduation? You must be so excited".

"I should be. But I have no idea what I want to do with my life. I had thought about vet nursing. Oh, I don't know." Grace sighed heavily, feeling at a loss. She suddenly perked up. "There is something I want to do more than anything."

"What's that?"

"Find my mother!"

The forlorn expression on Grace's face prompted Bonnie to hug her as she said, "I will do whatever I can to help you."

"Granny told me that mother had planned to visit your gallery the week she disappeared. Since she didn't get there, would you mind if I visited someday soon?"

"Of course, you can Grace!" Bonnie paused a moment. "Is there any particular reason why you want to see the gallery?"

Grace shook her head and said, "No, nothing in particular."

"I was on my way to the gallery when I noticed you sitting here. Would you like to come with me now?"

Sandy was anxiously waiting for Bonnie. She groaned with relief when Bonnie walked through the door.

"I'm so sorry, Sandy," Bonnie pleaded forgiveness for being late when she saw her worried expression. "I completely forgot about the appointment," Bonnie said, glancing at Grace.

"Never mind, Luvvy," Sandy replied, picking up on Bonnie's meaning, "You're forgiven. I shall take over from here while you make a few phone calls."

Gabe followed Grace and Sandy. He listened to their conversation as they strolled along the hall.

"I had no idea you were interested in art, Grace," Sandy chirred.

"I'm not really," Grace replied, nonchalantly. Sandy gave her a puzzled look.

"Oh, I like art and appreciate the talent that goes with it, but I can take it or leave it. Granny told me that my father was interested in art. His art collection is stored downstairs.

"OK, that's cool. To each his own," Sandy quipped, unperturbed.

'Take a look at Bonnie's work,' Gabe whispered in Grace's ear.

"You and Bonnie paint, don't you?" said Grace to Sandy. "I remember that at Mason's last barbeque a few weeks ago, you two were talking about an exhibition you were putting together."

Sandy smiled and thought, *'That was a tactful comment. She's up to something.'*

"That's right," said Sandy. "Would you like to see our work?"

Grace nodded.

"Then follow me."

As they walked down the hall, the noise of their shoes clattering on the polished wooden floor echoed around them. Grace giggled. "We sound like a herd of elephants tramping through the place."

"We do, don't we?" Sandy chuckled, as she entered a room off the hall.

"Here we are," she said.

"Wow!" Grace sighed, with admiration for all that she saw. One wall was covered with seascapes and the opposite wall, landscapes.

"All of these are Bonnie's' work," Sandy said, proudly looking at Grace. She was shocked by Grace's reaction. There were tears in her eyes.

"I've seen paintings similar to these before. Granny told me that she had my father's things from his office, packed away in our storeroom downstairs. She showed me his collection. Five seascapes like these are among them."

"Yes," Sandy said. "But Grace, Bonnie doesn't know that your father bought her paintings. Your father was my client. He made me swear to absolute confidentiality. I agreed." Sandy looked at Grace with pleading eyes. "Even after all this time, I've kept my word, just as your father had instructed."

Grace nodded. "I understand." She then moved in closer and ambled past the paintings, studying each one with the intensity of an art critic. "I really like this painting of the pelicans," Grace said, "They look real. There's life in their eyes." Grace paused and then her brow creased. "I can't recall seeing that many pelicans around the foreshore," she said glancing back at Sandy.

"Sadly, there aren't any more. But a small group of us are fighting to save the pelicans and Moreton Bay from total annihilation."

"It seems that most people are fighting for something going on in their lives, at one time or another."

"What are you fighting for, Grace?"

"To find my mother!" she replied without hesitation.

Gabe stood beside Grace prompting her. *'Sandy's husband was the detective who investigated your mother's disappearance'*.

Grace pondered that for a moment and then said, "Would your husband mind if I ask him what he thought about the way my mother vanished?"

Bonnie caught the tail end of the conversation as she entered the room. Sandy looked unsure how to respond to Grace's request and glanced over at Bonnie, who was nodding her approval.

"OK, hon," Sandy said, not convinced that this was the right thing to do. "I'll discuss it with him tonight. But ..." she flinched, "I have to warn you, sweetheart," she hesitated. "There are ... there are things that you might not want to hear."

"I'm sure there are, Sandy," Grace said, with false courage but holding her head high. "Granny has protected me all my life from the truth, whatever that is. She gave me a fairy-tale childhood, for which I am most grateful. But I think it's about time I grew up and faced the real world."

"What has your Grandmother already told you about your parents?" Sandy asked.

"Not much that makes sense to me," said Grace, and began telling them what she knew. "Father wanted to marry Bonnie, but she was still in love with her husband Gabe, who was killed. He got involved with my mother, she ended up pregnant with me and they married. Mother was unhappy because my father didn't love her. Now people think she ran away. Father died in the fire that burnt our home to the ground."

"What doesn't make sense to you, Grace?" Bonnie asked warily.

"If my mother loved me so much, as Granny had so often said, then why didn't she take me with her? That doesn't make any sense at all. And why would she just up and leave without at least telling one of her friends? We all have friends that we can confide in, don't we? I have." Grace paused and looked at Bonnie and then at Sandy. She saw something in the expression on their faces that alarmed her. "You both know something, don't you?"

At that moment the atmosphere in the room suddenly changed. Time stood still. Bonnie and Sandy somehow faded into the background and were standing motionless, like statues in the corner. The paintings on the walls seemed hazy. Grace was more fascinated and curious than afraid. She gazed wide-eyed around the room. A tiny group of concertina folds gathered across her forehead when she saw a familiar figure leaning up against the wall, smiling at her.

"Gabriel! What ... what are you doing here? I didn't see you come in. Why are you dressed like that? She paused. "And your hair? Wow!" Grace giggled. "Are you going to a fancy-dress party? You actually look really cool!"

"I'm Gabe. Gabriel's my boy."

Grace stared at him in disbelief. "How can that be when ...?"

"When I'm dead?" he finished her sentence.

"Yes." Grace said frankly and then asked, "Am I dreaming?"

"No. But you will remember my visit as a dream. I'm here because I've got something to tell you." Gabe pointed to a chair. "You'd better sit down. I don't want you falling in a heap onto the floor."

Grace sat down and waited.

"You seem like a strong kid, from what I know about you, so I'll tell you everything."

"You know about me? What do mean by that?"

"I'm keeping an eye on my wife and my boy – keeping them safe – you know that sorta thing. Don't ask me why I don't know. I'm just here. I get to know people well as I see them – measure their character, good, bad or indifferent.

You're OK in my book. Even after your old man murdered me."

Grace's hand shot up to her mouth in shock. "My father what?!" she shouted, as tears welled up in her eyes.

"He killed me! He thought Bonnie would marry him with me out of the way. Huh! That didn't go as he'd planned," Gabe shrugged. "What's done is done! Nothing will change that now! But as you can see, I'm OK. Your mother is OK too."

"My mother?"

"Yeah, would you like to meet her?"

"Yes, of course. Where can I find her? People said she ran away but I don't believe that. I think the reason she left was that she was ill ..."

"Look to your right, Grace," Gabe interrupted her. She slowly turned her head in the direction Gabe was pointing. Grace could hardly believe what she was seeing. The woman whose eyes had stared blankly at her from a photo album now glowed with love. She stepped forward to embrace her mother, who promptly vanished. Grace looked at Gabe, puzzled. "What just happened?"

"Your mother was telling you that she loves you, that she's at peace. She wants you to get on with your life."

"How did my mother die?"

That's not important now, Grace."

"It is to me!" she shouted at him, then paused a moment. "Wait! If my father killed you then he must have killed my mother too, right?"

Gabe nodded.

"But why? Was he insane? Am I insane too?"

"Whoooah there, kiddo! You're not insane! You have a kind and loving and generous heart. You're unique. We're all unique in our own way, Grace. We can all decide what kind of person we want to be. But before you can move forward with your life you have to forgive your father. If you don't forgive him, you'll be stuck in *yesterday* and

152

yesterday is so far behind you that it shouldn't matter anymore. This has less to do with forgiving your father, Grace. It has everything to do with healing your heart and your mind. Your future is in *your* hands now. It will be determined by the choices *you* make," Gabe said, then he vanished and everything returned to normal.

As Bonnie and Sandy were about to respond to Grace's question, she held her hand up to stop them before they could say anything. She told them that she had finally put the pieces together. The women were astounded when Grace revealed she now realised that only her father was implicated in Gabe's death and her mother's disappearance.

"I'm so very sorry for all the heartache and pain my father caused," Grace said, overwhelmed with emotion. She sniffed back her tears and continued ... "and I'm awfully sorry he robbed you of the life you and Gabe should have had together."

"How Grace? How did you come to that conclusion?" Bonnie asked, shaking her head in disbelief.

Grace shrugged her shoulders and wiped her eyes. "I don't know. My mind had so many thoughts swimming around inside of it and then, all of a sudden, the pieces of the puzzle fell into place. That seems more logical, don't you think? You knew that didn't you?" Grace asked, looking directly at Bonnie. "You knew my father was a killer?"

"Yes Grace, I did. The police told me years ago that they had found evidence on your father's body that confirmed he killed Gabe. But I didn't know about your mother. There's still no evidence to confirm her death."

29

Grace sat quietly in her bedroom, mulling over what had happened at the gallery. She was a logical thinker. There was a purpose behind everything she did, even what she thought. Grace could recall thinking, *'The choices I make will determine my character and my destiny,'* but she could not grasp why she had thought that. The possibility that she could be unstable like her parents began to niggle at her confidence, despite the reassurance from her grandmother and Bonnie that she was not unstable and neither were her parents. Her fear was on a treadmill, gaining momentum!

Suddenly, in the depth of her depression, Grace stood up and went over to the mirror. She stared long and hard at her reflection, looking for any sign of evil that might be lurking deep within her. She studied her fine features, clear ivory complexion, her long, lean shapely form and lustrous red hair. Hysteria ran through her mind. *'If Father was evil, then surely, I must be, too. Oh, I hate that I'm his daughter!'* she screamed in her head, *'I hate it! I hate it!'*

Edward caught a glimpse of Grace out of the corner of his eye as he passed her room. He stopped.

"Are you alright, love?" He called from the doorway. "Grace?" He called again when she did not answer. Grace turned around.

Edward was startled to see her face drenched with tears and went to her, trying to recall the last time she had cried. *'About seven years old, when her cat died. It must have been then,'* he thought, as he gently dabbed her face with the handkerchief that he had taken from his pocket. "Want to talk about it?"

Grace shook her head. "I'll be OK."

"I'm always here for you, love. You know that, don't you?" he said on his way out.

Grace gave him a weak smile and nodded. "Thank you, Edward," she said, "Yes, I do know that, you've been like a father to me for most of my life." Her smile brightened. "You taught me to ride my bike." She laughed out loud, remembering the event with fondness. "I was wobbling all over the place, about to crash into the fence, until you ran up behind me and grabbed hold of the back of the bike's seat to steady me. Thanks to you, I was riding like a champion by the end of the day." She paused thoughtfully. "And you were there with me when Sambo died. We dug his grave together," she said, looking at him through misty eyes and then laughed. "You even paid a tribute to him." She hung her head, overwhelmed with regret as if a heavy cloud had suddenly swept over her. The pleasure of those memories was marred by the realisation that Edward was not her father. "I wish you were my father, Edward," Grace said, holding back a flood of tears.

"Being your father would be an honour, Grace." Edward said sincerely, "Perhaps I should adopt you," he smiled.

Grace laughed. "Now that would be wonderful," she beamed brightly, "but perhaps it would be a bit confusing for some people."

"How so?" he asked.

"My father married to my Granny," she giggled.

"Oh, I see what you mean." He raised his eyebrows and grinned.

"I am thinking of changing my surname," she said, seriously. "Grace Anita O'Malley sounds rather nice, don't you think? After all, we are family now!"

"It sounds wonderful!" he smiled, with thumbs up.

Changing her name did help Grace to a small degree in dealing with the shame of her father's unforgivable sins. At times, the knowledge of what he had done still haunted her in her dreams. The nightmares were slowly debilitating her. She discovered that partying to all hours of the night with her friends helped her forget about everything for a while. The consequences of trying to forget by getting inebriated to the stage of passing out were soul destroying, especially when, in sobriety, the shame and nightmares returned.

Lilly and Grace were each other's confidants and often bared their souls to one another. Grace was there for Lilly, as all of their other friends had been when her cousin Max had not returned from his skiing trip in Switzerland some years ago. An avalanche had claimed his life and newsflashes about the incident were broadcast on the radio and television. The outpouring of grief was immense. Lilly adored her cousin. She was an only child and Max had filled the role of a big brother to her. He was loved and admired not only by his family and friends but by the community as well, for the support and time he gave to numerous kids' sporting clubs. On the day of Max's funeral, the church was filled to capacity, the many mourners standing outside in the searing heat without complaint a mute testimony to Max's popularity.

As they moved forward into the future, both girls had a heartache they carried with them that would remain buried within until they faced it.

Anyone observing Grace, Lilly and their other close school friends while sitting around the table laughing and chatting, as they sipped their wine and nibbled on tapas at their monthly catch-ups would be forgiven for not noticing the multitude of contradictions there. Behind each smile, was a battle to survive, one day at a time. Sometimes an anecdote shared might resonate with one or more of them, as an encouragement to hang in there and to keep striving. Life wasn't all that bad after all, because they had each other.

Over the years, an announcement of one kind or another was made at those gatherings: 'I'm an apprentice carpenter!" Carol Byrne piped up with pride.

The girls immediately cheered, "Good for you!"

"Cool! You can build a house for me, Caz".

Carol was the first to get engaged. Thereafter the women would meet to celebrate a forthcoming marriage, pregnancy or birth with squeals of delight and heartfelt well-wishes.

All of them were thrilled for Molly Childs the day she extended her left hand with a large, sparkling diamond on her finger and said, "Guess what?!"

"Yay!" cheered her friends. "You're getting married!"

Molly giggled and then proceeded to tell her friends all about her high-flying property developer fiancé. Molly was admired by her friends and of course, it was unanimous that she should be happy. Molly had left her dysfunctional home at aged fifteen. She got a job, found a place to live and still managed to attend school. It had been tough going for the petite teenager but Molly's determination to finish her education was paramount.

Although Joey Daily was thrilled for Molly, she sat quietly in the background nursing a fear that her friends would not be as jubilant for her as they were for Molly when she confessed that she was gay. It had been torturous for her, hiding the truth from them for as long as she had. All the same, Joey bucked up courage and said, "I have a confession to make." The group fell silent and turned their attention to Joey with enquiring eyes. She cleared her throat and said," I'm gay."

The women looked at each other and smiled. "We know," Lilly said, in a matter-of-fact way.

"And we don't care!" declared Grace, "We love you just the way you are, the beautiful soul that you have always been." The conversation then flowed on to other things.

As the afternoon turned into evening, they all decided to move on to one of the clubs in the Valley. "After all, it could be sometime before we get another free pass. So let's make hay while the sun's still shining! Or perhaps, it's while the moon's still shining?" One of them shouted. "C'mon let's go," and they all piled into a taxi bus.

They danced the night away with each other, laughing and having fun until two in the morning.

30

Tim Osborne stood beside the street van with large *FREE FOOD & COFFEE* signage all over it in huge colourful letters. He was handing out coffee and soup to a homeless group when Grace, Lilly and the others staggered past him on their way to the taxi stand. Neither Grace nor Lilly saw Tim. As far as they were concerned, he was just another homeless person with his cap pulled down over his eyes.

The street was crowded with other sozzled club goers, either on their way home or heading to another venue. Some had linked arms with each other for support as they dallied along the street, singing out of tune and shouting obscenities to anyone who passed. Most of the foot traffic steered clear of them.

It was cool at that late hour. A curtain of mist hung heavily in the air, lingering around streetlights, on vehicles, around structures, footpaths and the road. Neon lights shone brightly in shop windows and from buildings, throwing eerie shadows across the street and on to the wet asphalt.

The line at the taxi stand was long. Grace turned to Lilly and grabbed a hold of her arm. "I feel weird," Grace said, and then fell in a heap at Lilly's feet.

"Call triple O," Lilly shouted.

Tim turned around and looked in the direction of the taxi stand. His brain was processing whether or not it was Lilly's voice he had heard shouting. A crowd was gathering around someone on the ground. He left what he was doing and ran to their aid, shocked to discover that the person on the ground was Grace. He checked her pulse. It was weak. He looked up at Lilly. "How much booze has Grace had tonight?"

"A lot," Lilly replied, daunted. "We've all had a lot to drink. But Grace didn't eat much. What's wrong with her? Will she be alright?"

Lilly was too fraught about Grace to ask Tim what he was doing dressed in shabby clothes, hanging out in the Valley at that time of the morning. Tim was about to answer Lilly but the banshee wail of the ambulance, reverberating around the city's streets and stopping at the taxi stand, silenced him. The sound also dispersed a group of teenagers across the street, where a fight had been brewing.

"G'day Doc!" the first paramedic said. "What've we got here?"

Grace was now conscious and asking to go home.

"Not yet," Tim said, putting a comforting hand on her shoulder. "You're dehydrated. You need to go to the hospital to get checked over. I'll come with you, Grace. OK?"

Grace nodded, only because she was too weak to argue. While the paramedic lifted Grace into the ambulance, Tim made sure Lilly was safe to go home with her friends. "I'll call you in the morning with an update. Don't worry, Lilly. I'm sure it's nothing serious," Tim said, giving her a wave as he climbed into the ambulance.

At the hospital, Tim stood by Grace's bed, watching her sleep. He thought she looked angelic, the way her curls fell randomly across her face. He could not resist pushing some of them gently aside. She stirred but did not wake up. He was enjoying the moment and was glad he had not woken her. *'This is the first time we've been alone together,'* he thought with tremendous pleasure. *'It's only taken what, eight years?'* He smiled ruefully, *'Better late than never, I guess'.*

Tim had not heard Nurse Ann Simms come into the room. "Good morning Dr Osborne," she said, startling him. "A relative?" she asked.

"No, a close friend,' he answered without looking up.

'Hmm ... lucky girl!' she thought, raising her brows. 'I wouldn't mind if he looked at me like that!' Anne had her heart set on nabbing Tim for herself.

Grace opened her eyes while the nurse was doing a routine check. She was frightened and confused. "Where am I? What happened?"

"You're in hospital, Grace," Tim said, taking hold of her hand to reassure her.

"Tim?"

"You don't remember fainting in the street, do you?"

"No," said Grace, surprised, and shaking her head. "But I do remember being out with Lilly and our friends from school and drinking way too much." She paused and then gripped tightly onto Tim's hand. "Lilly! Is she alright?"

Tim nodded and smiled. "Lilly's fine. She was worried about you though." Grace grimaced.

"It's OK," said Tim softly. "I've already called her. She knows you're alright."

"I feel so ashamed," Grace said, turning her face away from him.

"There's no need to feel like that. You haven't done anything to be ashamed of."

As Tim spoke, Grace looked at him but was not listening. She was drawn to study him. She saw things about him she had not noticed before. His eyes were dark and warm and gentle. 'Why hadn't I noticed that? His voice is soothing and reassuring.' She looked at his hands. They were smooth and beautiful with long, artists' fingers, 'A surgeon's hands!' she thought.

Grace had not grasped that she was staring at Tim, nor did she realise that he had stopped talking and was looking back at her.

"You haven't heard a word I've said, have you?"

Grace shook her head. "Tim," she said, feeling awkward. "I'd like to go home."

"OK," he said. "I'll get things sorted out here first and then I can drive you. But I'll have to pick up my car from the Valley first."

Grace did not say much on the way home. What she did say struck a chord with Tim.

"I'm 24 years old and what have I got to show for those years?" Grace said, feeling at a loss. "Most of my friends are married and have children and I am still living with Granny and Edward. I can afford to get my own apartment, but still, I haven't," she shrugged. "Lilly met a guy at the club last night. We were the last two singles left in our group. He seemed nice and Lilly seemed to like him a lot!" Grace went silent for a moment and then sighed. "I need to go away for a while!" she blurted out unexpectedly, and then did not utter another word until Tim stopped at her front gate.

Tim suddenly felt heavyhearted. He did not want Grace to leave. He had felt there was a connection between them. *'On second thought, I could've been mistaken.'*

Grace turned to Tim. She gave him a puzzled look as she was getting out of the car. "I know almost nothing about you, Doctor Tim Osborne. Why is that?" she probed.

"You've never asked," he said.

"Hmm, well, one day you'll have to tell me," she said in a matter-of-fact way. Then she softened her voice. "Thank you so very much, Tim. It's ironic," she laughed, "Gabriel was supposed to be my guardian angel, but you ended up being the one rescuing me. Goodbye!" she said, and then walked slowly up the footpath.

Anita was waiting for Grace on the veranda. She waved to Tim as he drove off. "I've been so worried, Grace. It's unlike you to …"

"No, Granny!" Grace broke in. "It is so like me these days … it is so like me. Oh … I feel detached from everything and everyone. I don't know where I belong … or what I want. I have no one. I've had lots of boyfriends, just like my friends, but I can't seem to find that *one* special man the way they have. What's wrong with me? I have nothing to show for my existence." Grace exploded. She was on the verge of tears, but stopped herself and ran to her room.

'*What is happening? Why is Grace so unhappy?*' Anita was consumed with worry. '*Is she having a breakdown?*'

Edward saw and heard the episode from the lounge room. First, he went to comfort Anita. "Grace will be fine, love," he said, sliding a protective arm around her, gently guiding her to one of the chairs on the veranda. "Here, sit down and enjoy the view. I'll make you a nice pot of tea."

Anita moved like a robot. She was shocked by Grace's behaviour and deeply worried that she had failed her. She gazed out at the bay, but her heart was not open to appreciate its beauty today. Her mind was in too much turmoil to notice the wind forcing the dozen or so sailboats to almost flying over white-capped waves below the clear sapphire sky.

When Edward was sure Anita was comfortable, he went to check on Grace. He tapped gently on her bedroom door. "Grace," he called, "may I come in."

"Yes, Edward," she replied. "I'm sorry." She said the minute he entered the room.

"The wheels have fallen off the cart, eh love?"

Grace nodded. "It seems so." She hung her head. "I don't know how to fix it. Everything's topsy-turvy."

Edward sat down on a footstool and faced Grace. "I'm open to being a sounding board if you're up to it."

Grace sat crossed-legged on the edge of her bed, contemplating Edward's offer. She started talking, firstly about her happy childhood and then moving onto her teens. That, Edward thought, was where the change in Grace's life began.

"Look, love," he said, quietly, "I'm no psychologist, but I've seen enough things in my lifetime to tell me that all this drinking and carrying on you've been doing is about ... well, punishing yourself. You don't hate your father. It seems to me you've got a bad case of self-loathing. You're not a bad person, Grace."

She was about to protest but Edward held up his hand for her to listen and he continued. "Have you forgotten the little girl who shared her lunch with the child that was being ignored at school? The little girl who found a baby bird in a clump of grass and climbed a tree at her own risk, to put it back in the nest it had fallen from? The young woman who loves and admires her friends, who would do anything thing for any of them if need be? I could go on and on, Grace, to remind you of those acts of kindness, actions of the good person that you are."

Edward stopped talking a moment to allow Grace to absorb what he said. He continued. "Did you know that your father loved you more than anything?

She looked at him but remained silent. She shook her head.

"From what your grandmother has told me about your father," Edward said, "you were everything to him. That's why he gave her permission to take you to the UK. He knew you'd be safe with her." Edward paused, waiting for Grace to respond, when she didn't he said, "Your father was a complicated man without boundaries. Lord knows, love, your grandmother has punished herself long and hard enough for neglecting him as a child. As atonement, she put her life on hold and dedicated it to raising you. She learned to forgive herself and that is what you should do. There is strength in forgiveness." There was a short silence. "To put everything in a nutshell, Grace," Edward said, "the choices you make will determine your character and your destiny!"

Grace's eyes widened with clarity when she heard Gabe's voice instead of Edward's telling her that. An image of Gabe flashed into her mind and she instantly remembered where she had heard those words before - the day she visited Bonnie's gallery. At that moment all the pieces of the puzzle fell into place for a second time. She wanted to scream from the rooftops, *'I'm not unbalanced! Or insane! Or crazy! Or mad! Or evil! I'm sane!'* Instead, she gave Edward a face-splitting smile and said, "I get it!"

Grace went silent for a moment and then threw Edward a broadside question. "How do you know when you're in love?"

He stared at her in disbelief and then burst out laughing. "Ah well, now that's an easy question to answer," he sighed with delight. "You can be sure it's love when that person becomes more important than yourself, or anything else on this planet. Anyone, I know?"

"Ah well, now, that'd be tellin'," she laughed, mimicking his Irish accent.

31

Grace decided to take the plunge and move out of home and get her own place. After all it was now the IT age with the internet and mobile phones. The idea of living in trendy Teneriffe had always appealed to Grace. It was close to the city, to the nightlife and weekend markets, and only a short drive to the veterinary surgery where she worked.

An occasional dip into her healthy trust fund, left to her by her father to cover the extra cost of living away from home, was necessary. Her wages as a vet nurse certainly did not provide adequate finances to cover the rent on her new, swish lodgings, as well as to enjoy the social life to which she had become accustomed.

While grocery shopping, Grace noticed an advert on the store's noticeboard. *Evening Cooking Classes* was written in big bold handwriting. She took out her mobile phone and typed in the contact number. She made the call the moment she arrived home and arranged to join the class.

After a few classes, Grace discovered that she had a natural culinary talent and soon felt confident enough to host a family dinner party, reciprocating the dinner invitations she had received in the past. Anita and Edward were thrilled when Grace called to invite them.

"I hope everyone is healthy," Grace joked.

"Why is that darling?" Anita enquired.

"Well, just in case I accidentally make everyone sick. Don't forget, I'm still learning, Granny!"

"How many have you invited, sweetheart?"

"Oh, let me see … all up it's about a dozen … Lilly and Dean, you remember him? Lilly met Dean at the club. Daniel and Kay, Beth, Joe, Bonnie and Gabriel, Sandy and Samson, oops! I mean Eric. I forgot we don't call the detective that anymore. Oh, Tim and Bobby Taylor," she said. "Hmm, I don't think I've missed anyone."

"That's a lot of people to cook for darling. Is there anything I can do to help?"

"It's cool, Granny, thank you. I've got it covered."

"Very nice!" said Tim with admiration, looking around the room as he entered the apartment. Soft lighting surrounded the large, extended table propped in the middle of the open-plan kitchen-dining room. Name cards and menus were in place for each guest. The theme of the evening was Italian. Tim picked up one of the menus from the table.

Entrée: Polenta with wild mushrooms.
Main: Vegetable Torte and Mediterranean salad
Dessert: Panna Cotta, Strawberries with Balsamic vinegar

"Aww, you shouldn't have … all this just for me?" Tim teased while reading it. "I love Italian tucker!"

Grace playfully flicked him with the tea towel. "Get over yourself. Be useful and take the ice out of the freezer and empty it into the Esky."

"OK, chef. Where's the Esky?

"Here, under the sink!"

As the guests arrived, they all were wowed by Grace's creative talent in transforming her apartment into an Italian restaurant. During dinner, Grace leaned in closer to Tim and in a low voice said, "Do you remember the question I asked you the day you drove me home from the hospital?"

He smiled and nodded. "Now isn't the moment for time travelling … But," he said, testing her reaction, "we could discuss it tomorrow morning over breakfast."

"OK," said Grace, challenging him.   "I'm guessing you're a wiz at cleaning up after dinner parties?"

"I'm an expert!"

The relaxed chatter in the room was a reassuring comfort among friends. Gabe was leaning against the wall listening to Joe, Daniel, Edward and Eric talk about their last fishing trip. They were planning another on Eric's next day off.

"The boys should join us next time we go out," Daniel said, raising his voice loud enough for them to hear.

"You old men are retired and have all the time in the world to do as you please," Gabriel said, laughing. "Us young blokes have to work to keep the country going."

Eric chipped in to say, "I hope you're not including me in the 'old men' part?"

"We've paid our dues and then some," said Daniel. "You're as cheeky as your father ever was. I can still remember the day he came looking for a job ..." The room went quiet as Daniel reminisced.

Gabriel always enjoyed the tales Daniel told him about his father when they went fishing. He loved Daniel for that. *'I'm one lucky bastard!'* he thought as he and the others listened to Daniel. *'I've had good men looking out for me all my life. Pa, Daniel ... even my dad.'*

Gabriel looked over at his mother. She smiled and winked, reassuring him that she was fine with Daniel talking about his dad. Gabriel scanned the room and his eyes fell on Lilly and Dean. He frowned. *'Hmm, I wonder where those two are at.'*

Gabe was standing beside his son. *'Go and ask her,'* he whispered. So Gabriel did, the moment Dean left Lilly's side to refill their drinks.

"How's it goin'?" Gabriel said, playfully bumping Lilly with his hip.

"Fine," she answered with a smile, shoving him back. "Where's your latest squeeze?" she asked.

"Dumped again," he said, mocking sadness.

Lilly shook her head in disgust. "Your problem is that you attract bimbos who only see a handsome face, not substance. You'll never shine dating women like that!"

"Substance?" he laughed. "Now how can a self-centred, egotistical, moron have substance?"

"You're none of those things, Gabriel," Lilly fired back at him, shocked that he would say that about himself, even if he was being flippant.

"You're kind and generous and … and … will do anything for your family and your friends. Your looks take a backseat to your character with those who love you and know you well…"

"Wow, I'll definitely call on you when I need a reference," he interrupted. Lilly ignored the sarcasm. She felt sorry for him. He was extraordinarily handsome and physically perfect from head to toe to the point of being *beautiful. That* was an unusual description to use to describe a man, but there was no other apt way to describe Gabriel other than *beautiful.* Lilly felt concerned that he was wasting his life with brief liaisons. She had scolded him on several occasions, saying, "Meaningless relationships are soul destroying! You can do better than that!"

Gabe smiled at Lilly's comment and thought, *'You needn't worry about my boy, love. Since the day I was murdered, I've had been watching over him, hopefully guiding him in the right direction and protecting him from the bullies he's encountered since he was just a pup. I'm not about to stand by and do nothing when my kid is forced to defend himself day in and day out, just because he's got a pretty face, not while I could prevent it from happening. By crikey, I nipped the bullying in the bud from the start. The day Graham Jones and four others cornered Gabriel and Bobby on their first day of high school."* The scene ran through Gabe's mind like a movie …

"Where did you think you're goin' pretty boy?" Graham sneered.

"What's it to ya?" Gabriel replied.

"Oh, a pint-size smart arse!" Graham jeered, raising his hand, about to punch Gabriel.

Gabe was talking to Gabriel. *'This tough kid pees his bed.'*

"Wait!" Gabriel shouted. *"I think we should talk in private before you go thumping me."*

"Why should I talk to you?"

"Let's just say ... ah, it's in your best interest."

Graham looked around at his mates, puzzled. They shrugged. Then Graham said, *"Lead the way, dead man."*

"OK fat boy," Gabriel said, and Graham curled his hand into a fist.

"I wouldn't be too hasty if I were you," Gabriel warned him, *"or I tell your mates you piss your bed and your old man beats the crap out of you."*

Graham paled.

"Now if you leave me and my mates alone, I'll keep your secret. I figure your life is pretty much shit anyway, so why make things worse? Deal?"

Graham thought about what Gabriel said for a moment, and then he nodded. *"Deal!"*

The boys walked away in different directions.

"What the hell did you say to him?" Bobby was astounded. *"That fat arse could have wiped the floor with the both of us, with one arm tied behind his back."*

Gabriel shrugged and laughed. *"I told him that I'd make his life hell if he gives us any more trouble."*

Bobby's eyes were popping. *"Bloody hell, mate ... he ... he towered over you and you tell him ... shit man, you're insane!"* He laughed.

'Yep,' thought Gabe. *'I can protect my kid from physical harm. But it's up to him to work out his own matters of the heart.'*

"I had no idea Grace was so creative," Lilly said, changing the subject. "I guess nesting suits her. Look," she said, smiling, "I see Grace has found an apprentice."

Gabe noticed that Gabriel did not look over at Grace and Tim. He shook his head. *'Poor kid. It obviously hurts too much to see them together. He wouldn't even glance over at Grace and Tim. His eyes never left Lilly's face.'*

"How are you, really? Are you and Dean serious?"

As Lilly was about to reply, Dean appeared on the scene with their drinks in hand, ending the conversation.

"Well," said Gabriel, backing away, "I'll leave you guys to it. Catch you later."

Gabriel moved over to the couch where his mother and the others were discussing the latest shows which the Savoyards and the Mercury were rehearsing. Anita, Beth and Kay had been loyal supporters of both local theatre groups since they were formed.

The evening came to an end, and the elders groaned as they pried themselves out of their comfortable seats.

"I can't remember my body being so unwilling to move," said Joe, winking at Grace. "It must be all that food you forced me to eat," he laughed and the others agreed, thanking Grace for a marvellous evening.

"It's late, darling. We'll see ourselves out since you've refused our offer to help clean up. Good night," Anita said, closing the door behind her.

"OK, mate," said Grace, with authority in her voice after everyone had left. "You clear the table and I'll stack the dishwasher!"

Tim saluted. "Yes, ma'am!"

When they had just about finished Grace said, "While you're rinsing the glasses, Tim, I'll take a shower."

When he had finished his chores, Tim poured wine into two glasses and waited for Grace. She soon appeared in the doorway with an arm full of blankets and a pillow. She tossed them to Tim, picked up a wine glass, and kissed him on the cheek. "See you in the morning for breakfast," she said on the way to her room.

Shards of sunlight coming through the shutters and falling onto Tim's face woke him. He stretched and yawned, and for a moment he had forgotten where he was. A smile replaced the uncertainty. *'Ah, yes, Grace and the dinner party.'* He glanced at his watch, then threw back the blankets and went to the bathroom.

The sound of a closing door had woken Grace from a deep sleep. She rolled over to look at her bedside clock and then fell back onto the pillow moaning. "Aaaah, it's only 5.30."

Her eyes sprang open, remembering Tim was asleep on the lounge. She got up to check on him but he was nowhere to be seen. The blankets she had given him were folded in a neat pile on the lounge. *'Hmm,'* she thought, disappointed, *'We were supposed to have breakfast together. Maybe the hospital called him.'* She shrugged, too tired to worry about it, and went back to bed.

Loud knocking on the front door stopped her from closing her eyes. "Now what?!" she groaned, exasperated. "OK, I'm coming!" she called out when the knocking persisted.

"Tim! I thought you had absconded." She laughed.

He smiled broadly. "You're not getting rid of me that fast," he said, handing Grace the packages he was carrying. "I thought we would start with lattes and croissants before heading off to the cafe."

32

Lilly stood on the footpath of the foreshore, looking out over the bay and waiting to witness another spectacular sunrise. Moments later, long, spindly fingers of light sliced their way over the dark, obscure horizon.

'This scene needs music,' she thought, as the golden orb appeared to slowly rise out of water. When it was higher, Lilly closed her eyes and turned towards the sun and let its warmth caress her face. She did not want to think about anything at that moment, but thoughts of her future catapulted into her mind.

'Gabriel shouldn't have asked me if Dean and I were serious. Now I have to consider it. I didn't want to do that, not yet anyway.'

His question had unsettled her. Lilly knew she was not completely happy, not in the way she should have been. She had to finally admit to herself that there was something lacking in her relationship with Dean. She liked him, very much. She was not in love with him.

It was while watching the dawning of another day that Lilly began to understand that every day was a new beginning. She had the choice to use that to start again and again until she was living the life she wanted, or she could just stagnate where she currently existed. As she recognised that the choice was hers a sudden surge of excitement ran through her.

'I'm going to finish Max's trip and go to all the places he intended to see. I will live life for both of us.'

Grace and Tim headed for the little café just down the road from her apartment. When they arrived, at Tim's request, they were shown to a table tucked away in a quiet corner.

After the waitress had taken their orders and left, Grace looked at Tim and said, "OK, now will you tell me … what were you doing in the city dressed the way you were at that time of the morning?"

"First of all," he said, without any hesitation, "I want to marry you, Grace. That's why I'll explain the whys and wherefores, as Aunty Jean would say." Tim smiled at Grace's wide-eyed expression and continued.

"I was adopted, as you already know. But I know very little about my birth mother, just that she's part Aboriginal. My father was of Irish descent. The blended mix is why I'm so handsome," he joked. Grace smiled.

"The Osbourne's' adopted me at birth. Mum was a sad, sad woman, a broken woman really. She had suffered one miscarriage after the other. Her doctor suggested they should adopt, with the hope that would it help her get over the loss of her babies. It didn't. Mum literally drank herself to death. Aunty Jean, our next door neighbour, was my lifeline. I love her dearly. She saved my life. There was a loose paling in our adjoining fence. With her encouragement, I'd slide through it and go to her house when Mum drank herself unconscious. Aunty Jean's eyes were always warm and sparkly when she looked at me." Tim paused. "It's funny the things you remember about people when you were a kid," he said and then went on with his explanation. "It didn't matter to Aunty Jean that I was grubby and smelly. She'd wash my face and brush my hair into place. It was she who taught me to wash my hands and clean my teeth. She's an amazing woman," he said, with pride. "Aaah … and the cakes she made especially for me made me feel so important." Tim looked at Grace. "You know, I can't ever remember eating cake before having them at Aunty Jean's."

He fell silent a moment and then said, "Dad knew Aunty Jean was caring for me but he didn't say anything. Come to think of it, dad didn't say much about anything at all. He was just there. He was kind enough though. But I wanted to crawl under the house and hide when he would say, "Go and bring your mother home from the pub, son."

Tim shook his head. "Man, that was humiliating." He did not elaborate. He went silent for a moment again and then said, "But I survived it. Other kids have suffered much worse. That's the reason I was in the city at that hour of the morning. I volunteer to serve coffee and soup to the homeless. I couldn't help Mum but I can offer a kind word while I hand out coffee and soup, especially when I can see my mother's pain in some of their eyes.

Grace wanted to wrap her arms around Tim and say, "Oh you poor, poor man ..." She kept herself in check because she knew Tim did not want her sympathy. He was just answering her question.

"Well," she said, taking hold of his hand. "That explains all that beautiful compassion you have for people and why you're so protective of those you care about. I've always loved those qualities in you, Tim."

"You just love those qualities? What about me? Could you love me?"

"I love you and I love Gabriel," she said sincerely.

"I know that, but do you love me enough to marry me and have lots of babies."

Grace became serious. "I love you enough to marry you, but ... I don't want to have babies, yet. I want to travel first and we can do that together. I'm not sure about children because you'll be so focused on your career. I could be left to bring up the children on my own. To be honest Tim, I'm not prepared to do that. If we can't be a parenting team, then I don't want children at all."

Tim shrugged off Grace's concerns. "I promise you, Grace, we'll always be a team in everything we do!"

After Grace told her grandmother of Tim's proposal, she called Lilly.

"That's wonderful, Babe!" Lilly shouted down the phone. "I'm so happy for you and Tim!"

As they chatted a while longer, Lilly told Grace that she was going to end her relationship with Dean. "We've both lost the spark," she said. "But it's not just that. I have unfinished business in Europe. There are places I have to visit ... for Max and for me, too!"

"Oh sweetie," Grace said, with great affection "I get it! When do you leave?"

"Tomorrow!"

33

'*Time and tide wait for no ma*n,' as the saying goes. Lilly had gone to Europe. Grace and Tim were engaged, and Gabriel and his grandfather had formed a partnership and named the business, *Mason and Connor, Builders.*

Gabriel was well known to have a good head for business, using much of his natural, trustworthy charm and good looks as persuasion to secure major building contracts around Brisbane.

On the surface, Gabriel's life was enviable to those who knew him. He skilfully hid the ache he felt for failing to capture the elusive heart of the woman he dearly loved. There had been times he was tempted to tell Grace how he felt, but changed his mind because he was not sure if she felt the same about him.

'*There are some things in life you just know for certain,*' he thought with remorse for not having declared his feelings. '*I'll wait for her even though she's moving in another direction. But one day... if I get another chance, I won't hesitate to show her how much I love her!*' With that thought in mind, he made a conscious decision that there would be no more women in his life. '*I'm just not interested. It'll be Grace or no one!*'

Two years seemed to have passed within the blink of an eye. Grace and Tim had just arrived home from their honeymoon in Vietnam. Lilly was still overseas. In her last letter to Grace, she wrote that she was working in a London restaurant.

'*I've loved my time here, but I'm really missing home ...*' she went on, '*Don't laugh, but I joined an internet dating site. Ha! I've been chatting to this guy in Brisbane via email for over six months now and neither of us has seen photos of the other. It's rather exciting in a way. He goes by the name of 'Car Guy'. I'm 'Aussie Gal'. I really like him. We seem to have so much in common that I actually don't care what he looks like because we communicate so well. We love the same music, art, food ... he makes me laugh. He was very supportive during a drama I was having at work. It's strange. I get the feeling that I might know him, but I can't really say for sure. Anyway, I'm coming home to meet him. He has promised to meet me at the airport.'*

Grace kept reading the letter, looking for the date of Lilly's arrival. "Tim! Tim!" Grace called, running to him.

He looked up from his study notes with trepidation, ready to dash to his wife's aid. "Honey, what's wrong?"

Grace handed him the letter. "Lilly will be home Saturday ... I wonder who the mystery man is?" Her voice was full of excitement. "I hope he's as wonderful as you, and they'll be as happy as we are."

Tim nodded and then smiled. His dark eyes softened whenever he looked at Grace. "Especially as happy are we are sweetheart," he said, sincerely.

Lilly and her internet friend did not get the chance to exchange photographs before she left London. He told her in his last email that he did not need one; he would find her.

Although she had not mentioned any names, so much of her life sounded familiar to him: for example, the close brotherly friendships she has with her male friends, the backyard barbeques, and her closest friend who had recently married one of her childhood mates. He was hoping he was correct. On the other hand, Lilly worried that she might not find 'Car Guy.' Or he might not find her. She had no idea that he had an inkling of who she might be.

A couple of hours before landing, and while most of the passengers were still sleeping, Lilly grabbed a small bag that contained her toiletries, a cotton dress and fresh underwear and went to the toilet to change and freshen up. She needed a distraction. Her mind was racing, and in a quandary.

She set about stripping off and sponging herself down, not realising it would be so difficult. The toilet was no bigger than a postage stamp, but she persisted and eventually managed to wash and change into fresh clothes with a lot of huffing and puffing and bumping of her arms against the toilet door. At one stage of undress, the door almost burst open when she leant against it while drying herself with her scarf, but she caught the door in time. Lilly had not realised the length of time she had taken in the toilet until she was faced with glaring disapprovals from passengers waiting at the door. She smiled an apathetic apology. She was focused on what she may or may not face at the end of her journey. Her heart was thumping hard with anticipation of marriage and a family, for which she was now ready if Car Guy lived up to her expectations.

Going through customs seemed to take ages. Then suddenly she was making her way out to meet her future husband - she hoped. Lilly walked into the waiting area, stopped and took a deep breath. She looked left and then looked right, and then straight ahead. She beamed a face-splitting smile at the tall man with dark hair looking directly at her. His smile was as broad as hers. He was holding a huge bouquet of flowers.

"Hello, you!" She laughed out loud with overwhelming joy.

"Car Guy! Of course, you're a mechanic!"

She reached up and kissed him. He wrapped his arms around her and held her tight. "You're not disappointed?" Bobby Taylor asked shyly.

"Oh Bobby, did that kiss say I was disappointed? I've had a crush on you ever since I was a kid. I'm thrilled!"

Grace sat on the couch, holding the phone, toying with the idea of calling Lilly at home. She knew Lilly's flight would have already landed and 'Car Guy' would be there to meet her. *'But what if he wasn't? What if he got cold feet? Lilly will be devastated. No, no!'* Grace reprimanded herself. *'Don't be negative. It will be alright. She'll call me when she's ready.'*

It was indeed, alright for Lilly. She was delighted that her mystery man had turned out to be Bobby Taylor. They walked down to collect the luggage, hand in hand, smiling as if they were the first couple to discover love.

Both were preoccupied with thinking about the snippets of yesteryear as they travelled through the city. He was recalling the moment Lilly had caught his eye and how he had dismissed it because of her age, and she was recalling the thrill of Bobby winking at her the evening she met Grace. Lilly had thought it was just a schoolgirl crush, as he was always there in the background, but the thrill she got when she saw him since then had never waned. They glanced at one another and smiled. *'Yep, he's here, right beside me,'* she was thinking, *'there's no need to pinch myself.'*

Bobby's smile was one of satisfaction, glad that he had trusted Gabriel's advice for him to join the dating site. He recalled the conversation with clarity as it ran through his mind.

They had planned a day's fishing. Tim was on nightshift and was unable to join them. It seemed the fish had taken a holiday, so they sat in the boat and talked. Just general chit-

chat at first, and then out of the blue Bobby said that he missed Lilly. 'It's funny how you get used to people being around the town, and then miss them when they're not around anymore. They become part of the scenery … well, something sorta like that." Bobby shrugged.

Gabriel nodded. "Yeah, I know what you mean."

Gabe was there too, sitting back watching and listening.

Bobby looked over at his mate. The regret in Gabriel's voice was evident. "Ah gee, mate. I'm sorry."

"For what?"

"Grace."

"That chance has long gone. She's with Tim now."

"Has it?"

Gabriel looked back at Bobby and shrugged. "I just want her to be happy." There was a long silence, and then Gabriel said, "We're not talking about me. We were talking about you missing Lilly"

"What can I do about it? Nothing. She's living in the UK, having a ball by the sound of things. As you know, she writes to Grace. Tim passes on the news. You heard how much she's enjoying her time there. She may never come back."

"Go over there."

"What, to the UK?"

"Yeah, why not?"

"Nah, she might tell me she's not interested. I'm not that stupid to put myself in the firing line to be rejected. Nah, I'm not doing that."

"Well then, how about joining an internet dating site …

"Internet what?"

A few of the guys at work have been talking about it … you might meet someone else?"

Gabriel went into the procedure of how internet dating worked. "You write a profile about yourself, your hobbies, etc. and then you put up a photograph of yourself."

"The profile and hobbies seem OK, but I'm not too keen on the mugshot part. One look at this ugly dial and the girls *will run. I'll do the rest but no photo. If a girl doesn't like me for myself and my interests, then she can take a hike." He laughed.*

"Alright then, I'll give you a hand tonight to set it up."

"Great!" Bobby said, "Aaah, mate ... just one thing."

Gabriel smiled. "My lips are sealed."

Bobby gave him the thumbs up.

Still lost in her thoughts, it did not occur to Lilly to ask where they were headed. Her eyes lit up like beacons when she and Bobby drove into the Stamford Plaza carpark.

"I took the liberty of reserving a room," he said when they were stationary. "But I can cancel."

"Don't you dare, Bobby Taylor!" she smiled, "I'd never have thought of you as a romantic. This is wonderful! Ah gee, Bobby Taylor, this is amazing! You are amazing!" She leaned in closer and kissed him.

Their room was lovely. It overlooked the Brisbane River with an uninterrupted view of the Story Bridge. Lilly was in awe, never imagining that Bobby would think to do something as wonderful as planning a romantic weekend together.

She stood by the huge window looking out over the river, admiring the vista and marvelling at how leaving Australia, to travel around Europe had eased the loss of her dear cousin, Max. She smiled with gratitude, recalling parts of a verse from the Prophet. "*The deeper that sorrow carves into your being, the more joy you can contain ... When you are sorrowful, look again in your heart, and you shall see that in truth you are weeping for that which has been your delight.*"

Bobby joined Lilly at the window. He slid an arm around her waist and pulled her closer and kissed the top of her head. She looked up at him lovingly. "Am I dreaming? Are you really here?" She purred and then pinched him.

"Ouch!" he yelped.

She laughed. "I was just testing to see if you were real."

"I think you were supposed to pinch yourself," he said, rubbing the sore spot

"Oh, but that would've hurt!" she laughed, teasing him and then she turned and reached up and cupped his face in her hands. "That will be the first and last time I will ever hurt you, Bobby Taylor. The universe has brought us together. I have to respect that, and always be mindful of that because ... well, because I just simply adore you."

Bobby nodded. "Yes!" he replied, his heart pounding with excitement, utterly convinced that Lilly was the *one*. He did not have to rush anything; he wanted everything to be memorable. "C'mon," he said, leading her to the bathroom where the lights were dim. He pushed the door open and pointed to the tub. It was full to the brim with white foaming bubbles.

She turned back and smiled. "You're amazing. I love this!"

"Take all the time you need," he said and closed the door.

As Lilly disrobed, she noticed a phone on the wall with a very long cord. She could not contain her excitement any longer, she had to call Grace.

"Hi Grace it's me, Lilly," she whispered.

"Lilly! Where are you? Are you OK? You sound as if you are in a tunnel."

"I'm in the bath."

"What? Where?"

"I can't talk now. But 'Car Guy' is Bobby Taylor."

"What?"

"I'll give you all the details when I see in a few days. I have to go. Bobby's calling me. Bye!"

Bobby tapped lightly on the door. "How are you doing in there? Would you care for a glass of champers?"

Lilly giggled. "Come in," she called out and slid farther down into the bubbles so that just her head was showing.

34

After the phone call from Lilly, Grace grabbed her jacket, jumped into her car and dashed off to the hospital. Waiting until the end of his shift to tell Tim the news was not an option. She felt she would explode if she could not share it with him right away. She parked and then hurried over to the elevator and pressed on the button several times, willing the huge doors to slide apart. "C'mon, c'mon!" she mumbled impatiently.

The elevator announced its arrival with a ping and a swishing sound, and seconds later its heavy doors slid apart with a groan. Grace sighed with relief and stepped inside. She suddenly felt small, standing in the wide illuminated empty space that only hours before was a hub of activity, transporting staff, visitors, patients and trollies to various floors in the hospital. She quickly shook off that feeling, leaned forward and pressed the button to Tim's ward. She then stepped back into the middle of the elevator and stood erect and listened as it droned its way up to the seventh floor. The elevator gave a little shudder when it stopped, groaning again with the parting of its doors as if exhausted from travelling up and down the building all day long.

Grace stepped from the elevator into an almost deserted ward. Pockets of halogen lights bounced off the freshly polished linoleum. She looked straight ahead. At the end of the corridor, she saw Tim heavily engaged in conversation with the same nurse who had attended to her the night she fainted in the street. She could not recall the nurse's name. Neither of them turned when she arrived or when the elevators doors closed behind her.

An uneasy shiver attacked every nerve in Grace's body as if something awful was about to happen. They were not close enough for her to hear their conversation, but they were facing each other toe-to-toe, and the nurse was smiling and repeatedly touching her hair while they spoke. What Grace found alarming was that Tim seemed to be hanging on her every word and then suddenly, he laughed out loud.

'I could be reading this wrong', she told herself. 'But what if I'm not? And why do I feel so heartsore?'

The scene did not look innocent. Something was amiss. Grace quickly moved to the side, out of sight, even though they had not noticed her watching them. She leaned against the wall to steady herself, making a huge effort to suppress the tears that tried to surface, along with the rambunctious thoughts galloping through her mind. 'What should I do?' she wondered. 'Confront him?' Ignore what I saw?'

Before Grace had a chance to sort things out in her mind, Tim walked past and seeing someone out of the corner of his eye, leaning against the wall, he turned.

"Grace!" He was startled to see her there. "What's wrong?" He asked.

Grace looked up at the sound of Tim's voice, shocked to see him standing there, looking at her with his head tilted to one side, in the same manner as he did when confused about something. She lifted the corner of her shirt, dabbed her eyes dry and straightened up. "Fancy meeting you here," she joked.

Tim opened his arms, beckoning her to enter when he realised that she had been crying. "Want to talk about it?" he asked.

Grace shook her head as she stepped into his outstretched arms. "Not yet."

She snuggled in closer and Tim tightened his grip around her and kissed the top of her head. "All better now?"

"I guess so," Grace replied, having convinced herself that what she had witnessed was just an innocent conversation between two work colleagues.

"Ready to go home?" she asked with enquiring eyes.

As they headed out, the sounds of buzzers and bells, phones and machines in the hospital seemed louder than usual. Even the sounds from the city felt as though they penetrated the hospital walls – noise from every direction attacking Grace's brain. Her head ached.

"You look pale, Grace," Tim said, concerned. "I want to take you back to my office ... just to make sure."

"No, Tim! I'm fine." Grace said, much harsher than she had intended.

"Well, you're not driving home. It'll take only a moment to put my bike in the storeroom. Wait here," he said, which sounded more like a command than anything else.

Tim's tone of voice prompted Grace's mind to travel back in time to their wedding and the manner with which he took charge of everything – with such determination. She wanted to wait until Lilly returned from the UK. Tim had insisted they marry right away, and so she relented to please him because she loved him ... *'that's what you do when you love someone? Please them, isn't it? Then he had started talking about having a baby when I specifically said that I didn't want to raise a child alone as he already mostly lived at the hospital, working as many shifts as possible as it is. Just once, I wish he'd listened to me and stopped manipulating me to his way of thinking. We're supposed to be a team but we're not – not really.'*

When Tim returned to the car, he slid into the driver seat. He sat back and took a moment to study Grace; she seemed different somehow. He could not read her expression. He shrugged, dismissing it and cheerfully said to lighten the mood, "Let's go home!"

After that night, although Grace was not consciously aware of it herself, something within her had changed. She began second-guessing everything she did at work and even the simplest of tasks like buying a new dress became a challenge, which was so unlike her. She also had a nagging feeling that her future with Tim was not secure. The image of him and the nurse constantly haunted her in her sleep. However, by morning, she could not recall the nightmare, which left her exhausted for most of the day.

Grace brightened up when Lilly finally called her with news of her wonderful time with Bobby. They had made arrangements to meet that evening. Tim was still working and would not be home before ten. Grace would normally have left a note telling him where she was, but not this time.

"You look amazing!" Grace shouted with wide-eyed admiration over the restaurant chatter, the moment she saw Lilly walking towards her. They hugged; laughing so jubilantly that people stopped a moment to watch them and then went on their way smiling.

Noticing that something seemed different about Grace, Lilly observed her with a probing eye. "Are you OK?" She asked, curious to learn why Grace had lost the sparkle that was ever-present in her smile. "OK, hon, what's going on with you?"

Grace shrugged and laughed a little awkwardly, dismissing the question with a wave of her hand. "This is not about me," and leaned in closer, eyes bright with excitement, sporting a wide smile, and half whispered, "Now tell me all about your wonderful, exciting time with Bobby."

"C'mon Grace, fess up," Lilly said, adamantly.

Grace reached across the table and took hold of Lilly's hand and squeezed it gently, silencing her. "Not now, sweetie. I really need to hear something positive, and that my dearest friend is deliriously happy."

Lilly smiled. "Oh, I am so, so happy!"

"Then tell me everything, so I can be happy too!" Grace said.

"Well, from the moment I boarded the plane for the UK, I knew wholeheartedly that I was moving in the right direction. It was as if Max was by my side, guiding me along the way."

As Lilly shared her time in the UK with Grace, Grace in turn keenly scrutinized Lilly's every gesture. It was clearly evident to her that Lilly had reconciled her cousin's absence from her life and had found peace within that reconciliation.

"I'll always miss Max," Lilly admitted with a deep sense of loss. "He was a huge part of my childhood, which was such a wonderful time of my life. I simply can't dismiss that. Before I left Brisbane, I was trying to blot out my childhood memories because it hurt too much to be reminded that I'd never see Max again." Lilly paused a moment and then looked up at Grace and smiled. "The best way to honour my dear, dear, cousin-cum-surrogate-brother and best friend and our wonderful time together is to remember him and all the fun things we did growing up." Lilly paused again. She was examining Grace's face. Her brow creased with concentration. Both were silent.

"You seem different somehow, Grace, and that bothers me," Lilly's tone was serious. "I'm worried about you. Now, how can I be happy when my dearest friend looks positively miserable?"

Grace shrugged and looked down at the napkin she was twisting in her hands. "I think Tim is cheating." Grace finally admitted, then paused to stop herself from crying. She sucked in a gulp of air and looked up at Lilly, who had fallen back in her chair stunned.

"She's a nurse at the hospital," Grace added and paused. The noise around them rose up again, as Grace nodded, confirming her statement, she then continued. "I saw them together. They were too familiar with one another for their association to be just, friends."

"Are you sure? Lilly said, in disbelief.

"Perfectly! She was all giggly like a school girl fawning over a rock star, and Tim was responding with smiles and laughter."

Were you and Tim having problems?"

"No!" Grace shook her head so vehemently that her red curls danced wildly around her shoulders. "That's just it," she responded with wide-eyed confusion. "We were perfectly happy, or so I thought. We laughed and teased one another and kidded around the way we always had ... we made passionate love every spare moment we had together. Nothing was wrong. Tim seemed happy working extra shifts at the hospital. He said he wanted to learn as much as he could to advance his career. I didn't complain to him about the number of hours he spent at the hospital, even though I wasn't happy about it."

They both went silent. The chatter and laughter, the clanging of cutlery on plates, clinking of glasses in the restaurant, filled the silence between them. The noise became so loud that they both looked around the room simultaneously.

Lilly turned her attention back to Grace. "Do you love Tim?"

Grace nodded. "I do, but not the way I used to. The love I had for Tim waned the moment I saw him with that nurse. Afterwards, I desperately tried to convince myself that it was just an innocent encounter that I saw, but this nagging sense of betrayal won't leave me. I can feel the tear deep down in my heart."

"What are you going to do?"

I don't know. I keep thinking about the past two years of our marriage. They were wonderful, but as I dissect them, I've come to realise just how controlling Tim has been."

"What do you mean, Grace?" Lilly's expression was one of concern and curiosity.

"Well, for starters," Grace said as if things were finally becoming crystal clear. "I wanted you, my best and dearest friend, to stand beside me as my bridesmaid at my wedding. Tim brushed my wishes aside, saying that he wanted to marry me, now, that he didn't want to wait any longer. He knew I was disappointed that you were not there."

"Awww, sweetie," Lilly cooed, screwing up her face as she reached for Grace's hand. "I was so sad that I missed your wedding."

"Oh Lilly, there were so many other things that I'd ignored and eventually forgotten about until now. I was so dizzy and in love that I simply let him have his way with just about everything. Looking back, I now realise just how much it was all about Tim and what he wanted, and less about 'us' as a couple. It was *his* career, *his* dream of becoming a surgeon" Grace paused to look at up Lilly and sighed heavily. Tears were welling up in her eyes as she continued in a shaky voice, "Tim has never once asked me if I had a dream or what I had wanted to do with my life. I guess he took it for granted that I'd be his wife and the mother of his 'future' children, end of story!"

Lilly remained silent. She had no advice to offer Grace, so she said nothing. But in truth, Lilly was actually shocked to see Grace so unhappy. She sat opposite her dear friend and listened as she poured out all her pent-up emotions.

Grace half smiled, oblivious to her surroundings. "Well," she said, shrugging her shoulders, the palms of her hands facing upwards in a gesture of hopeless. "I'm a long way off wanting children. I told Tim before he asked me to marry him that I was unsure if I ever wanted children, and I certainly wouldn't have a child if he was not there to co-parent with me. I don't plan to raise a baby by myself, that's for sure! That's what I told him," she said adamantly. "And you know what?" Grace asked Lilly, leaning forward.

Lilly shook her head and shrugged. "What?'

Grace threw her arms into the air. "He brushed that aside too, with the promise that we'd always be a *team.*" Grace leaned back in her seat and laughed sarcastically. "Tim is a good man, but he hasn't got a clue about being a team player. He's a one-man band, always having to prove himself to the world. I've come to realise that I can't compete with that."

35

Sleep had evaded Grace. She lay in bed until first light, pondering the conversation she had earlier with Lilly over dinner. She knew what she must do. She turned sideways to look at Tim as he slept beside her. There was no malice in her heart towards him. She was numb. She pushed herself up on her elbow and observed him closely. He was sleeping soundly; his large frame sprawled out, covering most of their queen-size bed. *'Totally at peace with the world,'* she thought. Slowly she drew back the doona and went to the bathroom. Ten minutes later, Grace was on her way downstairs to the underground carpark. The area was deserted at that hour of the day, on weekends. Most of the residents in the apartment building were young and employed. They worked hard and partied hard and slept until mid-morning on weekends.

Grace's footsteps on the concrete echoed loudly while walking to her car, the pigeons sitting in the rafters scattering in fright. They flew aimlessly around the roof and eventually settled on beams above her car. Grace was unaware that her presence had disturbed the birds – her mind was focused on going to the bay, where she felt more at home and where she could unravel her thoughts.

Grace steered her car out of the carpark, oblivious to the day and its promise of perfection. The sun rose slowly, spreading its golden rays across the city, now slowly coming to life – and to the hint of a spring breeze dancing over the Brisbane river just meters from her apartment.

She was too distracted to notice that joggers seemed to appear from nowhere, zig-zagging their way through scattered groups of people, deflated tote bags hanging loosely from their shoulders as they headed towards the farmer's markets. Suddenly, several groups of cyclists came peddling along the main road that only minutes before was deserted, crossing onto her side of the road. She swerved to avoid them. At that moment Grace realised that she must be mindful of her surroundings or she could have an accident, so she took a circuitous route to the bay to avoid the heavy traffic heading south to the Gold Coast.

By the time Grace arrived at her destination, day trippers and locals had commandeered all the parking spots. She cruised along the esplanade in search of a vacancy and eventually saw reverse lights on a car about to pull out. She stopped, waiting for the vehicle to leave and blocking several cars behind her. She looked in her rear vision mirror and understood the frustration on the face of the driver, but could do nothing other than to stay put until her park was available. He angrily tooted at her as he drove on. Grace shook her head and muttered, "Yeah, have a nice day too, Mr Happy Face," as she cut the engine.

She sat back in the seat, wound down the window and drew in the bay air. A warm breeze gently brushed the side of her face as she viewed the world around her through the windscreen and opened window.

Everything seemed colourful – the grass a rich, deep green and the sky a cloudless sapphire. The shade of pinks, blues, greens, reds and yellows in the children's' clothing were radiant in the sunlight as they happily romped with their parents and pets in the park. Their laughter and jubilant shouts to one another made Grace smile. She looked to her left, farther down the foreshore, where vivid market tents fluttered in the breeze. Patrons wearing straw hats and caps and sunglasses, shorts, tee-shirts, long skirts and short dresses, strolled in and out around the tents, perusing the vendors' wares.

'I love this area,' she thought. *'I'm happy here. I should move back. I could buy that apartment up the road that's for sale.'*

Gabe was sitting in the back seat, listening to Grace's thoughts. *'But you are married and already have a life and a job near the city,'* he said.

Grace looked puzzled. She had heard Gabe's comment but imagined it was her thoughts. *'Now why on earth did I think that?'*

'Because you need to sort out your life, and decide what you really want. You can't just pull up stakes and pitch your tent someplace else without dealing with what it is that's troubling you. Running away from the truth only makes things worse.'

Grace dropped her head. She was about to start weeping but stopped herself. The world outside her car seemed so cheerful and she wanted to be cheerful too. *'I wish I knew what the truth is,'* she thought.

'Don't just sit here feeling sorry for yourself. Go and find Tim and ask him outright,' replied Gabe.

Grace responded by suddenly sitting upright, turning on the ignition. *'I'll ask Tim if he's having an affair. Hit him square in the face with it.'* As the engine idled, she suddenly felt deflated and unsure. *'What if he is?'*

"If Tim is having an affair," Gabe said, *"then he isn't the man for you. You could consider that there's something lacking in your relationship, something that neither of you can give the other."*

Grace pondered that thought for several minutes, the engine still idling until the beeping of a car horn caused her to jump. She looked over her shoulder and saw a questioning look on the face of a driver waiting for her to move. She responded with an apologetic smile as she backed out and drove off.

"Where have you been?" Tim shouted the moment Grace walked through the door.

"We have to talk, Tim," Grace said, bracing herself for what was about to come.

Tim took an uneasy step backwards. "What's this about, Grace?"

Grace observed her husband for several long seconds; he was perspiring and obviously uncomfortable as if he had just been caught with his hand in the cookie jar. He was looking at his feet instead of her. The answer to her question was clearly revealed in his body language. She was lost for words, which was so unusual for her. She wanted to ask him why, but no words would come.

Tears suddenly welled up and tumbled down her cheeks as her body began to tremble in fury. Tim moved towards Grace with outstretched arms, intending to comfort her, but she instantly raised her hand, blocking him and vehemently shaking her head. He froze in his tracks and remained there for several awkward minutes. He did not know what to do or say, so he said and did nothing.

When Tim realised that his presence was upsetting Grace, he quietly left the room. He went to the bedroom and quickly gathered most of his belongings together. As he left the apartment, the phone rang, muffling the sound of the door closing behind him.

The recorded invitation from Grace and Tim for the caller to leave a message was followed by several beeps, after which Anita's voice echoed around the room. "Hello, Grace! Hello Tim! It's me, granny. Just a quick call to say hello ..."

Grace sat sombre-faced on the coach, totally detached from everything around her. Negative questions consumed her thoughts, making her wonder what she had done to drive the man she loved into the arms of another woman. What had she done to push him hard enough to betray her, to break the promises he had made to her on their wedding day? *'This is my fault!'* she screamed in her mind. *'I'm the daughter of a murderer ... the daughter of a murderer who killed his wife and Gabe Connors! No man could love a woman with a history as dark as that.'*

Tim's betrayal had convinced Grace that she was worthless and she simply retired into herself.

When Grace failed to respond to her many calls, Lilly became frantic and called Gabriel. After she brought him up-to-date with Grace and Tim's situation she said, "I'm afraid for Grace. She hasn't returned any of my calls. Please ..."

"I'll meet you at the apartment," he said, cutting Lilly off midsentence.

Gabriel was pounding on the door of Grace's apartment door when Lilly arrived.

"She won't answer," Lilly said, with a tremor in her voice. "I was here just before I called you."

"Is Grace inside?" he asked.

Lilly nodded, fighting to remain calm. "Yes."

Gabriel dashed to the stairwell.

"Where are you going?" Lilly shouted at him.

"Outside ... I'll have to climb over the balcony to get inside." He paused briefly and then said, with a sense of dread. "I think you should call an ambulance." Then he was gone.

Gabriel knocked over a couple of pot plants in his haste to get into the apartment. The noise should have alerted Grace, who looked to be asleep on the lounge. She was not asleep but leaning back against a pile of cushions staring at the wall.

Lilly could hear Gabriel talking to Grace and banged on the door calling out, "Gabriel! Gabriel, is Grace alright? Let me in!"

Noting the desperation in Lilly's voice, Gabriel hurried to the door. "Grace isn't responding," he told her when she barged past him. "She's like a zombie."

Lilly froze and then turned around to look at him. "What do you mean ... zombie?"

Look for yourself. She's sitting there staring into space. Did you call the ambulance?"

Lilly nodded and then knelt down beside Grace and clasped hold of her hand. "Grace, Grace, what's wrong, sweetie?" Lilly said, almost in a whisper, managing to keep the panic she felt from her voice.

No response.

Lilly was about to break down, but Gabriel rested a reassuring hand on her shoulder.

"Are you OK, mate?"

Lilly nodded.

"Please hold it together a little longer?" Gabriel pleaded and took a moment to suck in a lung full of air. "She'll be OK as soon as we get her to the hospital."

As Gabriel was speaking, they heard in the distance the familiar high-pitched sound of the ambulance coming closer. They sighed and looked at each other, hope and relief reflected in their eyes.

36

The Emergency Department was a nightmare – a room full of patients who had been waiting for hours to see a doctor. Some hackles were raised and mutters of unfairness were expressed when the paramedics wheeled Grace in on a stretcher, with staff rushing to attend to her.

A gruff voice in the crowd called out. "Maybe I should go home and call the ambos ... seems to me that's the only way to get attention around here."

Minutes later, Gabriel and Lilly came rushing in. They headed for the enquiry desk. One of the paramedics, the driver, looked up from his paperwork and saw them. "Over here!" he called.

"How is she?" Lilly asked.

"The doc's with her now," the driver replied. He paused, and then asked, "Is Grace Doc Osborne's wife?"

Gabriel and Lilly looked awkwardly at each other and nodded.

"I can call him for you if you like. He's on..."

"No!" they said in unison. "I'll call Tim when we have more information," Gabriel said, balling his fist and holding back the urge to scream. *'That bastard is the reason she is ill.'*

"OK," the driver said hesitantly, narrowing his eyes. Feeling something was odd. He slipped away and made that call.

Gabriel peeked at his watch again. Another anxious hour had passed. He looked over at the entrance when the large glass doors slid apart for the hundredth time since they had been there. Anita and Edward came in. He waved to them.

"What happened to Grace? Is the doctor with her?" Anita set about to fire one question after another at Lilly and Gabriel.

"Darling," Edward said, gently wrapping an arm around Anita and leading her to a seat. "Let them speak."

"Oh, of course. I'm sorry, I didn't mean to..."

"It's OK," Lilly said, glancing sideways at Gabriel. He nodded. "We understand. We don't know anything as yet, Anita. We're still waiting for the doctor to tell us."

"I was beginning to worry. I hadn't heard from Grace for a few days. She normally calls. I left several messages." Anita looked pleadingly at Lilly and then at Gabriel. "Do you know why Grace didn't return my calls?"

Lilly looked uncomfortable. "Yes," she said, with a tremor in her voice. "Tim cheated on her. She was devastated."

Anita's eyes widened, in shock. "Oh, no ... did she ...?"

"No! No!" Lilly responded quickly. "Grace would *never* do that."

Anita released a heavy sigh and relaxed back into Edward's arm. Her hand shot up to her mouth when realising what she had implied. "Oh, dear God! What was I thinking? Of course, Grace wouldn't ... She's strong and full of life."

Edward noticed Lilly and Gabriel flinch. Their expressions worried him. He instinctively felt that there was something more going on with Grace than they were saying. Edward turned to Anita. "How about I get you a cup of tea, love?"

"Oh, thank you, darling."

Edward stood up. He moved over to Gabriel and said, "C'mon mate, I could do with a coffee, how about you?"

Gabriel's thoughts were elsewhere. He had not heard and jumped when Edward tapped him on the shoulder and repeated what he had said.

"Yeah, yeah, good idea," Gabriel replied and followed Edward.

"You're worried, aren't you?"

"Yes, I am. I'm very worried." Gabriel said, and then paused to steady his emotions. "Grace was *shallow breathing* when I found her sitting on the lounge. She was just staring at the wall. She was cold to touch and seemed lifeless. So yeah, mate I'm worried." Gabriel's eyes turned icy and his hand balled into fists when he turned to Edward. "I could kill Tim for betraying Grace. He knew how I felt about her. He knew I loved her and still, he pursued her."

"If you loved Grace as much as you say, then why did you stand back and let it happen? Why didn't you fight for her?"

Gabriel replied angrily without hesitation. "Because I was stupid enough to believe that Tim loved her so much to give her a good life ... and she loved him. I couldn't mess with that. I wanted Grace to be happy."

"I have to admit," Edward began, "Anita and I thought Grace was in love with you. We were surprised when she started dating Tim," he said, adding, "not that we had any misgiving about Tim. It was just that a day hadn't passed without her mentioning your name – Gabriel said this, Gabriel and I ... blah, blah, blah." Edward went quiet. "Now that I come to think of it," he said, breaking his silence, "I do recall something Grace had said that could have been the reason why she became interested in Tim."

Gabriel's brow rose in surprise and several fine lines formed across his forehead turning towards Edward. "What was that?"

Edward shook his head. "You might not like it."

"I'd like to know, regardless."

"She said she didn't think you were the marrying kind and that you'd probably get bored with one woman." Edward paused to watch Gabriel's reaction, then continued,

"It was said in an offhanded way. But you know what they say, mate. Many a true word said in jest."

Gabriel's shoulders slumped. "Yeah, I don't blame Grace for thinking that. My history with women wouldn't have encouraged Grace, or any woman for that matter, to have faith in me as a potential husband." He laughed out loud, but there was no humour present in that laughter. "I'm not giving up on Grace!" He was adamant about that.

"Good for you, son," Edward replied, slapping him on the back. "C'mon we should hurry and get those drinks."

The men were still discussing Grace's situation as they ambled back to the lounge, mindful of not spilling the steaming hot beverages they were carrying in paper cups. As they came closer, they saw a tall, lean man in a white coat, aged about thirty-something, talking to Anita. They picked up their pace. Although they were not close enough to hear the conversation, the expression on the man's face was grim and Anita was shaking her head as she rested her hand on her heart. She turned around and saw Edward and Gabriel. She reached out to Edward. "The doctor says Grace is dying!" she cried.

"She still has a chance," the doctor quickly added, "a slim one. That's better than none at all."

"What exactly is wrong with Grace?" Edward asked calmly, his arm around Anita.

"Nothing is physically wrong with Grace that we can see. We've done several tests, but she isn't responding to anything."

"What makes you think she's dying?" Gabriel asked.

"It was by chance that our resident psychiatrist, Dr Adams was in Emergency. I asked him to take a look at Grace and he was with her for over an hour. Afterwards, we discussed her case at length. Dr Adams is of the opinion that Grace is suffering from psychogenic death. It can be terminal within days; however, death is not inevitable." He paused a moment to watch the horror of his words penetrate their conscious minds, and then he continued, "Not if Grace can find a reason to live."

Gabriel stared at the doctor. "I don't get it," he said, bewildered. "A few days ago, Grace was happy and full of life, the way she normally is and now you're telling us that this, this ... psycho thing is about to kill her." He ran his hands through his hair in frustration. Tears were surfacing. "Why? What the hell caused this condition?"

The doctor put a comforting hand on Gabriel's shoulder. He shook it off.

"I'm not the one who needs your help," he said, clenching his jaw. "I just want you to explain how and why this is happening. Make me understand!"

"OK," the doctor said calmly, scanning their faces and stopping at Anita.

"First of all, it's not about suicide, nor is it related to depression. But giving up on life and dying usually, within days, is a very real condition often linked to severe trauma. Technically speaking, the recent trauma Grace has experienced could have triggered a change in the frontal circuit of her brain, the part that controls her motivation and her behaviour."

Edward drew Anita closer to him when she gasped. Lilly's eyes expanded in disbelief.

"This is a nightmare," said Gabriel, his voice full of anguish. "It can't be true. It just can't be."

37

The doctor knew this was going to take time. He looked around for a quiet corner. "How about we go over there?" he said, pointing to the end of the corridor. "We can all sit down and I will explain as much as I can."

They nodded and followed the doctor to an area where several seats were clustered in a semicircle around a low table. Everyone took a seat. The doctor sat on the edge of the table facing them. Four sets of eyes nervously fell upon the man in the white coat, clutching his pen and notebook. "Dr Adams," he began, "has given me a lot of information on psychogenic death, commonly known as *give-up-itis.* He explained that people with this condition regard death as a coping mechanism to escape the agonising stress of their situation. They are convinced that their situation is hopeless, withdrawing from life around them until they eventually die. Judging by what you've told me earlier, Anita, the breakdown of Grace's marriage was very traumatic for her, however, I feel that there is more to Grace's circumstances."

Anita looked drained. She was pale and utterly at a loss. "I've never heard of psychogenic death or give-up-itis before today. It is something new?"

The doctor shook his head. "No. According to Dr Adams, Dr Leach from the University of Portsmouth in the UK studied many cases on the subject as far back as the 1600s. They correlate with reports on the deaths of elderly people and hospital patients, POWs and veterans and even Grace's case."

The doctor paused as he searched each of their faces. "Can any of you shed more light on this, anything at all to help us understand why Grace is giving up?"

Edward thought back to the day he found Grace standing in front of the mirror, staring at her image. "Perhaps I can," he said.

All eyes turned to Edward. The hospital activity and sounds around them suddenly seemed deafening, and then the noise faded into the background as Edward began to speak. He cleared his throat, hesitating. "It might not be anything."

"Any bit of information will be helpful," the doctor replied quickly to reassure Edward.

"OK," Edward said, taking a deep breath. "It was a few years ago." He turned to Anita. "I was on my way to our bedroom. I walked past Grace's room." He shrugged and then looked at the doctor. "I had no idea she was there; I hadn't heard her come in. So you can understand why I was surprised to see her, let alone standing in front of the mirror. It was as if she was in a trance, staring at her reflection. I called her a couple of times before she responded. When she turned around, her face was soaked with tears. I was dumbfounded to see she'd been crying. Grace never cries. She's always happy. Her features were normally creased with a beaming smile." Edward went silent for a moment in an effort to keep his emotions in check. He then cleared his throat again. "Anyway," he continued, "I asked if she wanted to talk about it, but she shook her head. "I told her that I'd always be here for her if ever she wanted to talk.

Grace said, "I know. You've always been there for me."

Edward continued, "She began reminiscing about her childhood, saying that she wished I was her father. I said that I could adopt her. She laughed out loud, saying it would be very confusing for people if I adopted her. I asked why and she replied that I'd be her father married to her granny."

They all smiled.

Edward let his head loll. "I thought Grace was OK. Now I can see she really wasn't," he said in a voice cracked with emotion. Anita sat tight beside him, dabbing her eyes with a tissue.

While Edward was talking, the doctor scribbled notes as fast as he could. He looked up from his notepad at Edward when he had finished. "What makes you think Grace wasn't OK?"

Anita and Edward glanced at each other. "A short time later," Edward said, "Grace went a little crazy, partying, drinking, and staying out to all hours, that kind of thing."

"Drugs?" The doctor interrupted.

"A few recreational," Lilly chipped in and all eyes fell on her. "Nothing hard. It was our way of dealing with our issues at the time."

"Issues? What issues were they? Would you care to elaborate?" the doctor asked.

Lilly looked uncomfortable. "I'm sorry, I can't. I promised Grace I'd never utter a word of what she told me in confidence."

"Then I shall," said Anita. "Doctor," she paused, looking puzzled. "What is your name? I don't recall you ever mentioning it."

"Oh, I am sorry, Zac Thompson," he said.

"Dr Thompson, my son, Oliver, Grace's father, was an over-indulged child. My fault, of course, mine and his father's. Both are now deceased. What my son couldn't have he would destroy or do his utmost without any regard for others or the consequences of his actions, to get what he so desired." Anita sighed heavily with shame and then continued. "Oliver murdered Gabriel's father, Gabe, in pursuit of Bonnie, however an indiscreet moment with Carla, Grace's mother, changed everything when she ended up pregnant. It would seem that Oliver killed Carla too, but there's no actual proof to confirm that as fact." Anita paused, feeling uncomfortable at having to drag up the past.

Anita glanced over at Gabriel in apology for airing their dirty linen in public. He nodded his approval for her to continue. "It's a very long story, Dr Thompson," Anita explained. "I hope you have plenty of ink in that pen,' she remarked remorsefully and then began from the beginning while the others, with the exception of Gabriel, sat back to listen. He wandered away from the group as Anita began. She nodded to him, indicating that she understood. Gabriel knew the story inside out and had no desire to hear it again.

Gabe, who had never left Gabriel's side since he had arrived at the hospital, followed him, listening to his thoughts. *'I wish I knew what to do to help Grace.'*

Gabe replied, *'Find out what she loves. What's most important to her?'*

'I wouldn't know where to start,' Gabriel thought.

'How about her job? That's important to her, isn't it?' Gabe said. *'You could begin there.'*

'Yeah, her job. The animals. She absolutely loves all of them. Her boss doesn't know what's happened. I should call the surgery to let them know why she hasn't turned up for work. On second thought, I'll drive over there.'

Gabriel caught Anita's attention and mouthed that he would be back soon, and she waved to him.

When Anita finished revealing all the skeletons of her family's past, Doctor Thompson lifted the pen from the page. "That was an extraordinary story. Did your son have any redeeming factors?"

Anita gave the doctor's question some consideration. "Yes. I suppose there were a couple."

"What were they?" he asked.

"Oliver loved Bonnie. I know he was obsessed with her, but I do believe he loved her deeply and would have been a different man, a better man, had she loved him in return. Sadly, it was never to be."

"Why do you think your son would have been a better man if this woman had returned his love?"

"Gabe, Bonnie's husband, was an angry young man before he met her. I can recall people being afraid of him although he was the most handsome man I'd set eyes on. Gabe Connor reminded me of a time bomb, silently ticking away ready to explode at any given minute. In Bonnie's company, he was calm, and polite. The change in him was extraordinary. Like Gabe, Oliver was also besotted with Bonnie. She is an exceptional woman, beautiful and kind," Anita beamed.

"I imagine Gabriel must resemble his mother then, he ..."

"No," Anita interrupted. "He's the image of his father."

The doctor raised his brow in surprise.

"Gabriel inherited his mother's kind spirit. He's much like her in that way, but when you see Gabriel, you're also looking at his father. Gabe was an extremely handsome man, as is Gabriel."

"You mentioned that your son had two redeeming qualities," said the doctor. "What was the second one?"

"Grace. He adored her. Although he wanted Grace to stay with him, he realised that it was in her best interest that she went with me to the UK. I considered that an unselfish act of love on his part, doctor." Tears were brimming in her eyes. "He had no idea that he'd die in the fire. Grace would have burnt to death too, had he not let her go." Anita patted her eyes. "He trusted me to raise his precious child." She paused. "He also gave me a chance to be the parent to Grace that I should have been to him."

"Hindsight is a wonderful thing, Anita." Doctor Thompson said, thinking how her story had impacted him. He finally understood that his wife's complaints about him spending so little time with her and their son had merit. She would chastise him for buying their son toys to appease his guilt for neglecting him.

"Harry needs his father, not toys." She would say.

"I have a great deal of information to go over," Doctor Thompson said, now anxious to leave. "Grace is sedated at the moment. I suggest that you all go home and come back tomorrow. Hopefully, there will be an improvement in Grace's condition by then."

Lilly leaned forward and looked directly at the doctor, with eyes full of hope.

"What can we do to help Grace?"

He shook his head in a hopeless gesture. "Honestly, I don't know. There isn't any quick fix here. At the moment, Grace is hovering over a fine line between life and death. All I know for certain is that she needs to feel she has something to live for," he said. "If you'll excuse, I must go now," he said with urgency, "there's something very important I must attend to right away."

Doctor Thompson left the group and hurried to his office. He snatched up the phone and dialled his home number. The phone rang for what he thought was a long time. He impatiently drummed the desk with his fingers, while waiting for his wife to answer. He released a huge sigh when he heard her say, "Hello."

"Darling, I've been a fool for neglecting you and Harry. I hope you can forgive me."

"Well, I ...," she said cautiously, looking over her shoulder at the half-packed suitcase sitting on the bed. "I don't know what to say, Zac. I really thought we no longer mattered to you."

"No, no Baby. That couldn't be further from the truth. I'm so, so sorry."

"What brought this on?" she asked.

"I had an eye-opening experience today. I'll tell you all about it over dinner tonight. Can you arrange a sitter for Harry? I'd like to take you somewhere special."

"I can arrange that," she smiled, silently thanking God for answering her prayers.

Gabriel arrived at the vet surgery and parked the car. He took a few minutes to check his emotions before he faced Grace's co-workers.

The receptionist glanced out of the window when she heard a car enter the parking lot. She immediately checked the appointment book. No one was due. *'Oh no,'* she thought, feeling a little overwhelmed as the surgery was short-staffed. *'I hope this isn't another emergency.'*

When no one came inside, the receptionist got up from her desk. She moved closer to the window to see who it was, or if they needed any assistance with their pet. A man she did not recognise was sitting in his car. He looked distressed. Just as the receptionist was about to call one of the nurses, Kerry Davies appeared in the doorway. "June, what time is the next appointment? I ..." Kerry went quiet when she saw June's worried expression.

"What's wrong?"

"I don't actually know. There's a man in the parking lot. He's just sitting in his car. He looks dreadfully upset."

Kerry went to the window. "Oh my God!" she gasped. "I'll be back in a minute."

Gabriel got out of the car as Kerry came towards him. "Has something happened to Grace?" she asked, without her usual pleasantries.

"Yes. It's a long story."

"I've got time to listen."

June stood by the window watching Kerry and the man talking. Kerry's hand shot to her mouth. The man reached out and touched her arm. She was crying. *'Something awful must have happened for Kerry to cry. She's a tough gal, that one,'* she thought.

June scurried back behind her desk when they turned and hurried towards the surgery.

"Isobel is the kitten's name," June heard Kerry tell the man, as they walked past reception on the way into the Cattery. "She's fretting for Grace. She won't eat anything.

Isobel was barely alive when she was dumped on the surgery's doorstep. She's Grace's patient. They instantly connected. Perhaps if we took Isobel to the hospital to see Grace, she might start eating again. I don't know what else to do. Perhaps Isobel might bring Grace back too. It's worth a try."

"Yes, it is," Gabriel said, feeling more hopeful. "I'll call her doctor to see what he has to say. I'm sure it won't be a problem. He's just as anxious as we are to help Grace recover."

38

Tim thanked the paramedic for his call. He knew he could not join the others to find out how Grace was. He would have to wait until later when he was sure she would be alone.

In the meantime, he called his colleague, Dr Zac Thompson. "I think you should come by my office," he said to Tim.

When Tim arrived, Zac pointed to a chair close to his desk. "Sit down Tim," he said, closing Grace's case file which he had been reviewing. He clasped his hands together and placed them on top of the file. "I'm afraid it's not good news ..."

Tim was shocked to learn that Grace had given up on life. "I find that difficult to believe, Zac," he said, running his hand across his forehead and then through his hair. "Grace is passionate about life. Bloody hell, mate! She's passionate about everything. She doesn't just give up!"

"So her family and friends tell me. But her symptoms are textbook, Tim. She's not responding to anything."

"What about, Gabriel?" Tim said.

"What about Gabriel?"

"Did Grace not respond to him either?"

"As far as I know, Gabriel left the hospital without seeing her. Why do you ask?"

Tim stood up and paced the room.

"If you know something, anything that'll help with Grace's recovery, please tell me. It's crucial, Tim."

Tim stopped pacing and sat back down. He leaned forward in his chair. "It's only a guess, mind you." He paused. 'I don't think Grace is giving up because our marriage failed."

Zac gave Tim a puzzled look.

"Oh … I'm sure that's part of it. But I cannot accept it's the main reason for her totally withdrawing."

"Can you be more specific?"

"Well, yes, I think I can," Tim said.

The phone rang. "Excuse me," Zac said and took the call.

His brow went up as he listened. "Yes. Yes, I have no objections to trying that, Gabriel."

Tim's ears pricked up at the mentioning of Gabriel's name.

"OK. So you'll be here within the hour with the kitten. OK, Yes. Yes. I shall be there to observe Grace's reaction," he said, ending the call.

"I gather from that conversation that Gabriel's bringing a kitten in for Grace," said Tim.

The doctor nodded. "Ah, but this is no ordinary kitten. Grace and Isobel have a history. Isobel was close to death when she was left on the surgery's doorstep. Apparently, she responded well to Grace. The kitten was thriving until now. In Grace's absence, she refuses to eat." The doctor paused a moment. "Well Tim, if you intend to see Grace, you have less than an hour. May I suggest you do it now?"

Without another word, Tim got up from his chair and hurried to Grace's room. He found her sitting in a large comfortable recliner, staring out of the window. There were no lovely views for her to admire, as there was from her apartment balcony, just stark rooftop buildings and blue sky.

Gabriel arrived earlier than expected. Anger stirred deep within him at the sight of Tim sitting beside Grace, holding her hand. Before he could say or do anything, Gabe shouted, "Stop and listen, son!" Gabriel instantly stepped sideways out of sight and moved closer to the doorway.

"Oh, Grace. Grace, I am so, so sorry. Nothing is worth this, darling. I know I let you down. That's something I'll regret for the rest of my days, believe me," he said, hanging his head. He looked up at her and touched her cheek. "Grace, you were never in love with me. Oh, I know you did love me, in your own way. But not deeply or the way you love Gabriel. You're in love with him, and he is with you." Tim paused, gently massaging Grace's pale hands and then kissed them.

"Gabriel talked about you so often that I wanted to be with you – to know you. To love you the way he does. To have you love me back. I knew you were afraid that Gabriel mightn't be able to settle down. I took advantage of that. I couldn't help myself. It was wrong, so terribly wrong, Grace. My selfishness caused you so much pain. For that, I'm truly sorry. I was ambitious and imagined I'd conquer the world with you by my side. I was wrong about that, also. You mustn't give up now when you have so much to live for."

Tim turned suddenly when Isobel meowed. He got up quickly. "I was just leaving," Tim said. "Look after her," he said as he left.

Gabriel nodded. The kitten meowed again.

"Isobel?" Grace reached for her.

The kitten leapt out of her cage the second Gabriel unlatched the door, landing in Grace's lap. She turned several times in a circle before contentedly flopping down purring.

Zac Thompson entered the room just in time to witness Grace's reaction to Isobel. He clapped his hands in jubilation. "This is wonderful!" he said, wearing a smile that almost split his face in two, "perfectly wonderful!"

Grace held out her hand to Gabriel. He moved closer and wrapped his large hand around hers. She could feel the strength in his grip.

"I'll look after you from now on," he said.

Grace's eyes softened at the sight of Gabriel. She caressed his face with the back of her free hand. "I know," she whispered so only he could hear. "You're my guardian angel."

Grace suddenly laughed out loud. "I guess this really isn't the appropriate time to say it, but I'm very hungry," she said, "I feel as if I've just woken from a deep sleep. Isobel looks like she could be hungry too. She's lost weight."

Gabriel quickly produced Isobel's dishes and filled one with dried biscuits and the other with water. He placed the dishes and Isobel on the hospital tray. All three smiled as the ravenous kitten gobbled down her food.

Dr Zac introduced himself to Grace then said, "You've had a close call, Grace." His tone was serious. "It will take time for you to fully recover and of course, there will be therapy sessions, you understand."

She nodded. "Whatever it takes, doctor." Grace caught Gabriel's eye and winked. "I want to get better. I have so much to look forward to."

Grace stretched her slender frame and covered her mouth in an effort to stifle a yawn as she wriggled into a comfortable position in the chair. "We can talk later, when I'm lucid," she said and then up looked at Gabriel. "Will you stay with me for a while?"

Within seconds Grace was sound asleep

39

The Gallery phone was ringing.

"Will you get that please, Sandy?" Bonnie asked. "It might be Blake. Take a message if it is."

"OK," Sandy replied. "But you should be kinder to that poor man, Luvvy. He's worn his heart on his sleeve for you for over five years now. He's sweet and gorgeous," she said, then instantly changed to her professional and efficient intonation.

"Good afternoon, The Gal..., Gabriel!" Sandy shouted with delight at the sound of his voice. "How's Grace? Good news I hope?"

Sandy slipped her hand over the mouthpiece and called Bonnie. "It's Gabriel!"

Bonnie picked up the phone. "Hello, darling! How's Grace?"

Bonnie's emotions rose and plummeted like a roller coaster as Gabriel brought her up to date with Grace's progress. One minute she was mopping tears from her cheeks and the next she laughed with heartfelt joy.

"I am so relieved to hear Grace is on the road to recovery, sweetheart," she said, wiping away the last of her happy tears. "That's wonderful," she said when Gabriel mentioned he had overheard Tim apologising to Grace. "Tim's really a good man. Not perfect. None of us is. But still, he's a good man. It's a relief to know he's made peace with Grace. Time heals all wounds."

"Mum?" Gabriel said, wanting to move away from the subject of Tim. He was still angry with him.

"Yes, love?"

"Can I leave Isobel with you during the day? I'll pick her up and take her to see Grace in the afternoon. I'll take care of her in the evenings."

"Of course," Bonnie said with a laugh. "Starting a family already?"

Gabriel laughed too. "You could say that." He sighed heavily. "Words can't express how thankful I am to know Grace is going to be OK." He paused. "I nearly lost her a second time, Mum," he said. His voice cracked with emotion. Gabe moved closer to his son and rested a comforting hand on his shoulder.

Bonnie felt concerned. "Darling, are you alright?"

"Yeah, Yeah, I'm OK," he said, shaking himself. "I love that woman so much. I'd be lost without her…"

"Well, you don't have to think about that now." Bonnie interrupted. "Grace will be home soon."

"Yeah, you're right." He drew in a lung full of air and then slowly exhaled. "I can't dwell on the negative."

"That would be a waste of time, anyway," Bonnie replied. "Will you let Grace know I'll be in to see her some time tomorrow?" The conversation then flowed on to things in general before the call ended.

Sandy was in Bonnie's office like a shot after the phone call. "All's well that ends well, I presume?" she said, pulling up a chair to sit down.

"All's well," Bonnie smiled, and repeated all that Gabriel had told her.

Sandy put her hand on her heart. "Oh, Luvvy, that's so romantic," she gushed. "Looks like another wedding on the horizon."

Bonnie looked puzzled, "Another wedding?"

"Yes. Have you forgotten Lilly and Bobby's wedding next month? Those two are made for each other. Lilly will make a gorgeous bride," Sandy sighed.

"Oh, I had forgotten," Bonnie admitted, covering her eyes. "Momentarily of course. Anyone in my position would have, with all that's happened over the past week."

"Well, now that the dust is settling, you'd better grab Blake and ask him to escort you to the wedding, before Ella Frankston devours him. That woman has had her sights on him for a while now."

"Surely not," Bonnie replied, wide-eyed, with an edge in her tone, and her features fraught with anguish. "Ella isn't Blake's type."

Sandy placed her hands on her hips and gave Bonnie a penetrating look with one brow raised. "How much rejection do you expect that man to take? Oh for pity's sake, Bonnie! You like Blake Parker. What's not to like?" she said, raising her arms in the air to sing his praises Italian style. "He's tall, he's very attractive and amusing. He's also an amazing art teacher, which has benefitted both of us as well as the Gallery – and he's smitten with you, my dear. But," Sandy sighed in exasperation. "He's also human – humans need companionship Luvvy. It would seem," Sandy continued, in a low mischievous tone as she trotted off down the hall, "that Ella's ready to give that gorgeous man all the companionship he wants."

Long after Sandy had disappeared into her office, Bonnie stood in the hallway contemplating what her friend had said. She then went to the student's studio and peeped through the glass doors. Ella looked up from her painting and saw Bonnie. She smiled and waved. Bonnie gave a half-hearted smile and wave back. She liked Ella. She was fun to be around, but now Bonnie felt a little insecure, knowing that Ella was interested in Blake. A sudden sense of foreboding overwhelmed her. Bonnie turned around and dashed off to Sandy's office.

"OK, miss know-it-all", Bonnie said, standing in the doorway. "You're right. I do like Blake. But I'm afraid it's been a long ..."

"Awww, sweetie," Sandy cooed as she laid the pen she was using on the desk, cutting Bonnie off midsentence. "I understand. You're still in love with Gabe."

"No. Yes." Bonnie stuttered. "I mean, Gabe's in my heart and in my thoughts, but the reality is that Gabe has gone. I can't hold him in my arms. Is it wrong for me to want to be loved and to love again? Is it wrong of me to not want to be alone anymore?"

"No sweetie, it isn't wrong. It's perfectly normal to feel that way." Sandy said as a spark of excitement ran through her. *'At last,'* she wanted to scream from the rooftops, *'after years of discreetly inviting Eric's single colleagues to barbeques and family gatherings to meet Bonnie, she's finally found someone!'* "It's actually very right! Luvvy, just go and ask Blake if he will take you to the wedding."

"I can't."

"Why ever not?"

"What if he's now interested in Ella? She's so gorgeous and full of fun. Perhaps I've left it too late."

"OK then," Sandy said, softening her voice, taking care not to say or do anything that would entice Bonnie to change her mind. "I suggest you call him out of class right now and ask him. I saw Blake come in through the back entrance a while ago. He'd be there by now."

"What? No! I can't do that."

"Yes, you can. You're the boss." Sandy smiled and then thought about what she had just said. "Well one of the bosses," she corrected herself, laughing.

Bonnie was not paying attention to Sandy. She was weighing up the pros and cons of the situation. Suddenly she had a surge of unprecedented courage. She turned around and marched out of the office and down the hall to the studio. She stopped at the entrance, took a deep breath and then balled her hand into a tiny fist and gently tapped on the door.

Blake looked over his shoulder. He smiled and said something to Ella before moving away. "What a pleasant surprise," he said, pulling the door ajar.

She smiled awkwardly and fidgeted with the pen she was holding. "Could I have a word, Blake? Now if you wouldn't mind?"

Blake stepped out into the hall closing the door behind him. "Has something else happened? Has Grace had a turn for the worse?"

"Pardon? Oh no. Everything's fine. Grace is fine."

"You're trembling."

"I am," she said. "This is very difficult for me. I'm probably making a fool of myself. But I need to know something," Bonnie said and then paused.

A smile almost escaped Blake as he thought what a genius Sandy was. Her plan to have Bonnie believe Ella was interested in him had obviously worked. Bonnie is never nervous.

For a very long time, Sandy had been telling him all Bonnie needed was *gentle persuasion* for her to appreciate how important he was to her. Blake would not hear of it. *"Deception isn't part of my DNA,"* he had told her. But as time passed, he reluctantly agreed.

'I know Bonnie likes and admires you,' Sandy had said. *'She'll soon recognise that her feelings go deeper than friendship,'* Sandy grinned. *'I have an idea that'll shake her up. You'll soon know for certain, one way or the other, how she feels about you...'*

"OK?" Blake said, looking at Bonnie, "What would you like to know?"

"Are you interested in Ella? Yes or no?" Bonnie blurted out with fingers crossed behind he back.

"No, Bonnie. I'm not interested in Ella."

"Well then," she paused to steady her nerves. "I have a wedding to go to next month, would you like to ..."

"I'd be delighted to accompany you to the wedding," he said before she had finished asking the question. He took her by the hand. "We can discuss the details over dinner tonight. That's if you don't have other plans."

"Seven?" She said. "That'll give me time to see Grace."

Blake nodded, then leaned forward and kissed her on the cheek. "See you at seven."

40

Grace's recovery was slow. It had taken several months of therapy before she understood why she had lost her will to live.

Dr Thompson said to Grace during their last session, "Demanding unachievable perfection is doomed to fail. You're every bit a human being as I am. No human that I know of is perfect, far from it, so stop trying to be. Forgive yourself when you make a mistake. Believe me," he said, nodding, "when I say there are many more mistakes ahead of you," he smiled ruefully, "I'm speaking from experience, so learn from them and move forward. Everyone has the opportunity of starting again, with every new day." He paused and smiled. "May I suggest that you begin your day recalling the beauty in your life? Sure, there is ugliness in this world, but there is also so much beauty and love surrounding you. Just look into the eyes of the people who care about you, the animals you care for, even they have the ability to express love. Look at the sunrise. Watch the sunset. Look at the flowers ..."

As Dr Thompson was speaking, Grace felt warmth run through her, as if an invisible hose was filling her with energy and a profound appreciation of all that she had previously failed to see.

The doctor paused when he noticed a change in Grace's eyes. They were sparkling. "You finally get what I mean, don't you?"

Grace's expression lit up with the brightest smile, one the doctor had not seen before that moment. "Yes, I do, I totally do," she replied, getting up from her chair and extending her hand to him. Thank you, Doctor Thompson; I'll be forever indebted to you."

"It's my pleasure, Grace," he said warmly, standing to clasp her hand in his. "If ever you feel the need to talk about anything, my door is always open. But I feel you won't need my services any longer."

As Bonnie had predicted, with the passing of time, wounds healed. Although the friendship between Tim and Gabriel was not the same as they once shared, they were on speaking terms. Gabriel reasoned that the mistake Tim had made in getting involved with Anne Simms was punishment enough. That liaison produced a pregnancy. Tim aimed to do the right thing, to support Anne, but she wanted marriage – to be a doctor's wife. His response to her was, "I've been married. I botched that. I don't intend going for a second round."

Anne became impossible to live with, throwing one tantrum after another, whether at home or in public, she did not care where. When the slightest thing upset her, she would explode with obscenities, screaming about how Tim took advantage of her, ruining her life. "You trapped me!" she shrieked in an eye-popping, airborne-spittle rage, pointing at her swollen belly. "This is your brat! If you think I'm going to sacrifice my life for it, you've got another think coming."

Tim moved out of the house they shared before the turmoil affected his work. He was still puzzled as to what he had ever seen in Anne. She certainly was no beauty and had no extraordinary qualities about her. When it became known that he had had an affair with her, some of his work colleagues said, "Mate, you're supposed to upgrade ..." All he really understood was that he paid heavily for his stupidity. Although he could no longer tolerate the sight of Anne, love for his unborn child was growing. Tim was prepared to fight for joint custody, had she denied him the right to be a part of his child's life.

There was no fight. Anne wanted no part of him or the baby. She signed all the necessary papers and left Queensland the day after the baby was born.

Bonnie went to see Tim at the hospital when she heard what had happened. Tim was surprised and delighted to find her waiting for him, totally unaware that she had made it her business to follow his progress over the years. Jean Ryan, his caring neighbour who eventually became his foster mother, had recently passed away, leaving Tim without any family support.

"To what do I owe the honour of your visit?" Tim said, smiling broadly.

"I hope you don't mind, love," Bonnie said, parting her arms and reaching up for her usual hug. "I've come to see your dear little daughter."

Tim smiled and bent down into her embrace. "Of course, I don't mind, I'm glad you came. The baby's in the nursery," he said, beaming with pride. "She's so beautiful, Bonnie. I can't believe she's my daughter. Come, see for yourself."

"Have you chosen a name?" Bonnie asked as they strolled down the corridor

"Yes, I have."

"Well, what is it?" Bonnie laughed, "I can't read your mind!"

"Oh, sorry. Yes, of course, it's Rebekah."

Bonnie stopped in her tracks.

"Is something wrong?" Tim asked, looking concerned.

"No! No, Tim, that's beautiful. What made you choose that name?"

Tim shrugged. "It just came to me the moment I saw her."

They walked the rest of the way in relaxed silence. Tim held the door of the nursery open for Bonnie as they entered. He took a gown from the shelf and passed it to her.

She slipped it on and followed him over to one of the cots under the window.

"Here she is," Tim said.

Bonnie's eyes shone with utter delight as she looked into those beautiful, big familiar eyes, the eyes of her grandmother.

"Oh, Tim," Bonnie said, wrapping an arm around his waist, suppressing the urge to say that his daughter is the image of his mother. "Rebekah is just gorgeous!"

"She surely is," he said, standing taller.

"What arrangements have you made for Rebekah while you're at the hospital?

He looked blankly at her. "I haven't got that far as yet."

"Never mind," she said. "I'll be happy to look after her. It will be lovely to have a baby in my arms again."

"What about The Gallery and your work?"

"Oh, my office is big enough to set up a nursery. Sandy and I will enjoy being aunties."

Once the arrangements were made, Bonnie called Grace and Gabriel to tell them what she had in mind, knowing full well that they would support her decision.

"Whatever makes you happy, Mum," was their response. They both knew Bonnie always had a soft spot for Tim, but never knew why.

As the months rolled into years, it was inevitable that a close bond would form between Rebekah and Bonnie. The child was the glue that cemented family and friendships – everyone adored her.

Now four years of age, Rebekah was blossoming into a stunning version of her grandmother, with her long raven curls, soulful, dark eyes and long, lean frame. It prompted Bonnie to ask Tim if he had ever thought about his biological mother.

"Every day," he replied, without hesitation. "Especially now," he said looking over at his daughter. "I'd give my right arm to find her," he said and then shrugged. "I have absolutely no information about her – nothing, other than her being part Aboriginal."

Sometime later, Sandy was reading the obituaries in the local paper when she came across a familiar name. "Bonnie!" she called from her office. When Bonnie did not answer, Sandy realised she must be on the phone. She circled the name in the obituaries then went to Bonnie's office and placed the paper on the desk in front of her, pointing to the name with a huge red ring around it.

Bonnie gasped. "I'm sorry, I'll have to call you back," she said to the person she was speaking to, ending the call.

After reading the notice, Bonnie dropped the paper and picked up the phone. She dialled a number she had not used in so many years.

"Hello," said the familiar voice.

"Oh! What? I wasn't expecting you to answer the phone." Bonnie paused a moment and then said, "I'm so, so sorry."

Several days after the funeral, Bonnie asked her friend to meet her at the foreshore for lunch. "It's so good to see you again. I got such a shock when you answered my call,' Bonnie said, shaking her head in awe. She paused briefly and then said, "I'm sorry to hear about your mum." She paused again. "Although I never gave up hope that one day you'd return. I'm still surprised that you are here, sitting opposite me. Gosh, it's wonderful to see you! I can hardly believe my eyes." She smiled and continued, "A heck of a lot of water has flowed under the bridge in the past thirty-seven years, hasn't it?"

Rebecca nodded, her expression pensive. She laughed out loud. "Well, I had to come back. I still have to return those dozen or so handkerchiefs to you." Rebecca suddenly stopped laughing and she caught her breath. Her expression changed when she noticed a shadow behind

Bonnie. "Why haven't you married again, Bonnie?" she said, her voice deadly serious.

"Excuse me? Where did that come from?"

"Please answer my question."

"Well ... well," Bonnie stuttered, taken aback, looking blankly at her friend." I don't know. I haven't met anyone that I've wanted to marry. Oh, I don't know why."

"Is there anyone interested in you that perhaps you like?"

"Why all the questions?"

"Gabe's spirit is still with you, Bonnie," Rebecca said. "I can see him." Rebecca looked over Bonnie's shoulder. "Gabe," she said looking at him. "You must leave Bonnie alone. She deserves to be happy. She'll never be happy with you hanging around interfering in her life. She's safe. You can leave now."

"Rebecca. Stop! What are you doing? I'm happy the way things are."

"You can't be, Bonnie. It's not normal. It's unnatural! You deserve to experience love again. To be held. To be cherished."

"Stop!" Bonnie was almost in tears.

As Gabe went to move closer to Bonnie, Rebecca put her hand for him not to. He remained where he was.

"I'm sorry, sweetie. Someone had to slap you in the face to bring you to your senses. It might as well be me," she said, pulling from her bag a linen handkerchief which had once belonged to Bonnie. "Here," she said.

Bonnie made a little giggling sound. "The tables have turned," she said smiling through her tears. They both sat in silence for a moment.

"I know you're right, Bec. I really do want to have all of those things. There is someone, but ..."

"No but's," Rebecca broke in. "First thing is, you need to find another place to live – today! I'll come with you to help you find something."

Bonnie reluctantly agreed. "It will have to be this afternoon, though," she said. "I have a meeting in a few minutes. Bonnie sat taller in her chair and fired back. "OK, since its twenty questions hour. When do you plan to do something about searching for your son? What about Paul? He's divorced and his parents have passed away. He told me that he couldn't get you out of his mind or his heart. That he'd wished he had been stronger to fight his parents. He has so many regrets ..."

"I called Paul the minute I returned," she smiled.

"That's wonderful, Bec! Paul loves you so much. Now, what about your son? When do you suppose you'll start searching?"

Rebecca shook her head. "Not yet."

"Why ever not?"

"He might hate me for giving him away. There's so much to consider here. He probably won't want me upsetting his life. He ..."

Bonnie smiled with delight and leaned forward. "What if I told you I know where he is, that he would give his right arm to find you."

Rebecca covered her mouth with her hands as involuntary tears filled her eyes, spilling down her cheeks. Filled with incredulous joy, she reached across the table and clasped Bonnie's hand. "I wasn't going to return, but the spirits of my ancestors were calling me."

Bonnie had nothing to say in response to that, except to smile.

Rebecca dried her eyes and then looked pleadingly at Bonnie. "Are you sure he's my son?"

Bonnie nodded. "Oh yes. Tim, that's his name, is your son. Anita, Oliver's mother, used her contacts to get Tim's adoption information. She found out that you gave birth to him here in Wynnum."

Rebecca hung her head. "I'm so sorry I lied to you. I wasn't allowed to say a word to anyone."

"Water under the bridge," Bonnie shrugged, continuing, "Anita also found out that you were working as domestic help right up until you gave birth. So yes, I'm sure Tim is your child. He was about four years old when I first spotted him. There was no mistaking that he was your son. Tim has your beautiful, dark eyes. I got goose bumps when I saw him. A childless couple in Wynnum adopted him when he was a couple of weeks old. The poor little mite had a tough time for a while. Mrs Osborne, his adopted mother, never recovered from the loss of her babies. She ended up an alcoholic.

"Their neighbour, Jean Ryan, took care of Tim when Mrs Osborne was unable to. Jean adored Tim. After his wife's death and before he left the area, Mr Osborne made arrangements for Jean to foster Tim. Under Jean's care, Tim excelled. Sadly, Jean has passed away. You would have liked her.

"Gabriel and Bobby Taylor met Tim when they were twelve years old. Tim saved them from getting a beating from a bunch of roughnecks when they were travelling home on the train one afternoon after a football match – the trio has been mates ever since. Oh, by the way, Tim is a doctor."

Since it was no longer an issue, Bonnie felt it unnecessary to mention the falling out between Tim and Gabriel.

Rebecca relaxed back in her seat, astonished. "In the grand scheme of things," she reflected, "my boy was actually loved and cared for by his family, which tells me that we never really lose what we are destined to have in this life."

"Yes, Tim is family and so are you, Bec," Bonnie said, glancing at her watch. "We have to go!" she said, sliding her chair away from the table. "C'mon."

"Where are we going?" Rebecca inquired, bending to pick up her bag, revealing the tattoo on her shoulder.

"Follow me," Bonnie said, and then gasped. "What's that on your shoulder? It's beautiful!"

"This here?" Rebecca pointed to a delicate cyclamen colour flower.

"Yes."

"It's a plum blossom – I read that it blooms most vibrantly in the winter snow, that it symbolizes perseverance and hope and a transition of one's life. Perfect, don't you think?"

"Oh yes, yes, I do think," said Bonnie, smiling broadly. "C'mon, I can't be late."

When they left the café, Rebecca trailed a step behind Bonnie. She suddenly felt apprehensive crossing the street, down to the park on the foreshore.

In the distance, a tall, young man with blond hair was chasing a little girl with long raven curls around a huge tree. They stood out among the day trippers and locals. The sound of their laughter seemed louder than anyone else's. Rebecca stopped to watch them, feeling the need to imprint the scene in her mind. Her eyes never left them. Her heart thumped harder in her chest when Bonnie spoke to the tall man with blond hair. He looked over at her and then back at Bonnie. He smiled and then hugged Bonnie. He took the child by the hand and began walking towards her. When the child with the raven curls and the tall man reached her, the man opened his arms. "Hello, Mum!"

41

Gabe knew Rebecca was right. It was time for him to leave. *'After all,'* he mused, *'I've fulfilled my promise to protect my family. They're safe now; they don't need me any longer. Gabriel can well and truly take care of himself, Grace and his mother. Bonnie deserves to have another shot at happiness. Blake's OK. He seems like a good bloke, and Gabriel will knock his block off if he doesn't treat his mother right.*

'I'm proud of my son.' Gabe stood tall just thinking about him. *'Once that boy of mine had made up his mind to marry Grace, there was no stopping him. His plan to elope to Paris was a pretty sharp idea. Those two are made for each other, just like his mother and I are.'* Gabe corrected himself, *'were.'* He shrugged. *'I keep forgetting I'm dead.'*

Gabe stood by a tree not far from where Rebecca, Tim and her granddaughter were, observing them with interest. He was thinking that Tim was about to discover his mother was the highly respected Indigenous artist, *Nunyara* – meaning, *made well again.* She had embraced that name when she began painting. Rebecca was about to discover that Tim has one of her paintings hanging in his office and was a great admirer of her work.

'I guess Oliver did me a favour,' Gabe reflected, without regret. *'I was too damaged to last the distance. My demons were stronger than me. They would have eventually destroyed me or my relationship with Bonnie – I left this world a winner.'*